REASON TO BE

Reason to Be

a novel

R. A. Hinkle

BAD CLOWN
BOOKS

A Bad Clown Book
badclownbooks.com

REASON TO BE. Copyright © 2025 R. A. Hinkle

Cataloguing-in-Publication data

Names: Hinkle, R. A. (Robert Hinkle), 1998-, author.
Title: Reason to Be / R. A. Hinkle.

ISBN
979-8-9922149-0-1 (paperback)
979-8-9922149-1-8 (ebook)

LCCN: 2025901562

Cover design by Matt Crenshaw
Bad Clown Books colophon by Carson French

This is a work of fiction.
The contents of this book have as much claim on reality as a dream. Any references to historical events, real people, or real places are used fictitiously. Names, characters, and places are products of the author's imagination.
There is nothing in this book quite as important as your own life.

The author gratefully acknowledges Carcanet Press for permission to use excerpts from *The Poems of Rowan Williams* by Rowan Williams. Carcanet Press, 2014.
All rights reserved. Used by permission.

First Printing Edition
2025

For Mila Rose,

I'm looking at you right now and thinking of when Love
came as a baby to assure us of beauty and goodness and truth
...and now that you're a toddler,
the importance of being a little crazy

For your brother Wesley, too

Your sister is only a couple of years older than you,
but you'll have a lot to learn from her.
I learned a lot from mine.

Him: *How beautiful you are, my darling,*
How beautiful you are.
Your eyes are doves.

Her: *How handsome you are, my beloved,*
And so delightful!
Indeed, our bed is verdant.
The beams of our house are of the cedar tree,
Our rafters, the juniper.
...
I am the rose of Sharon,
The lily of the valleys.

...

I

She slammed the door behind her. I knew she was upset but said nothing. I put the car into first gear then placed my hand on her thigh. She tensed up. I moved my hand back to the gearshift.

We embraced that morning. It was the first time in a few weeks. The odd thing was, she initiated it. It was stale. It had been stale. We continued our marital routine to pass the occasional awkwardness of a new day and to keep me from getting frustrated. I know that's an uncomfortable turn of phrase in the current century, but I don't know how else to put it.

Over the years, we were both determined that we wanted to have children (though I'm not sure we ever asked if we should). It's been nearly a year since we gave up on getting pregnant. Neither of us mentioned we were giving up, not consciously at least, but there was an understanding. By understanding, I mean it seemed apparent her hope was abandoned. The last time I remembered her being excited about the possibility was months ago. We were at my cousin Reece's. They were out on the porch, laughing, glowing, giddy with the idea of raising kids side by side.

I reckoned if we were to separate, we would be grateful to not have subjected kids to the pervasive modern travesty of love dissolving. Then again, it must not be that modern of a problem, otherwise the Archbishop of Canterbury would still be Catholic.

The car behind me laid on the horn. I looked away from the Atlanta skyline to see the on-ramp light was green and pressed the accelerator. Our old beater of a car sputtered onto the interstate, backfiring every time the transmission changed gears. The smell of burning oil came through the air vents. It was a metallic silver Mercedes from the 70s. A diesel. Dad handed it down to me when I moved off to college. I had experience in fixing it, which is to say it broke down often. We could afford a newer car, but we lived in the city. We should hardly need a car at all, but that argument doesn't hold up too well in a city like Atlanta.

She used to beg me to find a newer car, but it was a classic. From a time when cars were made with real materials by real hands. And no cup-holders because 'there's no time for drinks when you're racing down the autobahn', as my dad would say. She didn't seem to appreciate that. Anyway, she no longer brought up the idea of getting a new one.

She stared out the window as if she were paying attention to something out there. I knew she wasn't. The entire ride, I didn't see her blink. I wondered if her thoughts matched mine, but I had a hard time believing she had any concern for what was going through my mind. Of course, all I cared about in that moment was getting through the afternoon traffic.

After pulling to a stop in the south terminal of the airport, I pulled her luggage out of the trunk and kissed her cheek. A tear formed in her eye as she hugged me. Then she grabbed her bag and walked away. She stopped about ten feet away, hesitated before turning around, and said, "See you soon." I nodded and sat behind the steering wheel and watched her disappear behind the automatic sliding doors. An airport cop blew his whistle at me to make my way through the orange cone jungle.

I drove north back through the city, once again fighting the deluge of traffic, and out to the farm. Dad met me at the door and muttered for me to come in. He poured me a beer and leaned across from me at the kitchen bar.

Mom came in a few minutes later and smiled when she saw me. Dad grinned, but Mom walked by him up the stairs to her room. I wondered how long their sex had been stale, too. Dad walked over and started fiddling with the sink, so I took a big gulp of my beer and followed Mom up the stairs.

"What's Johnny up to?" She asked. She was smoothing out the comforter on the bed.

"In the city for the weekend. Some leadership conference, I think. Charlotte's on a plane. I dropped her off at the airport before coming here." I adjusted my shoulder against the doorframe.

"Those leadership conferences are a waste of money and time. I wish he'd spend his weekends coming to see us."

"When you do what Johnny does, they pay you to go to those things." She shook her head and started folding clothes on the bed. I walked back down the stairs.

I found Dad drinking a beer of his own at the bar and sat beside him. He kept scratching the scruff on his face while looking at the wall to the right of us. I finished the over-hopped ale as we sat in silence. The yellow wallpaper with little black fleur-de-lis was peeling at the trim. My brother and I's high school graduation portraits hung in the center of the wall surrounded by family photos of people I had never met. There was one small photo of me and Charlotte at our wedding. She had this big toothy grin on her face. I was looking off into the distance with a solemn expression. My face was cleanly shaven. I looked so young. I followed the line of scruff down my neck with my hand. It was time for a trim.

With the beer put away, I went out behind the garage to the horse barn. Sally was there eating hay in her stall. Her brown hair was sleek and shiny. The groomer must have come in earlier that week. I threw my saddle on her and buckled it up before I led her through the gate to the pasture. Having hopped on her back, we strolled through the tall grass.

It was an unusually humid day for this early in spring. Yesterday's rain must've brought a warm front. The ground under Sally's hooves was half dried mush, slopping under each step. We passed through the open field to the west of the house, then followed up the edge of the woods, where the cows crowded together in the shade of the pine trees.

The sun was a finger width away from setting as Sally carried me back across the field and along the plot of land where mom tried her hand at a diversity of fruits: peach trees and apples, blueberry bushes, muscadines and grapevines, and figs. Most of her crop fell to the ground and rotted.

The past winter had been warmer than most, and many of the trees were well into flowering. Some of the peach and fig trees were already showing fruit. After sliding off the saddle, I pulled two small breba figs off a branch. I held one out in my palm, and Sally bit off a good chunk of it, chewed, and spat it out with a high blow from her nostrils. I laughed, took a bite out of mine, and then spat it out too.

I brushed Sally's mane until she laid down in the grass. From there, I leaned against her backside and watched as the sky in front of us went through her daily schizophrenic descent of colors toward darkness.

I hopped on Sally's back, and we rode back before it was too dark. She reluctantly trotted toward her stall. I told her I was sorry I had to lock her up and goodnight, then I went in the house and told Mom and Dad I was leaving. Mom gave me a hug and Dad followed me outside. He acted like he might say something, but he just stood by my door and shook my hand before I sat and drove away.

I didn't go home that night. I decided I wanted to stay out of the city while Johnny was there. His infectious positivity was too much for me at the moment. Instead, I went to my cousin's. She and her husband were good friends of Charlotte and mine. They greeted me at the door and Charlie asked if I'd like a drink. Charlie made a high-end cocktail you couldn't get at the bar for less than the bill that bore Ulysses. I told him an Old-Fashioned would be fine. I saw him grab a 10-year single-barrel bourbon from his shelf and forced a smile to let him know I was grateful.

We went out onto the back porch. It was wrapped in a bug screen with string lights hanging from the edges. Under the lights, the porch had a deep amber glow. The lumber that made up the porch soaked up the light, giving it a lively golden brown, rather than its typical dry-rot gray. Charlie pulled out two Cubans from his vest pocket and handed one to me. I never asked how he got them and always welcomed the offering. Charlie flicked open the lighter and held it to the tuck, I puffed till it was lit. We each sat and smoked away. My lungs exhaled all the air they carried that day, and I breathed easy.

My cousin Reece joined us. She had a glass of water and sat on the far side of the porch, away from the smoke. I noticed her face was gleaming and full, her cheeks showed a perkiness and plumpness. "You're pregnant," I said outright, and she nodded with a big grin on her face. I congratulated them and clinked my glass with Charlie's. They both beamed with ballooning eyes and fell into their own daze. I slumped down in the chair and sipped my drink, reviving myself before they could come out of their hypnosis and notice me.

"What name?" I stuttered.

"Hmm?" Reece looked at me as if she forgot I was there. "Oh! Well, if it's a boy, we'll name him Charles Jr." Air flushed through my nostrils as I held back from chuckling. It was a tired tradition.

"What?" Reece asked as Charlie grimaced in the corner of my eye.

"Nothing. And if it's a girl?"

"Dorothy. Dorothy Rose."

"That's an absolutely lovely name." I smiled.

Charlie sat in his chair with his head down, sipping his drink like he was licking wounds. Reece smiled back at me, but I saw the disdain in her eyes. I wasn't naturally cordial and refused to be a sycophant like the typical politician. They knew this.

"How's work, Del?" Charlie chimed in with that subtle sternness natural to every word he spoke. It made me feel like a project. Like the couple of years he had on me made him my elder. Reece nodded her head, thankful he broke the silence.

"I plan to quit soon."

"Is that right?"

I sat forward. "I can't keep doing this meaningless work for an *empty* organization." I didn't like how my voice sounded. Defensive. Wounded. Like I had to validate the statement.

"Empty, huh?"

Empty.

I nodded. "Charlotte's going back to work when she gets back from Seattle, and I'll put my notice in then. I'm not sure what I'll do, but her salary will be enough for me to not have to do anything. Besides, I was always better fit for keeping the home in order, and she was a better fit for work."

That must have been enough evidence for Charlie and Reece to assume we were giving up on getting pregnant, but they weren't the kind of people who would press, especially when they had their own good news to handle modestly.

***

I woke in their guest room still wearing my slacks from the night before. When I walked downstairs, Charlie and Reece were talking quietly, stopping when they heard the step creak beneath my foot. Charlie was sipping his coffee, scrolling on his tablet, while Reece was cooking pancakes.

Charlie acknowledged me, "Morning, Del. Want some coffee?" I nodded and Reece poured me a cup. I took a seat beside Charlie at the kitchen bar and started reading the town's monthly magazine.

"The Christians are really embracing pacifism these days, Del." I had one and a half unused degrees in religion, so Charlie liked to discuss these matters with me. "I read an article on the internet the other day by a pastor who calls himself a pacifist. He wrote that if he knew a baby was going to grow up to be a murderer as extreme as Hitler, he wouldn't kill him. I don't get it. Hitler killed millions. Sometimes it takes one death to save those millions."

Most people would be caught off guard–especially this early in the morning–by what Charlie was saying, but I sipped my coffee and replied, "I wouldn't kill that baby either, Charlie."

"You'd let him grow up and be Hitler then?"

I wondered if we've grown too far removed from the third Reich that we've made the Hitler metaphor into a synonym. Hitler is now the name given the devil incarnate, like Christ is God in the flesh.

"I wouldn't do that either."

"Well, you've gotta take a side. Which one are you pickin'?"

"I'd probably give him my job and let him die out that way."

Charlie set his tablet on the counter. "Del, this resentment of yours isn't doing you any favors." He started to sermonize me, using grandiose gestures with his hands. "Sure, you found out the life you idealized growing up isn't panning out the way you dreamed it would, but that's part of growing up. All you can do is accept it. You're responsible for your resentment. Not your job."

I took a sip of my coffee and Charlie went back to what he was reading on the tablet. Reece plopped a platter of pancakes in front of us, and Charlie immediately smothered his share with an ample amount of butter and syrup.

"What are you doing tonight?" I asked him.

Reece answered for him, "We've got to go shopping for the baby. That guest room of yours is getting a makeover. Well, it won't be yours anymore. No more room in the inn. We need your room for the baby."

I looked at Charlie. "Why don't we go out tonight?"

He looked at Reece. "If we pick the right paint and find the right cradle, you can go out tonight."

Speaking as if we didn't have a mediator, I told Charlie I'd pick him up at 7, then I tried to leave.

"Del?" Reece's self-assured and soothing voice called out to me.

"Yeah?"

"Help Charlie move your bed out to the street before you go."

"Yep," I replied, and followed Charlie up the stairs. We completed the task in silence, and I went on my way.

Charlie and Reece lived in a small, progressive town just outside of the perimeter. Every business in the town square displayed a pride flag, including the Baptist church. The CBD obsession had passed now that there were work arounds to getting THC and half of the beer list at the brewery I walked into seemed to experiment with different delta strains. Of course, I'm exaggerating. I ordered one from the other half of the list, paired with a fried catfish sandwich, and sat at the bar. It was only eleven in the morning when I went in, but others had trickled in by the time my sandwich was ready.

"That's not a war I'm willing to fight." I listened to the two men sitting on the stools beside me. I'd seen them walk in from the fire department across the street. They were dressed in navy shirts with the fire department's badge sewn on the chest. I assumed–as I watched them put down their lagers like the Fountain of Youth and order another–they had just got off duty.

"I would not call it a war," the smaller guy with caramel-tanned skin chimed back. He appeared to be of Latin-American descent, but I wasn't sure. If anything, his accent was laconic and monotoned, which is to say he had less of an accent than I did. He pronounced his words fully, with gaps of space between each line. I wondered how he became a firefighter in the Atlanta suburbs of all places. The town was mostly white, as Georgia towns tend to be the more north of the city you go. That is, except for a few concentrated pockets of Latin-Americans in, say, Dalton, or Norcross, or Asians in Duluth.

The brewery was no exception. Their black and brown skin stuck out against the flannels and beards of financiers and neo-Calvinists. They were both large men, their arms filling the sleeves of their shirts and then some, but the Black man was comparatively larger than his peer. Together they looked like Zeus and Poseidon, and I was just Hermes. Next to them, I felt like an underdeveloped freshman trying out for the varsity football team.

The "smaller" one continued, "This country is in crisis. If we go to war, we will lose. Divided countries always lose." He spoke of wars I had never heard of, the *War of the Triple Alliance, Chaco,* a liberal led revolt in Paraguay, civil war, the authoritarian *Stroessner,* all the sacrifices it takes to reach democracy. He stressed that word, *democracy.* It sounded like he had a good grasp of college history and social studies. I was curious how a college graduate becomes a firefighter. *Is that small-minded?* I wondered, as he lowered his voice to a sardonic whisper, *"Even something so important as democracy, can still be so fragile."* The way he knew so much of South American history furthered my suspicions he was Latino.

His friend pushed his stool back from the bar. "I wouldn't go to war for this country. We don't do that anymore. The only way half of the country would even go to war is if it were against the other half of the country. Could you imagine if we had another world war and one part of the U.S. joined forces with half of the world and the other part joined the rest of the world? Does that sound like a country that survives a war?

"If anything's true of our country, it's that the left and right are wed together. Whether they like it or not, divorce won't make things better. Trust me on that. And, for a short time, it'll make everything so much worse. They may hate each other, but they're husband and wife! They'll just have to learn to work together and leave this priggish impotence behind." He spoke with the authority of an army general in an old movie.

"Are you planning to join the moderates up the middle, then?"

"And be the disappointment of both parents?" Suddenly they became boyish comrades, slapping each other's backs and cracking up.

I had a hard time listening to them, partly because I couldn't hear most of what they were saying over the musician setting up and testing his equipment in the corner of the room, but also because I, too, struggled to imagine the U.S. fighting a serious war again. War doesn't make sense in the modern world. Even when our liberal government continued bombing countries in the Middle East, the common liberal–if they took their beliefs seriously–protested it as inhumane while the conservatives disapproved because their leader didn't make the call. The president pandering across party lines by bombing other countries doesn't appear indicative of a healthy country, but I liked to stay away from those conversations.

The firefighters were further into the bit as I gathered myself to leave. Zeus spoke with a deep and resolute voice, "Now is not the time to be apolitical or an *ideo-logi-cal* centrist." Each word was over enunciated and drawn out. "The best defense against nationalism is patriotism. We must revive the heart of Langston and Lewis and Baldwin."

"James Baldwin! You believe the ex-pat can retain their patriotism?"

"Oh, yes! Yes, yes, yes. To love an abuser, you leave them. Don't you know it's all connected? You must love your country to love the world, and you must love people to love humanity."

"Fair enough, but for some of us, this land birthed us. No matter how bad it becomes, we cannot leave. We know this land existed before we did. It is not the land that is damned. Whatever happens of this country, the land will remain." His partner was rolling his eyes as Poseidon grinned, adding, "Don't tell me the only American Indian you are familiar with is Chief Noc-A-Homa?"

"We call your people Native American now."

"How American of you."

"Columbus was not American."

"Touché."

They were laughing once again. One of them began another speech, apparently attempting to win at whatever these debates were, which seemed a regular occurrence. Having one upped the man of indigenous descent once more, Zeus signed the treaty with, "Now, where is my wife with the car?"

I paid my tab and decided, with apprehension, to go back to my place in the city. The interstate was backed up with weekend tourists trying to spend the day downtown. It took me an hour to get ten miles down the road. I pulled off an exit early and took side streets until I pulled into the parking garage under my condominium.

Our place was a one-bedroom on the ninth floor. Charlotte had an eccentric aunt who owned multiple properties around the city and rented this one out to us for a price we could manage. Her late husband had been a doctor at the university hospital, but he was no good with finances and gave his wife full control of their investments. She turned out to be as cunning as a serpent, buying up properties in neighborhoods pre-gentrification–I didn't admire the practice, but without her help, we wouldn't be able to afford living in the city. We basically paid the mortgage, which wasn't much because she bought it long before the housing boom of the pandemic 20s.

It was important for both of us to be in the city. I needed the constant noise of the traffic and construction to help me think during the day and to sleep at night. Charlotte says it helps her paint. Although, I haven't seen her pick up a brush in months, or years, really.

The clock above the stove showed it was two o'clock. I laid on our couch facing the city on the other side of the window wall. Cranes lined the burgeoning west side of town from southwest to northeast. Our cat, Amir–a long-haired, white Persian–jumped up on my stomach and made a bed above my head. He purred while I looked out across the escalating horizon. I had the smart speaker set a timer for an hour and picked up Amir, setting him on my chest so we could both be comfortable. I stroked my hand through Amir's thick, soft fur, and his purrs vibrated in response. Together, we drifted into sleep.

***

I awoke to a knock at the door. Amir darted off the couch as I sat up and checked the time: 2:30. I breathed an irritated sigh. Before I had opened the door enough to see who stood behind it, the stranger exclaimed, "Brother!" Then I saw Johnny standing there in a blue suede blazer and a white silk button up with the top button undone, exposing his shaved, tanning bed-tanned chest. His blonde hair sat on his head like sargassum, coasting over the crest of an ocean wave.

We'd both been blonde when we were toddlers and most people assumed we were twins. Johnny was just under a year younger than me, and our birthdays were situated where Mom was able to enroll us in pre-school at the same time. During the summer, the sun bleached our blonde hair like the color of unseasoned, butter-less popcorn. As we entered adolescence, my hair started to turn a darker shade of brown around the same time as the Autumn leaves. Johnny's hair stayed blonde.

He dropped his duffel bag and gave me a hug. I hugged him back with the one arm he wasn't squeezing too tightly. I invited him in for a drink. He turned down whiskey for water. I joked about him being pregnant, too. While I removed a glass from the cabinet and filled it with ice, he laughed and said he couldn't drink before his keynote.

"So, Reece told you?"

I nodded and noted that he must have known before me.

We went out on the balcony, and he leaned against the railing while he sipped on his water. The nerves in my spine turned on. My anxiety must have been tangible because he removed the glass from over the balcony and leaned against the closed wall.

"Want a smoke?" I flipped open my Victorian-esque cigarette case and held out a mini cigar. Johnny shook his head and chuckled, "You and your tropes." I was morally against cigarettes–though if I had a few drinks in me...my morals were known to loosen. Mini cigars were different. Romantic. I'd let myself have one about every day. Johnny turned my offer down, saying he didn't want the smell on him at the conference. I understood and decided against smoking myself.

"What's Charlotte up to this weekend?" He asked.

"Seattle for the weekend."

"What the hell is in Seattle this time of year?"

"I didn't ask."

"You let your wife fly across the country without knowing why she was going or who she was going to see?"

"I don't let my wife do anything. She does what she wants. She said she was going to Seattle, and I said 'okay.' Maybe she'll tell me about it when she gets back."

Johnny stood there with a disconcerted expression on his face. I knew what he was thinking, but I sat in silence to see if he would address it. He didn't. All he added was, "Seattle's fun, though it can get quite drab. I've been a few times–mostly for conferences. It's got a different mood than most cities. Good coffee, great art. You know what, I imagine Charlotte will find Seattle to be quite aligned with her temperament. I'll have to ask her about it next time I see her."

Johnny and Charlotte got along well–better than me and Johnny, better than me and Charlotte, really. One of the good things about being married to Charlotte was that she could be my placeholder when I didn't care to be present, whether it was a physical presence or a conscious one.

I asked him about the conference.

"It's been pure opulent bliss!" He began a long homily on leadershit, well, that wasn't the word he used for it. What was it? Leadership? Occasionally, he would sprinkle in the names of important people he assumed I had heard of throughout the conversation. I would nod to prevent him from assailing on a tangent about how said person is important and how he knows said important person. I wavered when he asked if I knew said other important person's book but bypassed his excursus by asking when he had to be back. He looked at his watch and said, "Oh! Soon. I should head out now."

I told him it was good to see him, and, after a pause, I knew I meant it.

"You too, brother. Tell Charlotte 'Hi' for me when she returns home. Honestly, Seattle can be great fun. You should've just bit the bullet and gone with!" I walked him to the door. He squeezed my arm and left.

I went back to the balcony and smoked. I had grabbed a poetry book on the way but couldn't encourage myself to read it. Instead, I stared off into the distance toward that non-existential realm where the earth and sky meet. My mini cigar burned away before I could enjoy it. I almost burned another one, but I thought better of it.

Just enough nicotine had made it to my brain that I was feeling its effects. All these neurons and all their energy, the nicotine did not create more energy; it seemed to make the energy behave. Sometimes. Sometimes it felt more like a storm of ideas rising up over the surface of my mind and demanding attention. I'd find I had the attention span for them, but there would be no linear coherence to why those ideas suggested they be categorized together. All I could do was hold them all together and see if anything started making sense. Usually, it felt like the little ideas, like children at a gymnasium birthday party, were doing somersaults across the wrinkles in my brain and laughing at me.

A lone sailor is in a real mess when a storm comes and blows the wind every which way. The wind is strong and powerful and refuses to be bound to the sailor's ends. They are stuck tacking at huge angles. This is a laborious process. It takes an awful lot of time and there's a high chance of stalling. The wind is not your partner but an opponent. You spend the day zigzagging at random, barely making progress with a wind that can change direction at a moment's notice, killing any speed you gain.

But if the sailor finds the wind to be in their favor, still as strong and powerful, the sailor strikes at the opportunity and lets it run. With one eye on the wind vane, the other marvels at the bowing jib revealing the shapely contours of their partner. The wind is a sailor's greatest enemy and the deepest love they've known. Anger and love are siblings born of passion.

It wasn't just any poetry book I was attempting to read. The book was *Les Fleurs du Mal*. Baudelaire in the original French. I hardly had a grasp on the language, but I was French. To some degree. I had minimal connection to my heritage. White people seem to lose touch with their old country heritage in fewer generations. That could be the Caucasian slogan: "We don't know where we came from."

We don't know who we are or if we're even a people. Not having a group is what makes us a group and we love being in a group. United by our lack of identity. And we will go to extreme measures to protect that identity. Of course, the Irish and Italians fought for a long time to hold onto their heritage, but across the 20th century some unseen magnetism pulled them toward whiteness, and you see it now. They may say they are Irish or Italian, but they don't know what they mean by it.

In our current generation, we can see it with Hispanic people. In some sense that word, Hispanic, was invented to erase different groups' cultural backgrounds while at the same time ensuring a category that meant 'not white.' If your country was colonized by Spain, that makes you Hispanic. And in America, we prefer it if you're from a country that was colonized by any other European country, for some reason. Also, it's easier to just consider Latin American and Hispanic the same thing. In other words, Portugal who? The cultures that come from the land south of the United States, and all immigrating cultures for that matter, face an immense pressure when they cross into this country: pass the heritage on, tell their ancestors' stories, and continue to be a people, or have the comfort and safety and the power of the white man.

I'm clearly being reductive here. It can be embarrassing to even bring up heritage in the South. It's a loaded word, and southerners don't always consider that heritage goes further back than America. They are often anti-English, anti-European, not considering that their lineage goes further back into the old world than it does in the new.

I am American, but I'm not sure what that means either. Personally, and I don't know how well this idea would be received by others, I think it means more for immigrants to "be American" than for those of us who don't know which family member brought us to this land. Precisely because they know what it means to be American.

America is the land of the immigrant and the stricter our immigration policies, the less we are acting like America. America is not the right to bear arms, not the glorification of the gun and its protections; it is freedom.

But we do not know what freedom is anymore. We've accepted a gross imitation. We think freedom is drinking a case of beer on a pontoon boat while firing off fireworks beneath the Stars and Stripes as she claps in the wind. Freedom may allow you to celebrate your freedom in such extravagant ways, but that doesn't make it a good application of such freedom. Freedom is responsibility.

The way we use our supposed freedom, God might as well have come down and told us this is our land, lay dominion to it. That is exactly what some of us believe. Freedom, as we imitate it today, is the right to exploit, consumption for the sake of consumption, exhume the dead and possess it to speak. I am not ignorant enough to think America has ever really known freedom. Arguably, George Washington understood freedom better than I do. The word freedom, in my mind, often conjures up the image of him crossing the Delaware, and yet he owned people. There is no turning away from it, no justifying it. True freedom does not lead to unfreedom.

But the immigrant knows freedom because they have known unfreedom. Not all of them, of course. America is not the only place freedom can be attempted. We do not *own* freedom. Freedom is an idea. It isn't real in any ontological sense. When we try to make it tangible, we end up on pontoon boats. Perhaps it is real on a metaphysical level, but I don't believe that is something we can know in our current state–if there even is any other state of existence that waits for us.

Christians often say they've been set free from the bondage of sin, and what do they mean by that exactly? What if sin is not real? Seriously, you don't have to deny the existence of God to question if sin is really real. Is sin real to God? What does being set free from the bondage of sin mean to a preacher who condemns porn and watches it every Sunday night? Is he a hypocrite or is he free? He certainly doesn't believe he is free to watch porn, but he does it anyway. Perhaps he is addicted. Maybe he has no self-control. Who chooses for him to pull up the incognito tab on his phone then? Perhaps in some spiritual sense he is free from the bondage of his addiction, but his body is not free from the effects. And any *orthodox* Christian should tell you that the body and spirit are one.

What I know of human existence today, every freedom we attain, a new bondage awaits us. Freedom is not real. Freedom is a goal. George Washington is the American archetype of freedom, and yet he was not free. He was enslaved to the subjugations of his own hand. All of us exist in freedom and unfreedom. The immigrant, then, comes here and finds true freedom, a freedom those of us born here cannot understand, especially if they escape a land of tyranny (another word we do not understand in America). But a new unfreedom welcomes them, too. Perhaps that new unfreedom is the slow dissolution of their heritage with each passing generation. Their grandchildren are damned to be American.

Next to the image of Washington's pursuit of freedom, where he stands confident above his men on that small boat, I see a small and wrinkled middle-aged, southeast Asian man driving a semi-truck, old model, gray from dust where it was originally white. He leans over the steering wheel, visibly tired. A small American flag stands upright on the dash, always in the corner of his eye. This man is real. I saw him once passing by on the interstate. I don't know his story. I don't know what freedom means to him. But that image grafts with your mind. One can't help imagining.

My last name is all the heritage preserved for me. I've hobbied at the French language to have some sense of connection with my ancestors. When our family dispersed from Louisiana, most of them moved to the Midwest and added an 's' to the end of Robert to sound more American, less offensive to their neighbors' tongue. Besides, "Roberts" sounds distinguished and ruggedly American. "Robert" just gets a lot of jokes from kids asking where the bear should row. But my father, his father, and his father before him insisted on keeping the name unchanged. This is how little morsels of heritage carry on.

I took two years of the French language in high school, and, every once in a while, I use that app that teaches you a language like you're playing a game. The game never holds my attention long enough to get further than anything I learned in school. One thing I know, and maybe this is more literary theory than grasping a language, *The Stranger* is absolutely dependent on the opening line reading "Today, Maman died." Or, as we say in the South:

Today, momma died.

When I read Baudelaire, I mostly rely on context clues and then, with a scrap piece of paper, I write my shoddy translations and stuff them in the crevice between the pages. I do the same with different mediums, too. Like Camus' essays in *Noces*, though that one I don't force a translation. I take the foreign tongue as it presents itself. Camus' French prose introduces itself to me as an unanswerable question. A locked door concealing a mystery I'm not meant to know.

Today, it seems I couldn't control the wind enough to make it through the poem's first line.

Sans cesse à mes côtés s'agite le Démon

Before I went back inside, I found I had it in me to pen my own poem. I often have original lines come to me, but I don't write them down. Not like I did in college. I don't call those poems, though. More so an angst with no medium but words thrown up on a page. For some reason, this time, I opened to the empty filler page at the back of the book and wrote a rigid, minimalist elegy on the concept of relating. I stopped after the fourth stanza and decided that the fifth, concluding stanza would only work if it resurrected the elegy itself. I shut the book on my four stanzas and took a long, hot shower, filling the bathroom with billowing clouds of steam.

***

The sun set behind us as Charlie and I rolled into the parking garage at the bottom of my building.

"It's a bit dense of you to always be driving out of the city to pick me up just to drive us right back in."

"I like to drive, and this way you don't have to deal with parking," I replied. It was true. Guest parking in the building filled up early on Friday and stayed that way the whole weekend. The pay-to-park decks followed soon after with people from Charlie's part of town coming into the city to blow off steam, paying twenty-five bucks for an evening and a high chance of a broken window. All of that could be prevented if MARTA went into their part of town, but they wouldn't allow it.

"Reece could drop me off."

"I like driving."

We parked in my designated spot and then walked down to the street. Three blocks from my building hid a speakeasy behind a record store. It was Charlie's favorite. Expensive, too. We only had access because he spent fifty dollars a month to be a member. Others could get in with the help of a hotel concierge.

We walked to the back corner of the store and pushed the 1920s replica sign to the side. The sign read "It's the Roaring Twenties, Y'all!" with a girl in a flapper dress holding her finger to her lips. A sign like that had no authenticity to it, no ability to keep a good thing secret, but charm is more appreciated than faith these days, and we're in a new sort of roaring 20s now. We don't care there was a global pandemic. We don't care about the economic repercussions or the increase of disastrous storms and fires. All of these apocalyptic happenings, the world could be ending and we don't care.

During our pandemic, people wondered how the Spanish flu could be so easily forgotten; now it all makes sense. We want normal and we want fun and we are uninhibited in showing it. There's an antsy-ness about us to enjoy life to the fullest by consuming our depressing means.

Behind the sign was the handle of the sliding door. Charlie scanned his card and waited for the lock to click, then slid it open, and we walked into the dark hallway. At the end of the hall, the bar-room opened wide, donned with low lit amber lights and deeply colored navy-blue leather couches with bronze bezels. The room cohered with the atmosphere. The bar itself had a thick bronze railing flowing along the grainy stained wood top. The glass shelving had light inserts that dimly lit the liquors displayed beneath them. The wall holding the shelves had a backsplash of antiqued mirror. I could tell by a quick glance that the aged and distressed look was faked, but it worked.

I sat next to Charlie on one of the blue couches. A waiter dressed in a white button down and black suspenders promptly took our order.

I ordered a Manhattan from the well, but Charlie interjected and told the waiter to make it top shelf. I shook my head but didn't object. Charlie ordered a 30-year scotch for himself and told the waiter to make it neat. The waiter ran off to the bartender while Charlie pressed back into the couch, crossing his legs.

"Would you ever cheat on Charlotte, Del?"

I didn't understand what he had asked at first which caused a glazed veneer to spread across my face. I replied, attempting to show I was capable of reflexive emotion, "What kind of a question is that, Charlie? Would you ever cheat on Reece?"

"My God! I would never! She brings more color to my life than any single person I have ever known. I wouldn't think about it. And now she's bringing me a child into this world. Oh, I am in a great debt to her. How could you ask me such a thing?"

"You can't be serious? You asked me first."

"Del, we both know you're a much different person than me. I haven't a clue if you would even find it immoral."

"Of course it's immoral."

My attention dropped from Charlie and moved to the people chatting each other up at the bar. Out of the periphery of my eye and the energy radiating from his direction, I could tell Charlie was seething.

A couple tore through the hallway donned in dangly golden diamanté and walked straight to the bar. I could tell they were from out of town as the male entrant surveyed the room and the spouse held up two fingers and mouthed "Martini."

Our waiter was back with our drinks, taking his time to set each drink on the whiskey barrel tables that were placed at each side of the couch. Charlie picked up the scotch and feigned a toast. Then he put his nose to the glass. He sniffed with his mouth agape and swirled the drink multiple times before taking his first sip.

I removed the cherry garnish and took a sip of my Manhattan when he asked me, "What if Charlotte was cheating on you? You just let her go to Seattle on her own. Who's to say what she's doing? Or who?"

My heart quivered.

"I don't let my wife do anything. She does what she wants," I replied. "But I do doubt that she would do that under our current conditions." Charlie raised his brow. "Even with our current situation."

Charlie sipped his drink, and I retreated to the restroom. The restroom was tiled in black across the floor and white across the walls. The lights gave off a purple hue, keeping the room dark and the sanitation cryptic. A candle flickered by the sink. It didn't cover up the smell, it joined it. The wall over the urinals was lined with newspaper collages in frames, showing headlines from a hundred years ago. One reads: PROHIBITION ENDED. The urinal flushed with excessive force. I had to jerk away from the splatter. The soap was a dry talc that powdered the air with haze. I added water and scrubbed. Staring back in the mirror, my hair was flopped over the front of my face. I took my damp hands and ran my fingers through my hair and back over my head, a little to the side to cover the recession.

I thought about the idea of Charlotte cheating on me. Maybe she had good reason to, the sex was stale. People cheat because they aren't satisfied. I wasn't satisfied, but I couldn't–well, I wouldn't.

Charlie stood up and apologized as I walked back to the couch. I noticed a gun was holstered under his blazer. He knew I didn't like guns. I accepted the apology, and we sat back down and finished our drinks. I had two more that night, Charlie had three, then we both took a shot of tequila, chatted up some people at the bar, including the two flashy tourists, then Charlie dismissed his inebriated self into the alley to smoke.

Normally, I would join him, but I had fallen into a conversation with the tourists, a married couple visiting from Chicago. They would later explain that she was from Atlanta and met her husband while he was studying at Morehouse. The husband had attained a PhD in some esoteric philosophy he seemed to avoid explaining directly and taught at the university in Chicago. They were in town for a lecture he gave the day before.

The wife gave me the impression she was simple. Vapid, maybe. Lovely, too, and relaxed. She wasn't open, but she wasn't reserved, either. They were almost as young as Charlotte and me–young thirties, though he looked a few years older than her–with no kids. I told them about Charlotte and how we lived in a building just down the street. I asked them where they were staying they said the hotel across the street.

"The W?" I asked.

The husband answered, "It used to be a W. Somebody else took it over."

"Ah."

I always liked the W. Dad and I stayed in a few of them during travels to different cities when I was growing up, for birthdays and such. I told them this along with the fact that I had even stayed at the W in Chicago.

They pretended to care, or maybe they were tipsy like me, and drunkenly open to the all the world offered them. They must have been because I invited them back to my place for a drink and they accepted. Before we made our way out of the bar, I excused myself to the alley to smoke with Charlie.

Once the cigarette burned and I had let out a hard pull, I told Charlie about my new friends coming back to the condo. He asked me their names. I told him I forgot. He shook his head and chuckled, then said he would figure them out for me, and we made our way inside to escort our new friends back to my place for more drinks.

***

Carolyn. That was her name. Her husband was Nathan. However, in my head I referred to him as 'the doctor.' She walked around my living room slowly, and I watched in earnest as she intently encountered my condo's interior. I noticed how long her legs were. The slit in her dress went all the way to her hip. The way she stood–legs crossed, her right heel perched behind her left, while she tried to make sense of the oil painting hung above the couch, a painting Charlotte wasn't particularly fond of being our main display–opened the slit to reveal the toned musculature of her leg, from her thigh through her calves, down to her ankles.

The sound of the men popping champagne came from the kitchen, followed by boyish giggling. Carolyn made her way to my bookshelf, admiring the titles that haunted me. She fingered the spines of the Russian literature section before moving to philosophy and sliding out a book by Martin Buber. She spent a long while reading from a dog-eared page, glancing at me occasionally as I stood stupidly, clasping my hands. She put the book away and asked me about the painting. I explained it was a family heirloom painted by a great uncle of mine who had stayed childless and single his whole life.

Charlie and the doctor came into the living room bearing French 75s for each of us, disrupting the conversation I was having with Carolyn about the inflammatory emotion of the piece. She told me she found it gripping but understood why Charlotte didn't. It's not that Charlotte didn't like it, she just didn't think it belonged as the center piece in our living room. I didn't bother explaining that to her.

We sat with our drinks, Carolyn on the couch next to me. The couch was an antique passed down from my mother. It was red and suede with mid-century modern dark wood feet and bronze bezels across the frame. The doctor sat in the chair next to her, Charlie in the chair next to me. The chairs were green and leather with mid-century modern wood legs and bronze bezels across the frame. They were also passed down from my mother.

Charlie was intoxicated at this point, and I was worried about what he might say. My instincts did not fail me. Charlie wasted no time to break in and say, "Del's wife is in Seattle cheating on him right now. Can you believe that? I don't blame her." He paused before adding, "I actually like Charlotte a lot. She's a good woman."

"She's not cheating on me, Charlie. Leave it alone." I urged him.

Carolyn and Nathan both sat forward. Carolyn had a devious smile on her face as she looked at me and asked, "Then what is she doing in Seattle?"

"I don't know," I said with a shrug.

The doctor blurted out, "How do you not know what your wife is doing on the other side of the country? You just let her fly to a different city without knowing why?"

"I don't let my wife do anything. She does what she wants." I snapped back with my eyes locked on his.

Carolyn threw her hand in the air and said, "Good on you! That's the way it should be." Her husband gave her a condescending look and she added, "You trust her, right Del?"

"Sure."

I noticed Carolyn was sitting closer to me now. The doctor didn't seem to care. Her posture leaned in my direction; her legs were crossed with her feet pointing toward mine. While Charlie and the doctor talked about God knows what, I shifted my seating, so my thigh subtly pressed against Carolyn's. No one noticed. With a smirk on her face, Carolyn was the only one to tell it was a conscious move. Even I hoped it wasn't. I didn't know why I did it, and I knew I wouldn't do anything more. I needed the touch of a woman whose mind lived on my own wavelength. I thought about Charlotte. She wasn't cheating and neither would I be–but I didn't move my thigh.

"My wife's pregnant," Charlie beamed. They raised their glasses, and I followed suit.

"Congrat-ulations!" Carolyn said, a master of repartee. "We've never really considered having kids, have we, dear?" She glanced at her husband, who was preoccupied with a print I had framed on the wall of a group of nuns smoking cigarettes.

"That's funny," the doctor muttered under his breath. "How about another round, Charlie? What do you say?"

The guys went to make another drink. Carolyn shifted her hand to my inner thigh. My biology went against my psyche as I looked into her eyes. Or, I should say, she looked into mine. A grin formed on her lips as her pupils followed mine while I subtly shook my head. Her hand remained. I was at odds with myself. She knew.

My phone buzzed in my pocket, so I pulled away to dig it out. It was Johnny. I stood up and walked out of the room to answer it, leaving Carolyn alone. Before I put the phone to my ear, I glanced around the corner of the hall to check on her. She was content with her own company. Unbothered, she shifted her gaze back to the painting, to the nuns, and back to the painting.

Johnny wanted to know if I was home and if he could stay the night. I asked him what was wrong with his hotel. He told me nothing, he just missed me. I replied that I was slightly inebriated and had guests over. He answered, "Even better! I'd like to down a pint myself." And he was on his way.

I walked back to the living room to see the men had returned to their seats. Their conversation carried over from the kitchen. Carolyn leaned forward to assert herself between the two men, but their eyes were locked together like freshmen roommates who'd just learned they both love Derrida. I sat beside Carolyn once again. Close but not touching. What I really wanted was to talk to her more.

The doctor revealed his current area of study revolved around Black humanism, and Charlie quickly steered the topic of conversation into pacifism. When Charlie asked if he was a pacifist, the doctor replied, "Not quite." Now, I couldn't understand why Charlie was so concerned with the growing appreciation of pacifist philosophy, but he became so passionate and loud and domineering of the conversation that I looked at Carolyn and raised my brow. She seemed to be pleasantly entertained by the conversation. No dog in the fight, just excited for blood. I didn't like blood.

So far, the doctor was in strong agreement with everything Charlie was saying, nodding and cheering, "Precisely!" like a populist politician with every point he made. There was no way they understood each other, but alcohol had a knack for creating imprudent characters, leading to new enemies, or, in this case, new friends. I sat there and sipped my drink, wondering when Johnny would show up.

"Well, Christ said to turn the other cheek, now, didn't he?" Carolyn asked as she unraveled and extended her hand to the air, turning her head, too, to offer up the other side of her face for our beholding. Charlie had turned his attention to pacifism infiltrating the Christians. She replied so matter-of-factly that I smirked out of impulse. She winked at me, and my heart lurched against my chest. Was this woman the dragon or the gold? I could feel my body inching toward her.

The only reply Charlie could come up with was, "Well, that's not what he meant!" That was always the argument. Who knows if he even said it, let alone what he might have meant?

"I agree with the religious on one point and that's that all of this is about love. At the center of it all, love. I just learned this phrase quite recently, pardon my poor German, '*Liebe ist ein welthaftes Wirken!*' Love, love, all the way down, boys, and love and fear are fighting, but love will end the war."

When she didn't translate, the men questioned, "German? What does it mean?"

She grinned in satisfaction.

"How recently did you learn that one?" I asked, knowing.

The energy was shifting. I was wonderfully inebriated and raised my glass.

"May the present carry on if only through encounter!"

Charlie and the doctor reluctantly put their glasses to mine and Carolyn's as she cheered, "Wax poetic, Del, wax poetic!"

The room quieted down as we took a moment to sip our drinks. The doctor seemed to have taken interest in me. I could feel his staring. It didn't seem like envy, at least not in relation to Carolyn. I leaned into my suspicions and took a jab.

"I wouldn't expect a university man to be so encouraged by violence," I said. Now Carolyn was the one with the smirk.

He pulled back in his chair, "I can't say I was, early in my studies. But even philosophers must grow up and live in the real world. Of course, I don't support war like these blazoned nationalists. It's not nationalist pride. It depends on who's fighting, in the end. Some wars must be fought to bring about freedom. Some things have to be burned down to bring about progress. You are a progressive, aren't you, Del?"

Finally, I saw Charlie squint his eyes, that look of a drunk man who feels as though he's been conned. He stayed silent, it was my question to answer.

"In many respects, sure. I'm certainly not a liberal. More so an idealist...but I'm afraid that's worse...but you, you call yourself a humanist? Dr., you are a contradiction!"

Charlie and Carolyn lurched upright with swelling, excited eyes. Even I was taken aback by the words shot out of my mouth like a bullet from a gun.

The doctor smiled. "I'm aware. Are you?"

A knock came at the door. I saw Charlie ease his hand onto his holster. I told him to relax, it was just Johnny. I opened the door and found everyone had followed me. There was a commotion of hugs and introductions. Johnny immediately took command of the room. I expected Carolyn to flaunt over him, but my judgement of her was wrong again. She was cordial, even engaging with him, but her energy still pointed at me.

Johnny took a shot of tequila and then another. To everyone's startled response, he replied, "I've obviously got some catching up to do," as he grabbed a beer. We returned to the living room and Johnny sat in Carolyn's spot on the couch. I expected Carolyn to sit on her husband's lap. I even offered to grab another chair from the dining table, but she denied it and squeezed between me and Johnny, forcing us to be pressed against each other.

I hid my discomfort for the rest of the cocktail party. Charlie had grown quiet ever since Johnny arrived. I imagined he knew Johnny would take the doctor's side now that they had realized their point of difference and avoided any more political chatter. He was outmatched and knew it wasn't worth picking a fight.

Johnny and the doctor got along okay, but it was clear Johnny and Carolyn had more charisma. Now it was the three of us caught up in the spirit of drunken connection. It was as if the couch sitters had slipped into a different room as we bounced between Freud and Audre Lorde, making connections only intoxicated people could make, none of us admitting we were not well versed in either of them. The doctor, who had probably read the most of the psychoanalyst and the poet-philosopher, didn't involve himself in our conversation. He must've been bored because he stood up and said he'd like to leave.

"I'd like to stay a little longer," Carolyn told him.

"I'm quite alright with that but I don't want you walking to the hotel alone this late."

"Del will walk me, won't you Del?"

I urged myself to say no, but all that came from my lips was, "Of course." The doctor left and it was now just Carolyn, Johnny, Charlie, and me.

We thought Charlie had gone off to the restroom but when he didn't come back for a while, Johnny went to check on him and reported he had passed out in my bed. We tried to think of a childish prank to pull on him, but Johnny decided we were above those kinds of things, and then he joined Charlie in the bed. I would be sleeping on the couch then, I reckoned.

Alone with Carolyn, we sat quietly, occasionally sipping our drinks. We were on to bourbon now. I knew few women who took their whiskey neat.

She walked over to the record player and looked through my small stack of old classics and new vinyl. From a pile of French records I'd gotten for cheap—they were mistreated and stored in torn up sleeves—she pulled out an Emma Liébel record.

Finally, I recognized the song that had been playing in my heart from the moment I laid eyes on her. Not Liébel, but the one that lay now exposed in the gap of Liébel. Not a record I'd gotten for cheap either, but one I kept in mint condition, unplayed, *La Javanaise*.

She placed Liébel on the turntable. The record spun and, with a casual trepidation, she placed the needle into the grooves of the vinyl. The sound emanated with a crack.

Pour rendre plus jolie toute la vie
Pour que tout s'harmonise se poétise
Des fleurs suffisent sans aucun artifice
Elles les ravissent et rajeunissent

She returned to the couch, and we engaged the lineaments of the other's face.

Votre robe Madame je le proclame
Vous fait une silhouette vraiment coquette
Mais incomplète

The sound of the song disappeared into the distance, a faint echo in the silence.

Il vous faut je le jure à la ceinture
Une parure

As I took in her image, I began to see the contours of her personality. I noticed the smoothness of her forehead where other women her age had wrinkled, her almond shaped eyes bearing the green of Canadian evergreens, her nose—small but pointed, and her lips, wide and heart-shaped, as full on the top as on the bottom...

Et séduisez-les coquettes
Auprès de vos gorgerettes

The music concluded with an abrupt scratch, leaving only the white noise of the record spinning. I mustered up the courage to tell her I would feel more comfortable if we walked to the hotel.

"You're scared of me," she insisted.

"Excuse me?"

"At first, you were intrigued with me, but now you think you have me figured out, and you're fearful of whoever it is you think I am."

"Not true."

"Then explain your change in posture toward me."

"I'm only afraid of myself."

Then she kissed me on the lips. I drew in to her sudden release. She stood and said, "I'm worthy of fear. Now, walk me home."

The street was dark under the impervious city's glow. We walked slowly, silently, her arm weaved in mine. I thought grossly of myself for my lack of discomfort. Carolyn was quite comfortable herself, asking me, "How'd you and Charlotte meet?"

The directness took me by surprise. It struck me that she'd used my wife's name. Using her name was strange and disorienting. I'd assume someone who had just kissed me would not want to name the 'other.' Instead, I would have expected her to choose the abstract and impersonal 'wife.' She said her name as if Charlotte was a friend and not a person she had betrayed.

"We knew each other growing up—went to the same schools and church. We dated off and on through the years, long before any mature person would consider it actual dating. She wasn't my first kiss, but I was hers. That always bothered her, I think. We went to different universities, though we had fallen off before then. I went out of state, and she came here to Atlanta. While I was at school, I guess I thought about her a lot and no other girl I dated at school seemed to compare. Graduate school brought me to Atlanta, though she had moved back home with her mom. Well, I went home one weekend, and Mom convinced me to go to church—I think it was Easter or something. Anyways, I obliged.

And she was there. I guess I was surprised she was there; organized religion was never her thing, but it felt like it had to be divine providence if it happened at church. We went to dinner that night and a few more nights during the next week. It seemed like the timing was right, so she moved in, and we hurried the wedding along to appease our parents. That's been our story for the past six years. Seven in June. We would have pushed it off till September, but Charlie wouldn't have come if it was during football season." I paused. "I'm not sure if that's a joke."

"And how long did you date before you proposed?" She tightened her arm in mine as if she needed support up the incline of the street.

"Well, she proposed. We were fighting because I told her I couldn't handle the stress our parents–mostly my mom–were putting on us to not 'live in sin.' I wasn't ready for marriage. I knew that, but I was stressed, and I wasn't going to kick her out. So, she says, "Let's just get married," and I say, "Yes." She moved in two weeks after we ran into each other at church. She proposed a month after that, and we were married two months after that. It was a small wedding. Charlie was my best man. Johnny was ordained by an online website just so he could marry us. Mom wanted the preacher from our home church to do it, but that's not what Charlotte and I wanted. Johnny is the closest thing to a secular pastor we know anyways, and it just worked out."

"Three months together and you were married. Do you regret rushing it?"

I hated her line of questioning, but I didn't find any ulterior motive beyond pure curiosity.

"That's what fools do, I suppose. I'm not one to have much regret. Things are the way they are, and it can't be changed."

"You sound like you haven't convinced yourself."

"The thing is, it doesn't seem like we rushed it. I fell for her at sixteen and never stopped for the years we were apart. I remember the day it happened. We'd snuck out from the beach cabin we were staying at with her mom's family. The morning sky was still dark. From the sand dunes, we watched the most majestic sunrise I've seen in my life. The gray sludge sky disappeared as if God woke up and blew the darkness away, replacing it with a golden light. For the first time in my life, especially amidst that teenage angst, I felt like myself, and it was special that Charlotte shared that with me.

"We went on a long drive after that, down the scenic route. I felt like a kid, and I felt okay with it. People always told me growing up how mature I was. I was an adult before puberty. So, I felt free that day. I could be stupid and mindless and unburdened. And in love.

"The ironic thing is how adult we were acting. She opened up to me that morning in a way she hadn't before. I did too, but it seemed like everything I had to say was abstract—sterile and existential. She talked about her dad. I didn't know anything about him or where he was, and she didn't really either because he was always moving. At that point, he'd lived in Florida, Texas, even L.A. But she missed him. I always took her silence on the subject as anger, but I realized then that it was grief. I fell in love with her that day in a most superficial teenager kind of way. But it was real too, and I know I will always love her. My mind was opened up that day to what was possible in life, with love. I almost feel like I've spent all my life chasing that moment, that feeling.

"It did feel like we started over when we came back together—we were different people after all, and those feelings persist today. It was that moment on the beach that brought us back together, and even if our love isn't the kind that's supposed to keep us together, that love won't go away."

Carolyn was quiet. We passed over a crosswalk. The pedestrian signal was broken and blinked the number '49' over and over.

Then she asked me, "So, what is the problem?"

As we reached the sidewalk, a driver laid on their horn. Not at us. Some other driver wasn't paying attention. I waited for the calm of silence to return.

"I wish I could put it to words."

I was thinking about that day, and the memory I wouldn't share. Of me peeing on the sand dunes—and into the wind. Charlotte laughing at me as urine blew everywhere. I wouldn't share it with her because it was weird and gross and the truest intimacy I've ever known, even if that intimacy seemed unrecoverable. Just a memory.

We arrived at the grand hotel bearing a large exterior elevator lit up with bright lights. A vibration of jazz rumbled through the street from the hotel bar, but it was subtle. The street was thick with silence. She looked at me and I looked at her. We continued walking.

Having walked for a block and a half without a word, I spoke out of a compulsive mechanism that activates when I'm feeling awkward and in my head, "I wouldn't sleep with you."

"That's not what this is," she replied, predicting my words.

"I like you too much."

"Yes, I know what you mean."

"No, it's like we understand each other. I don't like you; I respect you. You're attuned to the world the way I want to be. You pay attention. You're a person, self-defined. I want to be a person."

"Del," She touched my hand.

"It makes it all the harder to not want to, you know, but even more important we don't."

"It wouldn't be worth it as a one-time thing."

"Yes, exactly."

We crossed through the big iron gate and into the dimly lit park. It was closed, but that didn't mean anything.

"Nathan and I struggle to connect because he doesn't see me as an intellectual being. I feel he doesn't respect my thoughts because I'm less educated, and, though he'd never admit it, I'm a woman. That's why he took interest in you, actually. Because you're a well-studied man. But no, I don't have any degrees, but I read and I read, and isn't that enough?"

She had a crease in her eyebrow I took to mean she was really asking me. She needed me to affirm it was, in fact, enough.

"If I've learned anything from my education, it's that years of schooling can make a person a deep well of knowledge, but that doesn't mean they necessarily think better things. Books, on the other hand, while they can do similar things as a university education–they are a main part of the curriculum, after all–make us more human, don't they? I stopped reading books just to learn things from them. Now, I feel books provide me with the time to contemplate who I am and how I ought to exist in the world."

I believed this. That was part of the reason I dropped out of my graduate program. They taught me how to really read a book that first year, and that was all I needed. I respected the university system, but I didn't want to be them. If I'd graduated, I probably would have been tricked into doing my PhD. Then I would be a professor. Then I would never leave.

"Quite right." She turned to face me, and I thought she might try to kiss me. Instead, she kept her gaze locked with my eyes. "You're a complicated man, aren't you? Worthy of fear but there is no need. And you really are a poet under the influence, someone ought to call the police."

Though it was impossible, I felt sober. "I think I'm more akin to a cliché than a poet, but whatever you say."

She shook her head and said, "If only our ships had passed in the daylight before we wore our rings. You intrigue me, Del. I quite feel like neither of us are very well understood by anyone, but it does seem I know you and you know me."

"I love my wife."

"I know, but–"

"But?"

"But what does that mean to a guy like you?"

That phrase, *a guy like you*, tumbled around in my mind.

"I love my wife, Carolyn."

From where we stood, a dim white light glowed from a telephone pole over that controversial monument of the confederate soldier, hesitant to lay down arms, while the angel of peace towered over him. The light hit the top of Carolyn's head, though it was fragmented with shadows of the olive branch in the angel's hand.

"I know. It's just nice to be seen."

I walked her back to the hotel. We didn't exchange goodbyes. We didn't have to, but she kissed my cheek. I nodded slowly, her smile striking to the depths of my soul. Then she turned and walked away. So god-damned certain. She disappeared through the revolving door, and I walked away. At the corner of the next block, I turned back to see the exterior elevator glide to the top floor. The song felt over, but I walked in silence listening for its melody.

Hands in my pockets, eyes on the sidewalk, I wandered till I was home.

Amir was waiting for me at the door. He gave me a condescending glare, like he was mad at me for staying out so late. I scooped him up and laid him with me on the couch while I looked across the city covered in hazy lights. Soon, Amir was purring his motoring purr against my chest, and we were both asleep.

***

My head throbbed as I opened my eyes to the morning light. I could feel the shriveled blood vessels around my temple pulsating. It felt like a grandfather clock ticking against my brain. I vowed once again to not drink so much. Charlie and Johnny were still passed out on my bed. I drank a large glass of water and started the boiler to make my coffee. Once it finished brewing, I slid out to the balcony quietly, coffee and book of poetry in hand. My mind and gut were marked by a subtle dizziness. I glanced over my unfinished elegy from the day before. Then, I flipped to the dog-eared page and set to work on *monsieur* Baudelaire.

The demon sits with me excited to no end;
Unseen but known as to the air surrounding;
I breathe him in, my lungs fraught with fire
A red coal burning an unthinkable desire..

  I thought of Carolyn. I had no idea what to make of her. She seemed like a dream; not in an idyllic sense, but in a way that seemed only my unconscious mind could have imagined a woman quite like her. Embarrassment flushed over me as I reflected on the way I spoke to her. Like a teenager who thinks they're deep. Like me, as a teenager. She didn't seem to mind. I guess she, too, spoke that embryonic language that comes from my lips when I try to put to words what is better left as feeling. It didn't help *I was drunk*.

He knows my love for the Artful,
Appearing as her beauty, stealing her seduction
And, crawling within my dark chasm
Stirs my heart with romantic chances

  I wondered if Charlotte really was cheating on me. I wondered what she would think of last night's rendezvous. Of course, I would tell her. She wouldn't mind something so trivial as a kiss, but maybe she'd know it was more. Maybe she'd know that I'd met someone with whom she can't compete. But I love Charlotte. I'm dedicated to her regardless.
  Marriage. What an institution. Bless the God of Abraham for getting me into this state of affair.

He leads me thus, directly to God's cross
Perplexing and exhausting my aloneness, at the center
Of a Desert, empty and unending,

  She would return to work soon. And what was I to do? Suffer over more poetry? Try my hand as a writer? Spend more time riding with Sally? I hadn't a clue.

And blinded by his lingering, my vision sets on
Soiled clothes and bloody wounds,
And his holding open the vesture of Destruction.

I took some creative liberties toward the middle of the poem, but something told me, although I removed his exclamation, that Baudelaire intended the poem to land on destruction. Some other translations were more successful than mine but ignored this point, so I ignored them.

Johnny slid the balcony door open and joined me. He sat with his legs crossed, looking across the skyline.

"Last night was indulgent. Did Carolyn stay long?"

"Not really. I walked her home soon after you fell asleep."

"She was interested in you, Del. I hope you didn't do anything regrettable."

I wondered what he imagined us doing. "Nothing too severe, I can promise."

He raised his brow, but let it go.

"I think Charlotte wants a divorce," I said, adding, "She won't say so or ever do it, but she wants it."

"I wouldn't be surprised," he chuckled.

"That makes me feel better. How can you joke about this?"

"What do you expect, Del? You put no effort into having a connection with her. Are you even having sex at this point?" He paused. "I imagine you are, but I doubt either of you enjoy it. Have you spoken to her since she flew to Seattle? What man lets his wife fly across the country without caring why?"

"I don't let my wife—"

"Do anything. She does what she wants. Got it. Do you want to know why she's in Seattle? I called her on my way over here last night. Unlike you, I take an interest in other people's lives. She told me all about this mysterious trip of hers, but I don't think it's my place to tell you."

I stared at him in wanting, but only replied, "Okay."

"I've got to shower. I have to be at church soon."

"Church? You're trying that again?"

"No. The elders at the Presbyterian church on Peachtree Street are consulting with me and asked me to sit in this morning."

"Good for them to go beyond Christendom, but how could you possibly help them?"

"You never tried to be a part of a church in the city, Del. They aren't like home. They actually believe believable things."

He stood from his chair and began toward the door.

"Are they pacifists?" I pressed.

"Very much so. Not like you." An ulterior reply to an ulterior question.

"Are you calling me violent?"

"Take it how you want, but you certainly are no pacifist. You're convinced you are but call it what it is: you're apathetic. You don't see the hurt you could prevent, the hurt you've caused. I don't mean to be so honest, but I've got a throbbing in my head, and I care about you, brother. We don't have to be like Mom and Dad. We can both be whole."

I looked across the skyline to the edge of the earth.

The balcony faced west and had yet to be warmed by the spring sun. An occasional wind would whip through, causing me a slight shiver. Johnny went inside to shower, leaving me with goosebumps prickling against the undershirt I'd slept in.

***

I was captured in a strange occasion of presence soon after Johnny left for his church service. Still on the balcony, I lit a mini cigar and stared out at the city. Out in the distance, peeking through the green forest borough, what looked to me to be a golden cross on top of an Orthodox church reflected the sun into the corner of my eye. I expected people to start rolling in for Divine Liturgy, and for that small part of town to fester with vitality, but nobody showed, and the church corner remained inert. The tradition must be exhausted, and I wasn't bothered. The placidity of the city on Sunday mornings was one of my introverted reliefs. I thought I remembered the Orthodox church dome typically being gold, but this one was bronze. I wasn't familiar with the tradition much at all, though.

I always liked the idea of Atlanta. It is a city in contrast. When you're familiar with Georgia as a state, entering Atlanta is quite another experience. It feels as though you've been transported twenty years into the future. The city just continues to grow and progress despite its location, despite the fact that the rest of the state wants to go back to 1950, despite the fact that their state flag still bears a subliminal ode to the confederacy. A truly progressive culture, not excessive in individual liberty and committed to true equality. And not diseased with the moral posturing of white liberalism native to many of our other major cities. In many respects, Atlanta rose again like a phoenix after Sherman burned her to ashes.

And yet it is, too, a city in despair. Despair at not being itself. An unrealized vision. The people carry an energy for change, progress, no virtue signaling, just being about it. Yet the elected city leaders, who come from among the people, who promise to be for the people, whose platforms are based on 'the people know best,' keep telling the people they don't know what they are talking about.

But the city persists in spite of itself. Especially in our music. Some say Atlanta is defined by its rap. Rap is our sacrament. An audible sign of an inward disposition. The sign and the signified echoing from the perimeter and around the world. More than a sign, a symbol. Atlanta would exist without rap, but the world would not know it. The South always had something to say; in rap, we found our vessel. It feels weird saying 'we' as a white boy from the country, who mostly listens to folk or alt rock or an emotional piano ballad, but this is the culture in which I live. It defines me too. And I enjoy it when André 3000 picks up the flute.

It was no surprise to me that King made his home here, preaching at Ebenezer Baptist with his dad. He was a true pacifist with a strong moral vision. Maybe all of the pacifist talk Charlie kept bringing up was King's dream finally being realized, like an arch toward justice. Johnny was right though. I'm no pacifist. Just passive. The only thing I had in common with King was that I betrayed my wife.

I missed Charlotte. Memories played in my mind from when we were kids acting in love. She is the only woman I have ever loved, but she never was the one. I knew it when she proposed to me, and I said yes. I didn't want to say yes, but I had no reason to say no. And there we were, married for over six passive years, living in an apartment that served only as a convenience, working a job that only provided money. I couldn't think of a single job that would actually fulfill me. Maybe I can't be fulfilled. Not by my wife, my job, my life.

The traffic was building on the interstate below, cars would occasionally honk with impatience as people rushed into the city for another day of quick tourism. The blare of an alarm came from the fire station and the big red truck came flying out with urgency, separating the cars on the side street like Moses slamming down his staff to divide the sea. Thirty seconds later, the truck had made its way so far down the road that the noise was close to ceasing. As I watched it disappear into the horizon, the corner of my eye continued to be struck by the glare of the cross.

A moment of self-actualizing came without tears. I wanted to cry but couldn't. The tears rarely come. Often, I feel them form behind my eyes and remain there, weighing my eyes down, until the moment has passed and they retreat to wherever they came. I thought of the damage I'd done–what Johnny said–I don't know what damage I've done, but I imagine he's right. He's certainly right to suggest I could have prevented damage. Can a pacifist prevent damage? Maybe I don't understand pacifism. I imagine they'd be better referred to as peacemakers. But the act of making peace is not like throwing your unfolded laundry in the closet and hiding it behind the door. It's more like grabbing the bully from behind and holding on for dear life until he calms down and is able to talk to the scrawny kid who accidentally bumped into him. Peacemaking means getting involved.

My eyes lightened. I looked across the city, content with my deduction on peacemaking. Peacemaking means getting involved. "The time is always right to do what is right," came to mind. I couldn't remember who said it, but I wanted to do what was right. I just needed to figure out what 'right' was.

***

Johnny was gone by the time I stepped back inside. Charlie was sitting on my couch watching the late-night show from the previous evening, drinking coffee, and eating a bowl of granola.

He looked at me and I could sense a banal platitude coming as he opened his mouth to speak, but I cut him off, "Charlie, I've got to divorce Charlotte." Before he could react, I added, "For her sake."

He stopped munching on his cereal, then mumbled "Hmm." After swallowing, he added, "How come?" I pressed my hands against my side and took a seat where Nathan sat the night before.

"Because we're miserable together. We both want this, but she just wouldn't ever say so. I wouldn't doubt it if she were with some man in Seattle.

I wouldn't doubt it at all. Not that that matters. I all but cheated on her last night."

As if not hearing my last remark, Charlie replied, "Del, you aren't miserable together. You're miserable apart. You've never really been together. Maybe when you were kids, but you were kids!" He took a matter-of-fact crunch of cereal and dropped the spoon into the bowl of milk. A few small chunks of oat swirled slowly with the spoon's impact.

"That's certainly the romantic way to look at it, huh? What am I supposed to do with that? Would it not be a true divorce then, only a legal matter?"

"Oh Del, divorce won't solve your problems."

"Charlie, if we've never been together, what's the point of staying together?"

"Look, you don't know what it means to be married. The both of you have accepted this idea of marriage as a sort of long-suffering, where you live together and try not to get in each other's way until you die. That's not marriage."

"I suppose you'll tell me all about what marriage is, then? You've obviously got it figured out. Reece pretends to submit to you while you surrender to her every beck and call to avoid her tightening the leash."

"You're a foolish man. Absolutely ignorant! And childish. Reece has given me the life of my dreams. I couldn't be freer. You wouldn't understand, so send that nonsense to hell." He grabbed his cereal bowl and dropped it in the kitchen sink, then he left. He must have had Reece pick him up. I didn't hear from him for the rest of the day, and that was fine with me.

I took a long shower, letting the water hit me directly on the crown of my head while I leaned against the cold, tiled wall. The heat put me into a daze and fantasies began to roll through my mind. I imagined Nathan and Carolyn out eating brunch, laughing, 'in love,' but Carolyn still thinking of me. Remembering last night, I saw her again, staring at the painting on my wall, my eyes following the slit in her dress all the way up, she scaled the tips of her fingernails across her thigh to the beginning of the slit and began to lift it higher, higher, higher, revealing more and more of what was hidden underneath. We pressed into the couch, her hand on my inner thigh, I grabbed her hand to remove it and she led it to the slit and slowly moved it across her smooth soft skin, higher, higher, higher.

The water heater ran out and I was jarred back to the shower by the rush of cold water. After getting dressed, I texted Carolyn to see what she and Nathan were doing.

"Flying back to Chicago soon. Grab lunch with us!" She replied immediately.

***

We met at a Latin American restaurant on the block opposite their hotel and sat on the front patio. Carolyn was as animated as the night before. Her eyebrows stretched high behind her large, ombre-tinted butterfly shades. Her lips concealed in cardinal red turned up slightly at the corners, because for every emotion she experienced, she added a positive twist. The doctor struck me as more pensive than the night before. He was lacking the copious amounts of alcohol in his system required to blithely lower himself to our level of being. He didn't seem to care to be involved in our conversation, and any time Carolyn would ask him, "Isn't that right, darling?" he would join us briefly to say, "That's right," and then he would disappear again into the structure of the building across the street, or the conversation of the two gentlemen at the magazine stand.

I decided to share my new peacemaking strategy of divorcing Charlotte. This seemed to bring the doctor's attention back to us. I told them it felt like the right thing to do–for Charlotte's sake. Carolyn looked at me disconcertedly. The doctor chipped in, "Well, why not? It does seem like the right thing to do. You don't strike me as the marriage type, Del. Surprised you made it this long." Carolyn was apprehensive to reply, and I had the feeling she'd rather talk to me privately. The doctor seemed content with the conversation as Carolyn sat leaning all the way back in her chair, slowly sipping her gin and tonic.

After we finished eating, I insisted on paying the bill. It felt like the right thing to do, despite the unsettling fact that they were in a better financial position than me. The doctor cordially blurted, "Good man!" Then he ran off to the hotel to grab their luggage.

"It's not the right thing to do," she responded as soon as her husband had disappeared down the street, "And I won't leave Nathan for you, so don't be so foolish to even think of that."

"This isn't about you. Maybe I didn't care to deal with it before last night, but this problem existed long before you came around. We both need to be free from each other. And I'm starting to realize that the freedom is worth it."

"Oh, don't start with that shit! If you want to be free, then take your marriage seriously. My God, you didn't experience freedom when you were single, did you? So why do you think you will after a divorce?"

"And you're so free, then? Because you can kiss other men and your husband not care? That sounds like dissatisfaction on both ends to me." I paused before adding, "So don't give me a lecture." She winced. I had hit a point of distress.

"Ah, so that's his problem. The doctor is too engaged with his work. Too passionate about his studies and no passion for you."

"You amaze me, Del. I've never met someone so insensitive. I'd be content to tell you to go to hell, but I think you're already there."

"Why not leave him, huh?"

She sat with her arms crossed. Her face effused sincerity and pain. "No, I won't even consider it."

"Well, if you can't be honest with yourself then I don't trust you to be honest with me." I got up and walked in the direction of my building.

I had only walked a block, when she grabbed my hand and spun me around. I pulled her close and she pressed in. I grabbed the back of her neck with one hand and her waist with the other. Our bodies hovered delicately close. She pulled away slowly, leaning her head into my shoulder.

"He's never seen me. He makes me feel so simple–so plain."

"And what would a life like ours look like, the two of us, together?" A sharp pain tightened around my chest as this new life flashed through my mind. I saw us doing it all together, side by side, life and life abundant, and I felt Charlotte's presence following me everywhere like the ghost of our relationship. Her soft, cracking voice whispering in my ear, *Don't you remember when you saw it all with me?*

"No! You're speaking foolish again. Don't act like we know each other enough to throw our lives away. We don't know each other at all. I only trust you because I see myself in you. All of me I've neglected, manifested in you."

I understood what she meant. It scared me.

My phone vibrated in my pocket, but I left it unattended. I grabbed Carolyn's hand and led her into the alley. I placed my hand on the back of her head and pressed her body against the brick, letting my impulses drive as we kissed again and again, as she ran her fingers through my hair. She brought me closer and closer. I wanted all of her and I wanted her to have all of me, immediately and forever. At the same time, I saw the ghost. It was crying out, breathless and voiceless, stripped of its vocal cords and unable to dissipate into the light.

My phone rang through. I ignored it, but the caller rang again. I pulled away to pull it out of my pocket. I missed the call from Charlotte but read her text: Just landed. Meet you at the south terminal.

"Shit." My voice echoed through the alley.

"What is it?"

"My wife's plane just landed. I'm late to pick her up."

"Perfect! You can drop me and Nathan off. We'll be your excuse."

Charlotte would still be mad, but her anger would only show itself passively. I could manage that.

Too fearful to call her, I texted back: 'Promised friends I would drop them off at the airport. They're running behind, be there in 15.'

Carolyn ran off to grab Nathan while I retrieved my car. Thirty minutes later, I pulled into the terminal to find my wife waiting on a bench. Nathan and Carolyn hobbled out; I introduced them briefly. Carolyn acted as if she were reunited with her childhood best friend, giving her a hug, and telling her how she had heard so much about her. Charlotte offered a confused but genuine smile.

I hugged Carolyn goodbye, catty-cornered, the way friends hug, and she whispered in my ear that she would text me. I squeezed her gently with my hand and pulled away. The doctor had semi-engaged Charlotte in small talk about Seattle and the lectures he'd given at the university there. I broke into the conversation to shake his hand. His grip was firm. Then they grabbed their suitcases, said goodbye one last time, and–with a gloss to Carolyn's eyes and her lips curved up–walked away.

***

The car ride was quiet. Charlotte didn't ask any questions about my new friends, and I didn't ask about her trip.

As I pulled on the interstate, I slammed my hand on the steering wheel and said, "Oh! You won't believe it."

She turned away from the window and looked at me. Her face was empty.

"Charlie and Reece are pregnant!"

Her eyebrows scrunched but her eyes seemed to glimmer. "That's wonderful." She replied subtly and paused, holding the same disoriented face, then she returned her gaze to the other side of the window.

I pulled into the parking garage and parked the car. After grabbing her luggage from the trunk, we rode in silence up the elevator to our floor. When we entered the apartment, she went straight to the shower. I tossed her bags in the bedroom and joined Amir on the couch. Resisting the temptation to pour a glass of cognac, I decided instead to smoke a mini cigar.

My heart was beating rapidly, and my hands had a clammy tremor as I tried to light the tobacco with a match out on the balcony. I didn't think I would be nervous for the conversation ahead, but my body was telling me otherwise. I stood on the precipice of change, for good or bad, whether I acted or not, there would be regrets either way. But I had to act. I had to. I didn't know exactly what was necessary to say. I thought I may not tell her about Carolyn at all and simply tell her I wanted to separate. Thank God we didn't have kids. That mere fact convinced me that divorce would be the moral decision in this situation—for the both of us.

"We need to talk," she said, startling me to the point of dropping my cigar. I watched as it rolled to the edge of the balcony before dropping to the abyss below.

I looked up at her to see her wearing gray sweat shorts and a cami tank top. Her feet were bare.

I was able to find my voice and uttered, "Right. So, I agree." Finding the confidence to speak directly, I continued, "I don't think there's any reason to bounce around it, so I'll just say it. I think we should separate. It would be good for both of us. You, obviously, should keep the condo, and I'll figure something out. We aren't in love, Charlotte. I know you know this, but it's time we stop acting as if this life is good enough for us. For Christ's sake, I let you go to Seattle without even questioning why! We've never really been together, have we? It's just been a matter of convenience this whole time."

I turned to the skyline and took a breath. I opened my mouth to continue, but as I did, I turned back to see her. Her cheeks were flush and damp with teardrops. I shut my mouth.

She leaned her weight against the edge of the balcony door and hid her face with her palms, not making a sound, the teardrops leaking through. My ears hyper-fixated on and amplified the thudding sequence of tears splashing against the floor. I stared at my feet, feeling like a fool.

Then she replied, "Yes, I do think you might be right..." Her voice fought through her sniffling, "But I'm pregnant."

II

With my eyes set on the ceiling, the weekend rushed through my mind as one long trek up a mountain of enlightenment which ended with me slipping over the side of a cliff down into Gehenna. I was lying on Charlie's couch. Charlotte had taken the car to her parents, but I didn't want to be in the house alone. So, I called Charlie, and he brought me back to his place. The car ride was uncomfortable. Charlie had every right to deal with me shamefully, but instead he gave me a non-judgmental silence. Reece wouldn't look at me when I walked through the door, and she stayed in their room as Charlie and I sat on the back porch.

All I could see around me was the blackness of the room. My head hurt from the reservoir of tears that pressed relentlessly against my eyes as we sat there. Perhaps I cried, I don't remember. To my comfort, Charlie didn't try to say anything. I wailed about how foolish of a man I was. I felt worthless. Charlie walked over to me and placed his hand on my shoulder before saying, "You'll make this right," and went to join Reece in the bedroom. That was my attempt to do what was right.

My phone was cushioned between me and the couch. I grabbed it to text Carolyn. A text from her was already waiting for me. It read: 'We talked at the gate. I told him I wanted to separate... He said alright. What a man, huh? You were right, Del. I didn't go back to Chicago. I'm staying with my mom for now. Talk soon.'

I tossed the phone across the room and returned to staring at the ceiling.

My eyes opened to the sunshine peeking through the blinds. I couldn't tell if I had slept, but I felt rested. Reece was in the kitchen cooking eggs and bacon. There was coffee sitting on the ottoman still emitting a thorough steam when I sat up. Reece was quietly pacing around the kitchen as she cooked. While I was sipping on my coffee, Charlie came walking down the stairs as he tied his purple silk tie. He nodded to acknowledge me and went and kissed Reece in the kitchen. He took a seat at the kitchen bar and Reece placed a plate of food in front of him and another one in front of the stool beside him. I joined him, and we ate in silence. Reece returned to their room, while Charlie scrolled through the news headlines on his tablet.

"I was wrong about Christians being more pacifist these days. They aren't all pacifists. This pastor in Tennessee is calling for America to go to war with China. 'Cause they're communist, or something. Seems uncalled for. No reason to poke a sleeping dragon. Volatile, these Christians can be, huh? What'd they teach you while you were at school? Imperial arbitrariness or weak pacifism?" I don't know why he always had to ask questions like that. He knew how I felt.

"Charlie, you're a Christian. Why do you talk like they're someone else?"

"I'm not like any of them. My faith is personal."

"I see. Is that why you go to church on T.V.?"

"What difference does it make?"

"Do you believe in the resurrection?"

"I don't see why I shouldn't."

"Alright."

I asked him the pastor's name and had to keep myself from laughing. Of course it wasn't funny, but when irony's thrown on you, laughter is a natural impulse. It hadn't been two years since the reports of that pastor's abuses came out.

"The crusader Christ isn't going to die anytime soon," I remarked. Charlie seemed to like that, nodding his head slowly before going back to reading news headlines.

He finished his breakfast and told me he was off to work, patting me firmly on the shoulder. I had to be in the office in an hour, so I dressed in the sports coat and slacks I had brought and was heading out the door to grab better coffee.

"Del." Reece called from behind me.

I removed my hand from the doorknob and turned around slowly.

"I think we should talk before you go."

I nodded and joined her on the couch.

I didn't have a sister growing up, so Reece was the closest thing to a sister I knew. She fended for me in high school and introduced me to friends too old for me to have any business hanging out with. Johnny made his own friends, but Reece made me mine. One of them was Charlie.

Reece was also overprotective of me when it came to girls and, while she never felt she needed to protect me from Charlotte, she didn't care for her much either. She overcame her antipathy when Charlotte came back around after college and accepted her as family once we were married. I always knew that Reece wanted better for me, but she started to really love Charlotte and was just as loyal to her as she was to me.

So, as we sat on the couch, her face showing no sign of emotion, I wondered how she would react.

I felt my hands clam up as she opened her mouth to speak.

"How are you feeling?" I was disarmed by her recognizing my humanity. I naively underestimated how impartial she would treat me. Then again, I can't recount a time when she wasn't levelheaded in handling situations like this.

"Entirely confused. I feel my conscience has abandoned me."

She nodded. "You can't divorce her."

"And why not?"

She sat in thought for a moment. "You shouldn't."

"I can't think of a decision that isn't wrong, Reece. And I haven't a clue which is the lesser evil of the two."

"Why can't you stay with her?"

"We don't belong together." I spoke with certainty. "Charlie was right. We've never really been together. We don't even know each other. And when you've been together for as long as we have, there's a reason we don't. We can't. We live incongruent lives. You've always known she wasn't a good match."

"Oh, don't bring me into this. You didn't listen then so don't pretend to respect my opinions now. Besides, I was wrong. Being married to Charlie for so long has changed my mind."

"You doubted that you and Charlie were good together?"

"Only for a while. Just for a year or two while we were still figuring things out. We were young and full of dreams and sometimes I wondered if he could ever join me in building the life I wanted to live. But I was wrong. He has—and more."

"Well, the longer Charlotte and I stay together, the further the both of us move from our dreams."

"Don't be so dramatic, Del. You don't have real dreams. Your dreams are no different than the fantasies that come to mind when you sleep. Those aren't real."

I tried to interject but she continued, "You live in this abstract world in your head and the people closest to you just want you down here in this one. That's why you don't feel connected to Charlotte. She's a real person. In this world with the rest of us."

"Well, shouldn't I be with someone who also lives in the abstract world?" The image of Carolyn looking at my painting flashed across my mind.

"What a foolish thing to say. I imagine you already have someone in mind, huh? Go ahead and forget about her or you won't make the right decision for your child. Do not let her be in the way, Del. God, I should be mad at you! I am mad, but I hope you know it's because I care about you. And I care about Charlotte, too.

"But listen to me, this fantasy world you spend your time in is keeping you from living, so absolutely not should you leave her for someone who lives on the same plane. You're a prisoner to your conceptual world, not a ruler. If you were free, you could go in between, but you can't."

My face burned.

"Charlotte's real, Del. If you give up on her, you will give up on reality completely. I won't tell you what to do and I won't tell you to do what is best for the child because that decision is rarely what is best for the child. Do what is best for you and for Charlotte. That will be best for the child. For Christ's sake though, don't give up on reality. Grab it for once. Maybe then you'll find freedom."

Her eyes were glossed. My outward expression was glazed and stony, but my soul and my heart and my mind all agreed she was right. I stood up to leave and she hugged me. She was the sister I always needed.

"How are you getting to work?"

"I'm going to call a car on my phone."

"Just take mine." She tossed me her keys.

"Thanks. I'll bring it back soon."

"Yeah, yeah. I'm not going to be leaving the house much without Charlie. Don't worry about it."

I didn't have much time at the coffee shop, so while I waited for my pour-over, I texted Carolyn, "Can I call you after work?" Then I grabbed my coffee and headed for the office. My phone buzzed. I glanced at it quickly. It was Carolyn replying, 'Yes!'

Work dragged on like a rat paralyzed from the waist down. Our office met for a team meeting at eleven and it lasted until one. It could have been five minutes. Or an email. I couldn't recall a thing we discussed, so an email would have been better.

I did have the horrible thought that I would have to continue working here and sitting through these horrid meetings if Charlotte and I really separated. My stomach was growling, and I was frustrated by the time one o'clock came and my boss dismissed us for lunch. When I started out the door, my boss's voice called from behind me, "Del, could you stay behind for a moment? I'd like to have a word." I cursed under my breath and joined her at the table.

"I don't know what to do with you, Del. You're burnt. I've known this since my first week here. I've watched you struggle day after day to sit in your chair and hold your mental breaks under the surface, hidden from the rest of us." She was new in the role of the boss, but her background in finance helped her transfer into the position.

"What are you trying to say?"

She raised her brow and sat back in her chair, straightening out her pantsuit, and said, "I feel like you're done. You've been done. Honestly, you do phenomenal work, and yet you're completely disengaged. I couldn't imagine how good of a job you would do if you actually cared about it."

"How could anyone care about this work!" I drew back and stuttered, "I'm sorry. I don't mean to be so blunt."

"Why are you here?"

I didn't reply.

"Del, I want what's best for you and for the team."

My eyes rolled viscerally. She noticed but let it fall.

"I appreciate your concern, but I don't know what's best for me."

Time seemed to stand still as she stared at me. I kept my face as expressionless as I could. I breathed slowly and prayed for respite.

"How's Charlotte?"

Of the bosses I've had, none asked me anything about my personal life as often as Jasmine. She was probably the only one who remembered my wife's name.

I muttered, "Good. She just spent the weekend in Seattle."

"Yeah? What was she doing there?"

I still didn't know. Did she go there because of the pregnancy? I was curious now. Why didn't I ask her?

Jasmine watched as I disappeared into my mind.

"Del?"

"I don't know!" I cried out and threw my face into my palms.

Jasmine leaned forward on her elbows and let me grieve.

"She's pregnant though."

"Oh, Del."

"I don't think I should have told you that. Oh well."

"I'll keep the secret. I think you should take the day off. Sign on for an hour tomorrow but take the rest of tomorrow off too, okay?"

I nodded.

"We'll meet again on Wednesday. Go get some rest and think things through."

I sat and stared through the large office window. Off in the distance, I could see my condominium. I was there on the couch reading a book, Amir was on my lap. A record spun, humming a soft, reflective classical piece. Perhaps Bach's *Chaconne*. Charlotte was on the other side of the partition in the kitchen scrolling on her phone.

"Go home, Del." Jasmine came back into view. I nodded again and left.

***

I lit a mini cigar as soon as I reached my balcony. Then I texted Carolyn that I was free for the day and to call me when she was able. The afternoon sun pierced the walls of the balcony. It was hot. Sweat built along my arms and soaked into the breast of my shirt. I finished my smoke and went inside.

The phone rang shortly after I laid on the couch. It was Johnny. I wanted to silence it but slid my thumb across the screen.

"I went and saw Charlotte today."

The sound of my muffled gulp and exhalation through my nostrils was an adequate response for him to continue, "I'd like to see you soon so we can talk this through, but I wanted to call you first and see how you were doing."

I don't like phone calls. Never have. It eliminates too many factors necessary for genuine communication, body language and the like, resulting in awkward and dissonant back and forth.

"Charlotte's distraught, so I was hoping you might be as well."

Like that comment, I couldn't measure the balance of intended harshness and satire by tone alone.

I replied, "Mmhmm." It seemed like an appropriate response given the circumstances.

"Well, you don't have to pretend like you are on the outside for me to know you actually are. I'm your brother. You can't fake your feelings to me, and you can't hide them from me either. Why are you like that anyways? How do you feel things and still fake feeling exactly what you're feeling? That sounds exhausting. Anyways, I'm going to see Mom and Dad tonight. I'm having dinner with them. You should meet me there."

"I'll try," I muttered and ended the call.

I thought about taking a nap, but I wasn't tired. I didn't have the mental energy or nostalgia or any inclination for transcendence to read poetry, let alone translate it, so I picked up my worn-out copy of *The Stranger*. I could always relate to Camus' Meursault. Not quite in the way that I thought life was essentially absurdity without extrinsic meaning, even though it sure did seem like it. At least, I haven't found the meaning I'm predisposed to assume is there. Regardless, in Camus' narration of a man passive to social convention, I find alleviation from my own anxieties of feeling like an outsider, and I liked Meursault's smoking ritual. It reminded me of my own.

I didn't really understand the philosophy Camus intended, I just accepted what others said. In all honesty, I didn't care what Camus was arguing. I read him to be seen by the words on the page. I appreciated the brevity of the book, which is why I read it so often. I could finish it in an evening and never have to break the flow of the story by putting it down too soon.

'That evening Marie came by to see me and asked me if I wanted to marry her. I said it didn't make any difference to me and that we could if she wanted to.' I snickered painfully and tossed the book on the chair beside me.

I woke around 9 that night. I had fallen asleep on the couch. Amir was watching me from the cushion above my head. His eyes were telling me to stop being a lazy loaf and to feed him some dinner. "Okay," I told him, but first I checked my phone to see if I had missed Carolyn's call. The only notifications were missed calls from Johnny. He had sent a few texts as well. He was upset that I missed dinner.

In reply, I explained a nap interfered. Text bubbles instantly popped up and left. A second later a thumbs up emoji appeared. I told him I would come see him in the morning. To this he said he was already coming into the city and to meet for coffee at a shop a couple blocks from my home. I accepted and then stood from the couch and went to the kitchen to heat up a frozen dinner. But first, I opened a can of wet food and put it in Amir's bowl.

"You happy?" I asked him. He went to eating it without even a glare of gratitude.

As my meal spun around in the microwave under the dull yellow light, I texted Carolyn, "Are you still planning on calling?" It took her a few minutes to reply, "Not tonight."

I thought about calling Charlie; we hadn't talked since this morning. I realized how ridiculous that was, but it was a long day and we never really talked about the situation other than me vomiting my emotions in a confused, unintelligible stir last night. Now that I've slept and talked to Reece, I cared for his advice. I dialed his number and listened to it ring.

"Yeah?" came a tired groan through the other side of the line.

"Hey."

"What's up, Del? Reece and I are in bed."

Whatever gears turn in your brain that allow you to utter words, mine were locked in place and in need of oil.

"Del?"

"I'm incapable of doing right, Charlie. I give up. I'm willing to do anything to make this right, but how in the hell am I supposed to know what is right? Right? Staying with her could cause our kid to resent the idea of love and not want anything to do with it. They'll just think how terrible marriage must be. But how am I supposed to know that the kid won't have the same perspective if we separate? How could he believe in love then? How do you do it, Charlie? How do you keep choosing Reece?"

"Del, it's late."

"Sorry."

"It's fine. How about you come to dinner Wednesday. We can talk this through."

"Sure."

"Alright, goodnight then." I waited for him to hang up, but his voice came back apprehensively, "And Del?"

"Yeah?"

"The best thing to do for the child is whatever is best for you and Charlotte."

"Yeah, that's what your wife said."

"Well, she's right. I married smart." I could feel him grin before pausing, causing a silence that pricked me like needles against my skin. Then he added, "And I think you did too. I hope you'll come to see that. Goodnight." He hung up, and I was alone again.

I decided to go for a walk. When I exited the condominium, the cool air of the Georgia night swept against my face. I walked a few blocks, passing the hotel that Carolyn and Nathan had vacationed at for the weekend. Carolyn was the mystery I couldn't answer. Had she ruined my marriage or given me reason to make it work? There was no reason in leaving Charlotte for Carolyn; Carolyn would never be happy with me and I her. Right? Wasn't she just a dream manifested in reality? But I still wanted her.

When I returned to the condo, the painting on my wall arrested my attention. It always did, that's why I hung it where I did. But tonight, it gripped me and wouldn't let go. The black strokes intertwined with the red around the edges of the canvas in a circular motion. In the middle, a darkly-tanned figure cried blue tears over a brown cross covered in red oil splotches. This wasn't obvious, of course. It was an abstraction of color, but I could see it and most people could look at it and feel it. It was Christ, dead in the arms of his mother.

I felt the inevitability of death, death that even God couldn't escape. But this God didn't seem to try to escape death, I suppose.

Marriage sure felt like death, a death I could escape, a death I didn't have to experience to begin with, but I did. Christ resurrected though—whatever that says of death, I didn't know—and I didn't know if the resurrection of my marriage was right or the resurrection of who I could have been had I never married.

I smoked on my balcony in the light-polluted city. Then I went to bed.

I woke around 7 and texted Johnny I'd meet him for coffee at 9. Despite having avoided the place since Sunday, my home was a mess. I tidied it up and put everything in functional order before showering and preparing to see my brother.

He was standing outside the shop door when I arrived and grabbed my right arm, giving it a soft, assuring squeeze as his greeting.

"Hey brother." He opened the door for me to go in and patted my back as I entered the café. First, I was rushed by the strong smell of fresh ground beans, then the buzzing of baristas rushing to make all the crafty caffeinated drinks. The espresso machine wailed as it released bellowing steam, calming down with a slow 'tshhh,' as a barista slapped another portafilter with a fresh puck of tamped grounds into the machine's head.

Johnny paid after I objected weakly. Our coffee was brewed and handed over to us. It smelled like blueberries and caramel. We sat on the patio outside. It was a nice day, the sun was shining through the maze of skyscrapers and hitting me warmly on the face. I sipped my coffee and watched a young mother push a stroller bearing bald-headed twins in matching blue joggers.

"Where you at, Del?"

I looked at my brother and replied, "What do you mean?"

"Well, you're not with me in the world where your marriage is falling apart and your wife is pregnant with your child, so where are you?"

"Somewhere where I have less misery, I guess."

I responded to Johnny's silence by returning my gaze to the giggling babies in the stroller.

"I know you care about her."

"Yeah, doesn't matter if I can't act like it. She deserves someone who makes her feel cared for. That's not me."

"You sound like a child."

"What do Mom and Dad think?"

"Honestly, I wish I hadn't told them anything. Dad's as withdrawn as you are, so he understands. And Mom, God, Mom, I think she might be happy about it!"

We both laughed. There was nothing funny about it, but laughing seemed to be the only proper response.

"Well, not really," he continued, "The baby thing has her all confused and upset."

"Sounds right. She never did like Charlotte. You'd think she would, too. I couldn't imagine someone she should like more. She's dreaming if she thinks I should have ended up with a church girl. Could you imagine the hell that would be? Charlotte is the best she could have got. She should count her blessings, you know?"

"Oh brother, do you really think there's a partner out there for either of us that is good enough for our mother? My situation is obviously different. Not that I care what Mom thinks. Not like you do. I see how it might be more difficult for you, being the chosen one and all." He winked.

"And what's that supposed to mean?"

He took a sip of his coffee and shrugged his shoulders. "It's just, I shattered any possibility of being who Mom wanted me to be. Made her lower her expectations and made it easier for her to accept me. Maybe not accept so much, not fully, and thank God she's too passive to bring it up, but she's forced to accept I won't be who she pictured. You, on the other hand, she hasn't given up on your redemption. You still might save us all."

I shook my head. "You're so full of it sometimes."

He leaned forward and got serious. I tilted my head down but turned my eyes up to meet his stare. He met my eye with a gaze that made me feel like he was seeing all the secrets of my psyche. I had to fight myself to not let my eyes bolt away. I forced myself to grin. It was one of those grins that squeeze tight against the leather of your face, not wholly positive and seeming to carry the depths of emotion; a grin of acceptance that life is suffering, but you grin anyways because it's nice, for a moment, to connect with someone. It's a grin of misery, content for a moment of not feeling alone.

Johnny broke back in. "I was proud of you for marrying Charlotte. Truly. I think she brings out a side of you no one else can. A good side, too."

I winced. He could be so cliché sometimes. My grin faded as I looked at the coffee cup in my hands. I twirled it back and forth, watching the coffee swirl around, skating across the edge but not spilling over.

"I don't want to divorce her. I really don't. But neither of us are living the life we dreamed of living. We're still young. There's still a chance for us, but it means we have to go our own way."

"Nonsense, Peter." I couldn't remember Johnny ever calling me by my Christian name. Mom was the only one that ever did, and even she used it sparsely.

"What happened between you and Carolyn?"

"I don't care to talk about it."

"What did you do?"

"We kissed."

"That's all? And how'd that make you feel?"

He was leaned forward, frowning. I looked away.

"I felt free."

"Disgusting. You're not guilty at all about it? How's Charlotte going to feel?"

"I don't feel guilty. I don't think Charlotte will care–especially if we're separated. Honestly, I don't plan on telling her now that we're split up."

"Jesus, Del. You frustrate me so deeply. What are you doing? Do you have a plan? You need to think this through. Not by yourself either, you think like a child. But I'm too annoyed to help you. Not that you would listen to me. Go talk to Charlie or Reece, or even Dad, for God's sake."

He got up and left, leaving his coffee not even half drank. I went back to watching people walk along the sidewalk and paid close attention to a little girl dragging her dad down the street.

***

I went back to my place and ate a sandwich before hopping online to fulfill my hour of duty. For the next fifty minutes, I stared anywhere other than my laptop. Then, after a quick glance at the clock, I rushed to do an hour's worth of work in ten minutes.

The apartment felt small, drenching me in a fit of claustrophobic angst. So, I drove out to the farm. Dad met me at the door and unhooked the screen door for me to come inside.

"Where's Mom?"

"Running errands. Want a beer?"

It was half past one on a Tuesday, but I shrugged my shoulders and replied, "Why not?"

He pulled out a local IPA that neither of us really liked but was the closest thing that both of us would tolerate, and handed it to me. We cracked them open and clinked them together–a tradition we rarely skipped–and dad took a long swig while I took a small sip, trying to hide my recoil to the bitter hops.

I held the can awkwardly, fiddling with the pop-top with my thumb.

53

"So, Johnny told you about me and Charlotte?"

He nodded and took another long sip.

We didn't say anything for a while. We just kind of sat there, drinking our beers, knowing we couldn't change the subject, but not caring to talk about the subject matter.

"Did you ever think about leaving mom?" I figured we were already holding the deck, might as well put the cards on the table.

His face tightened up.

"That wasn't really an option for me. Would've been a waste of time to consider it."

"You at least questioned if you should've ended up with her, right? Doesn't everyone at some point?"

He bit his cheek. "I reckon. Would it have been healthy for me not to? Every man dreams of who he could've been, but those are just dreams."

"I–"

"Look son, I know my marriage to your mom hasn't been the best example for you or Johnny. And I can see why you'd want to leave Charlotte so you don't look like us in 30 years, but..."
He took another sip of beer as if he'd forgotten what the "but" was.

"Do what you want, son, but Charlotte's as good as they come, and I can promise you you won't find better."

"It's hard to believe that."

"Sure it is. But you're gonna learn it whether or not you believe it."
Swig.

"Remember when we used to ride together every Saturday when you were growing up? That was it, wasn't it? Damn, I haven't hopped on a horse in years. Why don't we go ride? You've been thinking too much, and I probably have too. Let's just ride around, get our minds off these things. What you think?"

"Couldn't hurt, I guess."

We went out and I saddled Sally up and led her out of the barn. Dad had a white-haired horse named Bucky who was notorious for throwing everyone off but him. The horse has calmed down over the years. Having heaved himself up in the saddle, I thought how nice it was to see my father up there so high; confident looking, sturdy. Still as strong as I remembered when I was young. Bucky looked content to be rejoined with his owner. The horse let out a giddy snort before Dad clicked his heel to the beast's side and we started strolling through the pasture.

I felt connected to Dad in our silence. We didn't share a word, communicating occasionally by pointing out a rabbit rushing through the tall grass toward its home, or noticing the growth of an interesting tree. The longer we rode, the closer I felt to him. It was nice not having to talk and yet feel like we were working on our relationship. I didn't have a relationship like that with anyone else. Everyone else always needed to know how I was feeling to relate to me at all. We were like dogs to each other. Man's best friend, never needing to talk, only needing to spend some time.

The horses trekked up a hill in the middle of the cow pasture. At the top of the hill rose a tree, high up in the sky, with thick, sturdy branches shooting off in every direction. I used to climb that tree almost every day when I was growing up. I'd bring a book and snacks and navigate my way up the branches as high as I could go and then sit there, reading and thinking about all of life's great expectations. Mom would have to send Johnny out to call me down for supper, otherwise I would stay there until I was ready to go to sleep.

Sometimes I would even take naps up there, locked in the branches. This scared Mom half to death. She would lecture me about how dangerous it was, but I always felt safe up in the tree, like it was holding on to me just as tight as I was holding on to it.

Dad and I tied our horses off at the end of one of the low hanging branches and then we sat at the base of the tree, hoping to cool off in the shade.

It would've been nice if we'd brought the beer with us.

"I admire you, Dad. I know you think I'm scared of turning out like you, but that wouldn't be too bad, honestly."

"We've got a lot in common, Del, but I'm not worried at all that you'll turn out like me. You've got too much of your mother in you."

"How so?"

"You've just got a sense about you. The way you think, hell, I don't really understand it, but that's the way I feel about your mom, too." I looked at him, but he was looking off in the other direction.

"She's the one who would've left, you know. I don't know why she didn't, but anytime she talked about it, you knew she wasn't gonna leave for herself. She really would have left me if she thought it was best for me. But, like I told you, I wouldn't have been any better without her. Honestly, it's probably God's fault she stayed with me. He's got her convinced that divorce is hardly ever a necessary evil."

"She really does listen to that guy, huh?" I pointed up above us and dad chuckled while nodding.

"And I think you do, too. In your own way. You both always connected to spiritual things. It made me curious."

"You think I'm spiritual? Dad, I haven't been in a church building in what, three years? Haven't prayed since, and I'm pretty content to just say that the guy up there doesn't exist."

He laughed. "Del, I think we both know He doesn't exist, but something might, and you can't help but believe in that something. I wish I had faith like you do."

"Faith! You're talking nonsense. I don't have faith in anything."

"I remember when you were going off to school and people used to ask you all the time, 'what were you going to be?' Do you remember what you would say?"

"Somethin'. I'd just say I would be somethin'." Something about the way I said "somethin'" made me realize how strong my accent was with Dad.

"Exactly. What you'd be didn't matter, all that mattered was you knew you'd be. And you could've been too. You didn't have to be nothing, but you could have been anything. You saw a world that no one else could see. It always amazed me. I guess that's what faith is to me. Being able to imagine a world that doesn't exist yet."

He pulled out a flask and took a sip. I tried not to laugh at the irony of it all, and then I took it out of his hand and took a sip too. Then we sat up off our asses, untied and mounted on our horses, and paced back to the barn.

I was sad to lock Sally up again, but I told her I was coming back soon. I thanked her as I brushed her snout. Dad shook his head at me and said, "Only spiritual people talk to an animal like that."

At the car, Dad opened the door for me. I sat down. He blocked the door from closing.

"Son, I'm proud of you no matter what you decide to do. But listen to me, I don't blame your mother for who I am. It's my own fault I'm so reserved and passive. I'd be like this, maybe worse, if I had been without your mother. You aren't gonna be like me, and you don't have to be like me. And you don't have to leave Charlotte to keep that from happening. And maybe you should know this too," he looked me in the eye as a tear rolled over his five o'clock shadow, "I'm happy."

I nodded my head so he knew I understood. He nodded his head more down than up, slammed the door closed, and waved goodbye. I started the car and watched him walk back to the house while I rolled out in reverse. The gravel creaked in a rhythmic staccato beneath the turning rubber.

On the ride home, I was convinced I should try to make things work with Charlotte, or at least talk to her. I thought about calling her to see if she'd meet me at the condo. Instead, I texted her, telling her I would be there if she was up for talking.

I returned to the condo to find the door was cracked. I assumed Charlotte had beat me. Breathing in a deep well of air, I pushed the door open and walked inside.

***

Carolyn was sitting on the couch, holding a glass of whiskey. She was reading my book of poems that I had left on the coffee table. The first thought that crossed my mind was that she wasn't as attractive as I remembered. Maybe it was the bags under her eyes, but her face was still strikingly structured. The lines of her figure captivated my attention.

"Hi." I cleared my throat. "How did you get in?"

"The code was your anniversary. That wife of yours sure didn't want you to forget, huh?"

"You've done your proper stalking of my social medias then." I edged closer to her and wondered if she could sense my frustration or if she thought I might be glad. I did not tell her I set the code.

"Why are you here?"

"You didn't call."

"So, you broke into my home and–" I paused and went to the decanter and poured myself a drink.

"I thought you'd think it was romantic. Are you not pleased to see me?"

"What if my wife were here?" My voice raised against my will like a snake striking from the pit of my stomach. "Are you trying to turn my life into a greater hell than it already is?"

"I really thought you'd be glad to see me. Besides, I can tell Charlotte hasn't been around. Her mom seems happy to have her home." My mother-in-law was particularly active online.

How was she keeping herself so composed? The more it became obvious I was rejecting her, the more she seemed self-assured and...sly. Was she happy about my distress? I took another breath and lowered my voice.

"I am glad to see you." I took a seat in the chair with the back to the window wall.

Her eyebrow raised and I knew we had both entered the game. She had only one move to make, and I would lose, but playing seemed like the only option.

I continued, "You must understand that I've got a great many things to think through."

"Of course—I understand! You do care about her, Del. I know this. It won't be easy to leave her, and divorce is hell no matter how cooperative your ex-lover decides to be. But it can be you and me now. I'm thrilled at the possibilities! We'll travel and you'll write and I'll read it. I'll wear all the fancy clothes and dazzling jewelry and they'll wonder 'who is this couple and why are they so happy?' Me and you, Del, partners, creating the loveliest life imaginable. Oh, it could be dynamite. Don't you think?"

I did think. My heart was excited, too, but she continued on.

"Why are we both childless? Don't you want to bring a person into this world and see how they do? And we'll raise them right, classy and adventurous, and they'll be happy to have such joyful parents that really love each other absolutely. You've got too much of an artistic mind to not want to create a being! What better art than your own offspring? A blank canvas for them to decide who they'll be and we'll provide the color. We can start tonight—why put it off?"

She didn't know the news. I was so caught up in her words that I didn't remember until now.

"Carolyn, Charlotte is pregnant."

Other than her blinking eyes, her body froze. Then her face turned red, and she muttered, "That bitch!" She jumped up from the couch and started pacing. "She planned this all along. She's trying to trap you now, Del. I bet that child isn't yours. You're impotent is what I think, and I think you think so too. You're going to fall for that, then, that she's having your baby?" She faced the window.

"Why am I here? Of course, you'll stay with her now. I'm a fool. I left Nathan for you. For you! And we were happy before you. Of course, I don't love him, but he provides for me more than you could. I can't believe I let you entangle me in this childish fantasy."

Her ravings caused my stomach to turn but I sat motionless. I caught her eyes dart to my painting. Immediately, she stomped over and yanked the massive canvas from the wall and slammed it into the bar cart. My decanter crashed against the floor, sending glass and whiskey across the room. The canvas was torn. The nails were ripped from the wooden frame. She held the mangled flesh firmly below her waist.

In all the commotion, I heard a soft sigh come from the other corner of the room. Carolyn cut her eyes to the open door where Charlotte stood. She dropped the busted painting and left, brushing her shoulder firmly against Charlotte on the way out. My eyes met Charlotte's. Her eyes laid low like two doves in mourning. I stumbled to find the words to say, but she turned and left. I had managed to find another way to lose.

I sat in my pity and wondered if I was the victim of divine vengeance. Who the hell was Carolyn to show up at my home like that? I barely recognized her. She was manic. Her eyes were saturated in betrayal. And yet, I knew this was all my fault. I bore the responsibility. My passive nature was pulling everyone around me in a swift descent toward hell.

Then, I remembered why I texted Charlotte to begin with and realized nothing had changed.

I chased after her into the parking garage, but she wasn't there. Over the edge, I saw her stopped at a stop sign with her blinker on to turn right. I rushed through the stairwell and out into the street, catching her at the next corner. She slammed the brakes as I ran around the front of the car and yanked the door open.

"Del! What the hell. What are you doing? I can't do this right now. For God's sake, why was that woman in our house? I don't want to know. I'm leaving. How could you?" She grabbed the door handle, but I stepped in the way.

"Charlotte–" I started.

"What?"

I didn't know what to say.

"Charlotte..."

"Damnit, Del. I'm in the middle of the street. Say it or don't, I've got to go."

My hand was trembling against the door. She looked at me, but I couldn't look her in the eye.

"Look, I want to make this work. I want you. I want our child. I realize I've never given myself to this relationship. I've never let you in..."

Tears ran down her face. She pulled the door closed and drove away.

III

Jasmine called me into her office shortly after I had settled in at work. My head was pounding and my throat felt scratchy as I sank into her faux raw-hide leather chair.

I could tell my eyes were glassy as I forced a smile.

She leaned forward on her desk, impaling the two-dimensional image of her against the wall of leadership books.

"How are we doing today?"

I shrugged, "Fine... Better."

"You promise? How is Charlotte?"

I didn't answer.

"Maybe I should send you home again... Or maybe work will be good for you." She raised her eyebrows hoping I would comment. I didn't want to work but it was better than moping around the house by myself. "I'll stay. There's no reason for me not to be here. I promise to be productive."

"I don't need you to be productive as much as I want you healthy, okay? Go home whenever you feel like it but stop by my office before you leave."

I nodded and returned to my desk.

Work consumed me enough to take my mind off my sorrows. It was even slightly enjoyable. I was able to focus enough to see how much more effi-cient my work could be by categorizing a trend in the data to show clients. This made the menial side of my job smoother, and it would make the clients happy. It was a win-win. It was so simple, so minute a change. That somebody else hadn't realized it sooner didn't make sense. I emailed my team to let them know what I discovered and soon they were coming one by one to my office to tell me how much it had helped them improve their work. Some of them described the ways they were able to build on what I did. It felt good to do something new. The improvement gave me a motivation I hadn't felt in a long time.

I worked through lunch and when five o'clock came, I was thor-oughly satisfied and packed my things. The communal office space was empty when I walked through toward Jasmine's office.

She was there, leaned back in her chair, reading a book–a novel.

"Where did everyone go?" I asked as I eased back into the cushioned chair, not allowing it to absorb me, sitting up straight instead.

"Around 10, their productivity shot up. I sent them home before three because they had finished enough work for the rest of the day. I wanted to let you do what you needed to do so I stayed. It was nice to do some leisurely reading for once anyways. How did it feel to work today?"

"It was nice–"

"How do you do it?" She cut in before I could put a period on my response. "You see things that no one else sees. Do you realize what you did today? You may have improved our capacity to serve clients by 15, maybe 20, percent, which dramatically increases our performance and our profit margin. In a day. Corporate will be pleased. You're better than holding the S&P."

I grinned through my teeth. My palms were sweaty.

"Honestly, it doesn't even feel like I did anything. I just happened to notice if I put a category around–" Jasmine had her brow raised. I muttered, "It just worked."

"Look at me, Del. No one else 'just happened to notice it.' Give yourself some credit. You don't know how pleased I am."

"Thank you."

"No, thank you. I should promote you, but I don't think you'd take it."

The pit in my stomach grew to the size of a baseball. I wasn't sure if I would take it either, or if I would stay at the job altogether. I figured it would be best to not think about leaving just yet. There were other problems for me to work through. This job offered consistency for now. Consistency was good. I stood up and told Jasmine goodnight. She told me the office was open for me tomorrow even if no one else came. I told her I'd be there.

I headed to Reece and Charlie's for dinner.

***

Dinner was quiet, but it felt normal. Charlie grilled steaks and we drank wine. Reece sipped her water and had a smile on her face the whole time we were eating. I couldn't figure out why. Charlie looked at her once and her smile grew, then Charlie shook his head as if he were telling her to calm it down. We didn't talk about Charlotte or Carolyn, but I did tell them about work. Charlie congratulated me and said, "See Del! You can learn to survive this world just like the rest of us." I tensed up but I knew he was right.

"Well, if my disagreeable ass can send a company's efficiency through the roof in a day, maybe I can have a healthy relationship with society after all."

Reece replied through laughter, "You're so full of it. You are society! If society needs outsiders like you to function, that makes you a part of the society. How's that feel? Being outside of society is exactly how you fit in!" Her and Charlie laughed, but I took this very seriously.

After our plates had been scraped clean and resting in our guts, I helped Reece clean up the table and started running the warm water to do the dishes. She tried to stop me, but I told her she needed to sit on the couch and worry about getting fat.

"Oh, I can't wait! I've bought so many dresses to accentuate my bump." She looked down at her stomach and rubbed it, whispering, "I can't wait to show you off."

As I ran the soapy sponge across the dishes, Charlie returned to our pacifism conversation. It seemed like we'd be having it the rest of our lives.

I asked him, "Charlie, do you want us to be a Christian nation?"

"Well, I think so. They've got the best principles."

"Alright then, so why are you so obsessed with pacifism? Why do you care if the Christians are becoming more pacifist? Was Jesus not a pacifist?" I shuddered as I remembered Carolyn's response about turning the other cheek.

"But war is going to happen, Del. We can't just let people come on our land..." I had to keep myself from laughing at 'our land...' "We can create peace by showing the rest of the world who's in charge. If a Christian nation is submitted to, then the rest of the world will have to submit to peace! War is inevitable so we might as well make it as just as it can be."

"We can talk about *just war* if you'd like. I'll tell you what Augustine said about Christians and war. He was no pacifist, yet even he said that the church should be a refuge of immunity for the *enemy*. And to honor Christ, those captives of war should find their Christian enemy to be compassionate. Is that how America handles war? I'm not so sure you want America to be a Christian nation so much as you want Christianity to be an American religion. I'd give the pacifist Christians some grace. Maybe they're just trying to correct hundreds of years of misrepresenting their Christ as a warmongering hero."

That shut him up. My education came in handy from time to time.

He poured himself a whiskey and gave me the cold shoulder. I couldn't keep from smiling. It felt good to speak my mind a little bit, and this carried over to the couch where all three of us sat. I looked at Reece and said, "Now, you're gonna tell me what you've been all giddy about tonight." I took a confident gulp of wine.

"Let's just say I have a very strong intuition that everything is going to be okay. And for the first time, 'okay' feels like it might even be better than whatever 'okay' was before."

"What makes you think that?" I leaned toward her and pressed my elbows against my knees.

"Well, I don't think I'm at liberty to say, but Del, there's been a change in you and you know it. It seems to me that you've finally taken ownership for yourself–it's like you're a real person now. Well, almost, but I'm hopeful you'll get there."

"What does this have to do with Charlotte?"

"Don't even worry about that–I mean, of course, you should worry about that, but it's not important to what I'm saying." I could tell she was veiling the truth, but I didn't bother to press her.

"Alright then, tell me... how do I win Charlotte back?"

"Don't be silly. You haven't lost her. She's bearing your baby, do you really think she'd–Never mind, that's not a good reason and Charlotte knows it too. She needs space and you do too, but you haven't lost her. She wants to raise that child with you and she's not going to give up easily, but you're going to have to fight for her, and the first fight is leaving her alone for a while. Think you can do that?"

"When can I see her again?"

"How about you go and see a therapist and then we'll think about y'all seeing each other again, okay? I am hopeful for the two of you, Del. Excited, really. But it's going to hurt a lot for y'all to heal and to finally see each other for who you are. I know you hate work, but it is going to be a lot of work. Hard work. And you'll do it, too. I don't doubt it."

She smiled at me, and I gave a suppressed grin in return. I didn't want to get my hopes up. I still didn't know what I was hoping for.

Charlie had been silent for the entire conversation, pretending to read on his tablet, but he stood up and announced, "Alright Del, I'll take you home."

"Has Reece been talking to Charlotte much, then? She seems to understand my situation better than I do."

Charlie continued looking straight at the road ahead with both hands on the wheel.

"Oh, come on Charlie, are you still upset that I shut down your silly rants against pacifism?"

He still didn't say anything.

"Charlie, can you blame me? Religion has twisted up the entire world because of thinking like that. Thinking it can be used as a sword. Religion has been abused as justification for killing people that look nothing like us, but that's not what religion is about. The sword does not bind together. And that's exactly what religion is about, the binding together of each of us. If only that were the prominent thinking in the West, I might still be considered religious." That's not something I had ever thought to myself, so my words came as a surprise. I would have to keep thinking about that.

"Do you really think I care this much about pacifism to be mad at you? I don't need to be preached at. Be real, you're the only person I know who ties their feelings to these abstractions as if they were real life. That's not why I'm mad."

I waited to see if he would continue.

He did. "I'm mad because these kinds of ideas are the only thing I can get you to care about. Could you imagine if I could get you this excited about your marriage? Or your job? You wouldn't be having the problems you're having now if I could. Well, if you could. It's not my job to make sure you have any libido toward life."

"You don't think I care about these things now? You've seen me fight to get Charlotte back–why do you think I still don't care enough?"

"Look–I do think you care, but I know you. You'll be passionate about her for a month, or however long it takes to get your relationship back to enough normal that you can sleep in the same bed. Then, you'll retreat to your mind until your apathy toward reality leads you to cause all this havoc again. I'm not as hopeful as Reece, Del. I'm not seeing any light at the end of the tunnel. Maybe a glimmer here and there, but glimmers are often an illusion."

"You may be right. I don't want you to be, but you might be, and fair enough, I shouldn't be naïve as much as I can help it. Okay, Charlie. Well, I don't know what to do. I am going to take Reece's advice and find a therapist, okay? Don't you think that will help me?"

"Sure, but you can't leave it up to a therapist to fix you—you have to want it yourself."

I felt provoked and blurted, "That's where you're wrong." I looked him in the eye, "I'm tired of being told I need to be fixed. I'm not broken just because I can't accept life the way you can, Charlie, so stop telling me that."

"If you're not broken then what's the problem?"

"I'm just not broken."

Charlie parked the car on the side of the street. I went to grab the door handle.

"Listen, Del, fine, you're not broken, but you aren't normal either. I hope you go to therapy and it helps you learn how to live with yourself."

I nodded. "Me too."

He leaned over and hugged me in an awkward way, but I didn't resist. I leaned in and put my only free arm around him, then he patted my back before I stepped out of the car.

Glass was still scattered across the floor and the rug was soaked in booze when I returned home. I hadn't bothered to clean it up the night before but decided I'd be better off not to put it off any longer. Besides, it was still damp, and I didn't want Amir getting any ideas. I laid the rug out on the balcony, then I moved the splintered painting to the corner wall out of the way and began to sweep up the shards of glass in the living room, and later shards that had found a way into the kitchen, too.

My poetry book was open to the back page. Carolyn had read my poem. I wondered how it made her feel. My eye shifted to the busted canvas sitting against the wall. Maybe she knew the last stanza, too.

I grabbed a beer out of the fridge and sat on the balcony. I stared blankly at the lines I had written and the lines I hadn't, wondering if I had the courage to finish it. Then, remembering my promise to Reece, I grabbed my laptop to search for a therapist.

***

"The problem is I can't be fulfilled by her. She'll never be enough for me. And I don't mean for that to be a criticism of her in particular, I just don't think anyone will ever be enough. I thought someone like Carolyn could be—but I realize now how wrong I was. Well, it's a problem because I don't want to leave her, but Charlie is right. It seems inevitable that I'll sink back into whatever it is that pulls me out of reality. That's my problem, I'm detached from the world everyone else seems to be a part of and I can't relate to them."

After a week of searching and sending emails back and forth between therapy offices, I sat on a black leather couch across from Beatrice–Bea, as she introduced herself. She had good reviews and was one of the few who didn't counsel 'from a biblical worldview,' so I figured I'd give her a chance. Her skin was tan, eyes brown, and her hair was a deep brunette cut to her shoulders. She must've been in her late forties, but in better than good health. It was possible she was much older.

There was something about her. She was compassionate just as she was stern. Sitting in her presence made the air feel light. That, and the Buddha in the corner, and the painting of a blue mandala on the wall. She sat up straight with her legs crossed and rubbed her left thumb in a rhythmic circle on the print of her index finger as I sat and rambled to her. It wasn't distracting to me, although I did notice it and questioned the possibility that it was hypnotic. The first thirty minutes had gone by so quickly, and I had shared more than I anticipated I was capable of, that it was easy for me to imagine I had been hypnotized.

"And why do you think it is someone else's job to fulfill you, Del?"

"Well–" I stammered, "It's not, but that's not what I mean."

"No, that's exactly what you mean. Has Charlotte ever done anything that would cause you to resent her? Is she disagreeable? Unattractive?"

"No."

"So, don't you think it's a waste of time to worry about someone else being enough when the problem seems, quite obviously, to be about you not being enough?"

I bit the inside of my lip while scratching the side of my leg, trying not to make eye contact with her.

"Okay then, now that we have the problem refocused," She continued, "let's talk about why you feel so inadequate."

"I don't feel inadequate," I stammered, "I feel misplaced."

She tilted her head and raised her eyebrows reflexively as if she disagreed. I barely glimpsed the expression before she returned stoic and said, "And what does that mean to you?"

"Like I don't fit in this system, you know? Like the social system. I want to have a healthy committed relationship, but 'Western romance,'" I made air quotes with my fingers, "has made that impossible. If it's not flowers and long nights staring into each other's eyes, then it's not love. Well, I don't want that."

"Does Charlotte want that?" She went with it, not seeming to mind I had shifted the focus away from myself and back onto my relationship with Charlotte.

My head dropped to my shoulder. "Huh?"

"Is 'Western Romance'" –finger quotes– "what Charlotte wants?"

"How should I know? She doesn't tell me what she wants. God, she's the only person on this planet more passive than me."

"Tell me about your relationship before you were married. How did you meet?"

I told her the same story I had told Carolyn a couple weekends back. We grew up together.

"What was your relationship like before moving off to college?"

My mind blanked. Bea gave me space to think. Slowly, the memories began to creep in.

"Well, it seemed like we always had a summer fling. We'd spend the summers doing everything together. But she took school seriously and I had sports, so we didn't have time for each other during the school year. Usually around August or September, we'd start fighting like hell because we couldn't communicate, then we'd break up. Summer would come around and we'd fire it back up again. And each summer, it felt like the first time we'd ever been together. I would look forward to summer every year. I'd start getting nervous around April 'cause I couldn't wait to try to win her back, never knowing if she would take me. But she always did." I felt a grin form on my face and looked down in embarrassment at the floor.

"Did you date anyone else during the school year?"

"Yeah. Nothing as serious though."

"Del, I need you to communicate better, okay? I don't want straight answers. I want all the thoughts that go circulating through your mind. Don't hold back."

I nodded.

"Tell me about the other girls you dated."

Having inhaled a deep breath, I shrugged and said, "I dated popular girls. The cheerleaders. The ones with rich dads. Any girl that wouldn't date just any guy. But I could get them to fall for me."

"And what we're those relationships like?"

"Boring. I used them for the convenience of being in a relationship. And they used me to feel like they actually had depth."

"Oh? What do you mean?"

"It wasn't only convenient. Dating those girls proved to me that even though I was different, I was just as good as anyone else. If not better. But listen, I wasn't full of myself. I always felt insecure. And I knew those girls didn't actually like me. They liked what I represented, but they never saw me for me. I could never shake that feeling, so I ended the relationship. And it was always me ending the relationship. Being able to date the girls I dated never made me feel better about myself. I felt worse, actually."

"So, since you think had these girls seen the real you, they would have rejected you, would you say you felt inadequate?" She gave me a toothy grin. I held back from swearing at her.

After absorbing the jab, I laughed and said, "Yeah, I guess so," and eased into the couch.

"Del, would you consider yourself a feminine man? Not womanly, you know, but feminine."

I chuckled. "I think I know what you mean. And sure. I mean, I'm comfortable with feminine things: poetry, tea, even warm baths and a glass of wine. I'm not sure if these are feminine qualities, but I do know many men are uncomfortable with these kinds of things, so does that make it feminine? Maybe."

She nodded in a way that seemed to signify "maybe" was the right answer. I continued, "I don't really get along with other guys very well either. Especially in groups. They all seem to be interested in investing and vacations in the Caribbean and guns."

"Hm, I find it of value that none of these so-called feminine traits seem to be connected with the modern romantic view of life women often portray in 'Western Romance.' You don't seem to be gushing with emotion, at least, not as far as I can tell. Maybe the glass of wine in the hot tub might make you start to open up with yourself, huh? However, the things you do enjoy signify to me that you feel things very deeply. I can't imagine you could enjoy poetry if you didn't. How would you describe your relationship to your feelings?"

My eyes shifted to the books that lined the wall behind Bea. Books of different colors, widths, and textures; bindings of leather, paper, cardboard. I returned my gaze to her, waiting, not rushed. Patient.

I was her patient. That word sat at the back of my mind as I searched for words that could be organized in a sentence that would explain something sentences made up by an organization of words had so far been unable to explain. How do you explain the ineffable void one feels where one knows meaning exists out in the world and also exists within you, those two meanings could not possibly be brought together, though they may flow from the same source, but even to think of this reality, to contemplate the explosion of meaningfulness that imbues all things, material and immaterial, creatures and objects, lessens the meaningfulness of it?

"I can't say. I wouldn't know what words to use." I added, "It seems to me that the feeling is always going in and never going out."

"Expound on that some more, will you?"

"It seems like all of these colors are floating through the air, reds and greens, yellows and blues, purple, orange... and they sink right into my body, my soul, maybe. But whenever I try to release the colors, all that floats out is gray."

"So, you feel deeply but you don't feel capable of expressing it, yes?"

"Something like that."

"That's very perceptive, Del. I want you to keep thinking about that until our next session. I'll see you on Monday, if that works for you. I think with your current situation we should meet twice a week until significant progress has been noted, okay? Separation from a spouse, even if it's temporary, is disorienting and destabilizing; we'll meet at that frequency to help keep you stabilized.

"I'm extremely hopeful for you, Del. You should see some of these other patients I have to help. You're doing okay, okay?" With a wink, she added, "and I have no worries we will be able to help you learn to live with yourself."

I thanked her and stood up to leave. She stood up too and shook my hand. Before letting go, she added, "Now, I want you to think on one more thing until I see you on Monday." I found her eyes and signaled for her to go on.

"And I ask this of all my clients to help them ground themselves in their unique lives. I want you to consider your *raison d'etre*." She spoke the

French phrase natural and smooth. The way it liaisoned together like water flowing down a stony brook with a soft, resolving landing in that final 'r.' I realized France must be her heritage, too. Even more than mine. I understood why I found her so formidable at first. Her independent confidence and European certainty intrigued me. Yet, like her tongue, her directness was more like a pillow than a knife. Nonetheless, I felt assured I was safe in her office.

"Do you know what that means?"

I said, "Yes, of course. You can't tell it from my appearance, but my family is French. Distantly, on my father's side."

To which she replied, "Well, of course, I should've known with your last name. I've been saying it all wrong in my head. Alright, Mr. Robert," she said my last name with a raspy accent, nasally and pushing out toward the front of her mouth. "Then I will hear about your *raison d'etre* on Monday. I look forward to it." She patted my hand before releasing it, and I walked out the door.

Although I rode MARTA to Bea's office, it was only a mile from the condo, so I walked Peachtree Street on my way home. I called Dad to see if he and Mom would come down for dinner. He told me he would ask her when she was home and hung up the phone. He confirmed almost immediately, so I texted Johnny and told him he was invited as well.

It was too late to plan something to cook so I decided to order take out. I stepped inside the Chinese place just a block from the condominium and told them my order to pick up in about three hours. The lady behind the counter told me it would be easier for the both of us if I placed the order online. She handed me a menu with the website on it before sending me out the door.

Amir was waiting for me when I arrived home. He didn't care to see me. All he wanted was for me to fill up his food and water bowl. I gave him what he wanted, and he bunted against my leg in thanks and started dining.

I was sitting on the balcony, about to light up a mini cigar, when my phone buzzed. The name that lit up on the screen sucked the breath out of me.

I'm in the city and would like to stop by and chat.
Let me know if you're around. Sarah.

It was just like my mother-in-law to sign her name in a text.

I thought about lying and saying I was out of the city for the evening, or just flat out ignoring her. I didn't have it in me to see her. I didn't know what I could possibly say to her, and I couldn't imagine she had anything positive to say to me.

For some reason, I grabbed that poetry book and read my unfinished poem. Reading it felt like a prayer unto itself. I asked *whatever was out there* what to do and my conscience told me what I already knew. I texted her back that I was home and could meet her. She replied that she would be up in ten minutes. I cussed under my breath and started boiling water for tea–hoping to approach her with an olive branch.

Exactly ten minutes later there was a knock at the door. I edged myself off the couch and walked across the room. After a deep breath, I grabbed the handle and turned it slowly.

To my surprise, she immediately embraced me in a hug.

"I felt like you may need that, especially from me. I can't imagine the anxiety I've caused you. Are you making tea?"

I nodded.

"Lady Grey for me, please."

I poured the hot water into the mugs and tossed the tea bags in while she made her way to a living room chair.

She looked at the bare wall behind the couch. "I really did like that painting. It wasn't in the proper place, but it was a masterpiece even still. Shame it's been destroyed, but let's not talk about that, shall we?"

I handed her the cup of tea and took my seat in the chair opposite her.

"I hear you've started therapy."

I nodded.

"I'm glad to hear it. I think we all could use some therapy these days, don't you?"

"Maybe."

"Oh, quiet Del, I've always loved your presence. So deep in thought all the time." She sipped her tea.

"So, no need to beat around the bush, and I know you're not one for idle chat. Tell me, how are you going to make things right with my daughter?"

I stared past her through the window wall where a glimmer shimmered through the glass.

I shrugged and said, "I'm not sure."

"Certainly, with all of that thinking you do, you've thought about it? Have you not?"

"Sure."

"And?"

I paused. "I'm not sure."

"What does your therapist think you should do?"

"We haven't gotten that far yet."

She sipped her tea again. "I see."

We looked aimlessly in the other's direction.

"Do you love her?"

"Of course I do."

"What's holding you back then, Del?

I could feel a glaze filling across my eyes. It was hard to look at her. I knew I shouldn't look away, so I began to look through her. The stillness of the room became like a painting as Sarah, in an old-style yellow dress with a flowery pattern sewn across the top portion, became one-dimensional with the chair and wall behind her.

"You're a good kid, I just," She burst into tears as though bursting through a canvas, "You're torturing her!"

I handed her a tissue and she patted her eyes.

"I'm sorry, I know you don't intend to hurt her. I don't know why. I feel like a damn fool trying to care for you as much as my own daughter, but I see no good reason to come here and curse you when you're going to be the father of my first grandbaby." She set the soiled tissue on the coffee table and picked up her teacup.

"I assure you that Charlotte misses you," she took a sip. "She hasn't forgiven you though, and she won't for a good while. I don't think she should for now. Since you don't seem to have a plan yet, I suggest you keep this therapy thing up. I think you should go to church, too."

I rolled my eyes.

"Oh, don't you do that! I don't care what you think about church honestly, Del. Just go to one—it can be one of those mainline ones with all their blasphemies for all I care—just go."

I promised her I would try one out and she stood up to say goodbye. "Alright then," she exhaled as I stood up to see her out. She hugged me again, said bye, and left abruptly. I stepped out on the balcony to smoke.

Not too long after my mother-in-law left, Mom and Dad knocked on the door. I heard the knock and realized I had forgotten to order the food. I forced a smile onto my face and opened the door wide.

"Hey Mom."

"Son." She hugged me like I was a dog on my deathbed.

"Del." Dad nodded and gave me a more encouraging hug and patted me on the back.

I led them to the living room and told them I had forgotten to order the food.

"That's fine, just order it now and Johnny can pick it up on his way." I did what Mom said and then grabbed two IPAs from the fridge.

"This one's Atlanta local," I said as I handed it to Dad.

We popped the tabs and knocked our cans against one another. I tried to hide my face's reaction to the bitter beer, and I could tell Dad tried doing the same.

"That's smooth stuff," he said, while examining the can.

I spun my can around in my hand to join in the investigation. Craft breweries always had interesting can art, which made up for the deficient palatability of bitterness that accompanied the hoppier beers. I noticed the brewery donated a small percent of their profit to help lgbtq youth in unstable housing situations. Dad's eyes were probably too aged to read the fine print. He'd pretend not to notice, regardless.

Mom asked me how I was doing, and I told her I was seeing a therapist so it didn't matter how I was doing, only that I would be doing better, hopefully. She didn't like that response and then she asked me, "Is he a Christian therapist?"

"She's not."

There wasn't much conversation after that, and we sat around staring at the walls. Dad and I shifted from staring at the walls, to our beers, at each other, and then back to the walls.

Johnny finally knocked at the door. I opened it for him, and he came prancing in, arms loaded with Chinese take-out. Behind him stood a distinguished man with smooth, dark brown skin, wearing a tight-fitted sport jacket, a clerical collar, and a grin. He must have been in his mid-thirties.

Johnny rushed to set the food down and then introduced the man.

"This is Adam. He's a minister at the Presbyterian church on the corner of Peachtree."

Son of a– I glanced at Mom who had a curious grin across her face.

I shook his hand. He grabbed it like ministers do, patting it with his free hand. His hands were soft and delicate, but he shook firm.

"Wonderful to meet you," he said. His voice soft, too, but resounding.

Mom became extra-cordial in the presence of the minister and tried tending to his every need as if he were a guest in her own home. She fixed all our plates of food for us and made sure everyone had a drink to go with it. I pulled a chair from the balcony so there would be enough seats at the table. Mom asked Adam to pray.

"Chinese food is already blessed," he told her with a chuckle, and then he picked up his chopsticks and thrust lo mein into his mouth. Dad said "Amen," picked up his fork, and followed suit.

We all started eating besides Mom, who was visibly disturbed. She prayed quietly to herself and then started to eat slowly, twisting the lo mein on her fork, dropping it, and swirling it again.

"So, Del, Johnny tells me you've found yourself in a distressing situation."

Inappropriate timing from a man I had just met, I thought. It was just like a preacher to pry.

"I guess so," I replied.

"I was in a similar situation. Except my wife wasn't pregnant. We did end up divorcing, but we were able to stay friends." What kind of preacher speaks so openly about divorce? I wondered if there was anything Johnny hadn't told him. "I imagine that's not very helpful, actually, so I'm sorry to bring that up. I have a knack for saying too much in the company of new friends. I guess I wanted you to know I can relate to you."

I shrugged.

"Did you divorce your wife, or did she divorce you?" Mom asked. Now Adam was being asked the inappropriate questions.

"It was mutual," he stuttered, before smiling uncomfortably yet graciously at Mom.

"Why would a churchman get divorced?" she followed up. Adam and Johnny shared a glance.

"How long you been a preacher?" Dad asked.

"I don't know if I've ever been a 'preacher,' but I went straight through seminary after college and became ordained. Of course, I preach from time to time, but mostly I offer spiritual guidance to the community. Are you and your wife church-goers?"

"We've gone to the same church for thirty years now," Mom piped in. "Our pastor has changed three times since we've been there, and we really like the new one transitioning in. He's a real Bible-preacher."

Adam smiled, "That's good." He was sincere enough to fool them, but I could see behind his eyes that he did not find this encouraging at all.

"Del, what about you? What do you think about all this 'church' stuff?"

I imagined Johnny had already told him about me. I'm often a talking-point for non-religious people who are trying to talk to religious people. They'd usually say something like, 'I knew somebody who used to be really religious, was gonna go into ministry and everything.' It wasn't a question I liked talking about in front of Mom. There wasn't an answer I could give either way that wouldn't cause her concern. Better to keep the bliss by ignoring it.

"Del's very religious," Dad chimed to my surprise.

"Is that right?" Adam looked at me.

"If he says so," I replied.

"Del went to school for ministry, didn't you know?" Now Mom answered for me.

Adam's eyebrows raised. "I did not."

"It was wonderful to see Charlotte at our mid-week service last night as well! Her and her mother brought a delicious soufflé."

And just like that, we were the perfect Christian family again. My wife was back in church on my behalf, and all we needed to do was figure out this little scuffle and hurry back into God's will.

Adam noticed my irritation and changed the topic, "Johnny tells me you're a market research analyst, how did you get into that field?"

"He's not just an analyst, he's a manager. A whole team answers to him," Mom said.

"Obviously my studies in religion prepared me immensely." I smirked.

Adam chuckled. "I do appreciate good tongue in cheek humor, but I feel like there's some truth in that. Did you read much of St. Augustine in your studies?"

"Ah, of course! No, I think you're right. I've been trained to see what people truly desire."

"And manipulate their religious desire for monetary gain. Good man!" The table laughed at the minister's quip.

"You joke, but that is what the job feels like at times. And maybe I'm wrong to not care. You know, they've studied this–I had to read an article about it in school–the people that love these tech companies have a religious devotion to them. These tech products produce the same brain activity as someone, like say Mom right here, would have if she saw a painting of the crucifix."

"Or, like you would have while looking at the painting that used to hang on your wall," Johnny added.

"Yeah, possibly. Anyways, yes, my religious training has certainly trained me well. I've climbed the ranks over the last few years and now I supervise a team of analysts that do most of the dirty work for me."

"Interesting. Would you ever consider marketing for a church?"

Mom perked up and her eyes grew big as she leaned in on the table. Johnny had a smirk on his face.

A buzzing noise began in my ear. One of those random noises you never see coming and you don't know what's causing it. I looked it up once before. Tinnitus is what they call it in its more severe forms, but that's all I could find on it. This wasn't tinnitus. I could feel my heart rate increase and wondered if my senses were adjusting to the increase in blood flow. Now that was a hypothesis. The increased blood flow caused my ears to perform more efficiently, hearing new frequencies, like a dog hearing a dog whistle. What a silly thing to think.

I looked Adam in the eye and rubbed my chin. I finally said, "No, I don't think that would be appropriate," and excused myself to the balcony.

The sun had set. Clouds covered the profusion of colors the sun had left behind.

Adam opened the balcony door and stepped out, leaning against the railing.

"I'm sorry I asked such an inappropriate question. I don't know why I felt compelled to do so." He scratched at his neck. "I swear this collar possesses me to pry too much, too quick. I am sorry."

An ambulance soared through the traffic below, followed by a police cruiser.

"And I hope you know I don't intend to involve myself in the current difficulties you're dealing with, but Del," I glanced at him, "I do want to offer myself to you if you ever need a stranger to just listen to you. I won't even offer you advice, I'll just listen." He pulled out a soft-pack of cigarettes and offered me one. I turned him down.

"Do you mind?"

I shook my head and said, "Just don't let my mom see you. You're already on thin ice for not blessing the food."

We smiled. His eyes were amazingly bright. They were magnetic. I couldn't help myself but stare. He lit a cigarette and inhaled. Leaning over the balcony and facing the westward view, he exhaled and the smoke rose slowly about him, and when he turned to face me, it veiled the light reflected in his eye. And though the smoke obstructed his view, I felt a weight in my stomach that his eyes could see through the apertures of my soul.

I left him on the balcony to see Mom and Dad out. I was warming up to him and didn't want to be rude, so I told him I would be back.

Johnny was with Mom and Dad in the kitchen. They were talking in muffled voices. Mom saw me and said, "Alright son, we've got to be going. Sally needs her medication." I wasn't aware of any medications she was on, but I let it be. Mom hugged me and stepped into the hallway. Dad gave me a sincere look and grabbed my forearm.

"I love you, son." His eyes were glazed, and I was deeply aware of how much he meant it.

"I love you, too."

He hugged me and joined Mom in the hallway. Johnny closed the door after we said goodbye once more. "Can you believe that preacher was smoking?" Mom's voice came through the door. Johnny and I laughed.

We went to join Adam on the balcony, but he was walking in as we were heading toward him.

"I've got to head out. A parishioner needs me at the church." He stayed true to the high church language that I found so garish but endearing. "Del, it was lovely to meet you. It would have been nice to have a deeper conversation. Your university studies interest me greatly. I do hope to see you again." He shook my hand then gave Johnny a long hug.

As he was heading toward the door, I asked, "Adam, are you a pacifist?"

He turned and, with a sincere nod, said, "An aggressive one, too." Then he left.

Once he was gone, Johnny and I sat outside. He pulled a couple of Churchill's out of his jacket pocket, and we lit them up.

"You're incredible, Johnny, just incredible."

Johnny gave me a prideful display of his bleached white teeth and puffed his cigar.

"It makes me sick, really. Mom thinks you brought that minister of yours to help me. How you play your games with her amazes me. So, how long have you been seeing him?"

A cloud of smoke filtered from his mouth as he replied, "We're not together. We're just friends. Besides he's sworn himself to celibacy, some personal calling he feels that I don't understand. Even still, if we were, I don't think he would take the collar off, and I would have nightmares after of being left behind. I do like him though. He's sincere, isn't he? And Mom was clueless, aha! I do love it–oh if she knew–she'd, oh, it pains me to think of her response, actually."

"I did like his presence. He had a way about him that just absorbed any tension in the room."

"People used to say the same of you."

I took a hard drag on my cigar. It burned evenly. The balcony was masked in a smoky haze. We were near silent for the time it took to smoke half the thing.

I came out of my head and said to Johnny, "I'm gonna pour a whiskey, want one?"

He nodded. I set my cigar on the ashtray and went inside. I grabbed a bottle from the cabinet where I stored my most expensive ones. Bottles that were gifted to me at special occasions, or bottles Charlie had decided he didn't need. This one was a 30-year-old scotch. I never was much of a fan when it came to scotch whisky, but it had the quality that fit the mood. And Johnny loved scotch. It was the only whisky he'd drink neat.

I came back with the scotch as Johnny was ending a call. All I heard was, "I'll tell him," before putting his phone away.

"What was that about?" I asked him, handing him his glass.

"Sally's sick. Mom says they have to put her down."

"What? I rode her last week. She was fine."

"She seems to have ruptured her stomach. Sounds unbearably painful. It's not going to heal, Del. The doctor recommends it."

My face remained stiff as I stared off into the skyline. A tear slid slowly down the left side of my cheek. It felt like a boulder rolled onto my gut. It was hard to breathe.

"They said they would wait for you if you wanted to be there."

I took a sip from my glass, my eyes still set on the horizon.

"I can drive you."

I took another sip and nodded.

***

The horse doctor was there when we arrived. She was standing with Mom and Dad outside of Sally's stall. It was dark beyond the yellow haze of the barn lights. Dad was leaning against the wall, drinking a light beer. Mom rushed over to hug me as I was walking up. Her cheeks were puffy and red, snot was running from her nose.

"Oh Del, I know you love her. You and that horse were inseparable. She basically raised you."

She pulled back to wipe her face across her shirt.

"She was a better mom than me, wasn't she? I let a horse raise my son!"

I didn't know what to say. This was not the moment. Still, tears were crashing up against the dam wall. I told her no and then went and sat by Sally. She was lying on her side. She cocked her head slightly to acknowledge me and then went back to breathing heavily. Johnny and the vet convinced my parents to give us space and they all went up to the house.

I stroked Sally's mane rhythmically and she shifted her head slightly enough that it pressed against my thigh.

"You're a good horse, Sally. The best. Mom's right, you did raise me. I wish she could say that without being so damn self-deprecating, don't you?"

Sally let out a feeble snort.

"Why'd you have to do this now? Don't you know I'm already in an emotionally fragile state?" I let out a small chuckle as a tear escaped my eye.

80

"I do love you, Sally. I really do. How'd you go and do that to me? Here I am thinking I'm incapable of caring for another human being and your horse ass has me bawling my eyes out. Look at you! You made a depressed man cry. Well, now I've said that out loud. I don't know if it's true, Sally. The evidence seems to point in that direction. But I've always been a little off, don't you think? Just seems so much more pervasive now these days. But you know what? Whenever we'd go riding through the field, you calmed me down. You always did. I could always come find you when I felt my lowest and you'd give me the strength to keep going. I think we may have an unhealthy relationship, Sally. I'm more dependent than I thought." I chuckled again.

Then, I threw my body onto the straw ground and wrapped my arms around her. At once, the dam wall was broken open.

"You're a good horse! The best. Now, I'll be alright, you be alright too, okay? I don't have the strength to let you go, Sally. You're gonna have to be my strength one last time, okay?"

Sally sat up on her side and nudged me with her nose. I sat up and clenched my arms around her neck.

"You're a good horse, Sally. The best."

My tears were raining from my face, enough to dampen Sally's mane. I didn't feel like I could let go, but I didn't think I'd ever feel like letting go, so I slowly started to release my grip, petting her slowly as I did.

"Del," a soft, familiar voice called from behind me.
Charlotte held her arms out and I fell right into them. She held me tightly as I bawled into her shoulder.

"I know, love. I know."

I saw the horse doctor standing on the porch talking to Charlie. He must have brought Charlotte over. The horse doctor looked over at me, and I nodded my head to let her know I was ready.

I sat crisscrossed on the ground with Sally's head in my lap, and Charlotte sat next to me with her arm locked in mine.

Mom, Dad, Johnny, and Charlie sat around Sally's body and petted her as the horse doctor stuck a needle in her side. I stroked her mane and told her it was alright. She blinked a few times before they closed for good. She was gone.

I sat with her lifeless head in my lap. Johnny and Mom were sobbing. So was Charlotte. Dad stood up and patted my shoulder, leaning down to hug me. His eyes were glassy and red. Then he walked up to the house, alone.

Johnny and Charlie followed him shortly after. Mom was talking to the dead horse like she could understand her, and it didn't seem like she would stop any time soon. I shifted my body to move Sally's head from my lap, but Charlotte grabbed me by the forearm and motioned for me to stay. She stood up and brushed the dust off her clothes. I watched as she walked up to the house. Slow. Steady.

"It's alright. It's okay." Mom ran her fingers through Sally's coat.

"It's alright. It's okay." She said this a few times.

I faced the wood stall, spaced out, while Mom prayed, "Lord Jesus, thank you for this horse. Thank you, God. Thank you. Thank you."

Then she stopped praying and turned to face me.

***

"Well Doc, I've had an emotionally taxing few days to say the least."

Bea leaned forward in her chair. "How so?"

"I guess the height of it was Sally dying." Tears were welling up behind my eyes as my mind flashed back to Sally's lifeless head lying in my lap.

"Sally, yes, your horse." My eyebrow arched in, but I nodded.

"You wrote about her quite significantly in the personal biography I had you fill out. Tell me more about Sally. Why was she special to you?"

"She—well," my hand had a slight tremor, and I had to take a breath to prevent myself from sobbing uncontrollably. "She made me feel like I wasn't alone. How silly is that? The fact that she was a horse makes me feel even more alone now. The only human connection I had wasn't to a human at all, but to a horse."

"It sounds to me like you had a relationship with this horse not unlike many people have to their dogs. A sort of man's best friend, don't you think?"

"Sure. But it was more than that. Sally made me feel free. She had a mind of her own and yet she always made me feel in control—"

"And what does that mean?"

"Like, we'd go for a ride through the field, and she'd make it so obvious where she wanted to go, but she wouldn't go unless I agreed. And the thing is, I never disagreed. You'd think once she realized this, she'd stop asking and just do it, but she always waited for me to lead her where she wanted to go."

"That makes a bit of sense. Enough at least. Tell me more about this freedom she brought you."

"I mean, I didn't have to be anything to Sally. She just wanted to spend time with me, and that was enough. I didn't have to make money or say the right things or say anything at all. Just being there was enough for her. All I had to do was exist. That was freedom."

"And what causes you to not feel free?"

"Just about everything else that has to do with life. I guess my parents were the first to choke my freedom. They wanted me to be clergy, at least that was Mom's hope. Oh, I'll have to tell you about Mom. Well, you should see my faith now. If I hadn't felt that pressure, it might have saved me from apostasy. And it would have saved me from using words like apostasy. Christ, I can use some pretentious words sometimes."

This made Bea giggle. "So can I. The pride of knowledge really grabs a hold of us, doesn't it?" She pointed to the three degrees hanging on her wall, and I knew exactly what she meant.

"Yes. Definitely. Well, then I married Charlotte, and she never seemed to impose any rules on me, but I still knew there were rules. And with rules, pressure. Obviously, some rules are good. Like don't cheat on your wife, that's a good rule. Broke that one."

"Do you think kissing Carolyn counts as cheating?"

"Of course it does! I betrayed Charlotte with that kiss. What was I thinking by doing that? Well, I was in a different place, I guess. Completely lifeless. Perfect timing on Carolyn's part to show up and animate my life so quickly."

She nodded, "I want to go back to how Charlotte made you feel less free. Is that an appropriate way to phrase that?"

"Sure."

"Okay, then tell me about some of these unwritten rules that Charlotte brought to your life."

A globe sat on the desk behind Bea. It wasn't a large globe. It was one of the ones that used different browns and tans rather than blues and greens. I stared at that globe for a moment while I tried to find the words to say. Bea noticed my attention seemed to be preoccupied and shifted around to see what was distracting me. She walked over, grabbed the globe, and laid it on my lap.

"Play with it if you must. Do you think it will help you focus?"

I shrugged and twirled it in my hand.

"The rules, god, I feel so selfish, but the rules I despised, well, one example would be I had to talk. Like, if I didn't say a certain number of words in conversation with Charlotte every day then I've broken a rule. Isn't that ridiculous? She never said anything about it, but I knew I had to make sure to talk to her enough. It's so frustrating because I don't have that much to say."

I thought back to the weekend. I was sitting on my balcony smoking a mini cigar. An untouched glass of whiskey sat beside me. The sun was setting. The clouds reflected a deep peach orange, and the horizon was a soft lavender, and I felt alone. Wind swept around and cooled the air. I was trying to read. *Nausea* by Sartre. It seemed fitting. Though I couldn't get into it. It wasn't the first time I'd tried to read it, and the wind kept blowing the pages around, frustrating me. And then I looked up from the book at the empty chair beside me. I'd hoped Charlotte had been there. I wanted to read alone in silence, but I wanted her there too. If she were there, I could still feel alone and not be lonely.

I brought my attention back to Bea.

"I see. So basically, the unwritten rules of a healthy marriage." Bea smirked.

"Yes. How does anyone not want to break them? That there are these unspoken universal laws to follow is beyond me."

"This isn't unusual, Del. Many people have these same frustrations in their marriage, and with work, and life in general. I hope you know that. My God, if that wasn't the reason I became a therapist in the first place. I didn't know how else to deal with this situation we've been thrown into. This thing we call existence. So, what we have to do is reframe it. We must learn how to have a functional relationship with these important unwritten rules. Some rules do quench our fire, Del, but some rules set us free."

I held the bottom of the globe stand and shifted it back and forth in my right hand. The globe would spin in either direction depending on its relationship to the gravity of the real earth below.

"So, tell me about your mother. Something has happened with her since I saw you last, yes?"

I set the globe down on the side table and leaned forward with my hands crossed. "Well. We had a conversation. A weird one. And the fact that Sally's head was still dead in my lap only added to the strangeness.

"Oh, and I have to tell you what Johnny did. He brought a gay clergyman to our family dinner! Mom was utterly clueless. She was so excited to have him there. Johnny assumed she would think he brought him to help me—I don't think she trusts you to do your job," I quipped.

"But no, he just brought him there because he likes him. If Mom knew, she'd point right in his face and condemn him to hell as a heretic and a sodomite."

Bea chimed in, "Well, she will eventually find out, won't she? Johnny doesn't plan to hide his relationship forever, does he? I wouldn't see that working out too well."

"Oh, they aren't dating. Adam, the minister, has chosen to be celibate. Johnny says they're just friends and that's all he wants."

"I see. I'd love to get to know your brother more. Another time maybe. Tell me about this conversation with your mom."

"Yes, well, she was crying and stroking her hand through Sally's backside, and she looks at me and says she failed me. She blames herself for how I've turned out. I don't know what she meant by it. Maybe because I'm emotionally withdrawn? Or because I cheated on Charlotte? Or that I just don't seem to function well in society. I'm sure that's mostly it, but she probably blames herself for all of it. Don't you think?"

"Sure. It's not unlikely for a mother to doubt her parenting skills, especially when their child is full of anguish and turmoil. And you didn't turn out to be the saintly church goer she raised you to be. She must carry a lot of guilt. I know the pathology of those kinds of religious parents. The dualistic-thinking kind. If you don't turn out one way, they feel they've failed."

"That's exactly right. So, I tell her she hasn't failed, and I start thinking of the anthropology books I've read that talk about how little the parents influence their child's development and, really, it's the society around them that creates them, and I almost start to tell her about this but then I realize that wouldn't be helpful at all."

"So, what did you say?" Bea put her reading glasses on and grabbed her notebook and clinked her pen. Then she gave me her full attention.

"I told her I was alright. I had a lot of things to figure out, but it wasn't her fault. 'This is the risk of life,' I told her. And then I thought of that damn painting Carolyn smashed. And I thought Mom looked a lot like Mary and Sally looked a lot like Jesus, dead in her arms.

"I told her she did a good job raising me. She tried her best and it was good enough. Then I told her I believed turning out like I did, though not exactly how she wanted, was a sign she'd done a good job. Because that meant

I felt comfortable to become my own person. It was more important that I be comfortable to become myself than become what she wanted. That's the sacrifice she had to make, and she made it. I told her that once she could accept the sacrifice she'd made, we could really start to have a good and healthy relationship. She cried a lot. I was crying a lot, too. I didn't really know what I was saying but I guess it helped.

"She stood up and left Sally there, and I finally laid Sally's head down slowly to the earth. I got up to hug her and through her tears, she muttered, 'I do accept you.' It was awkward–we hugged for a while–but it was genuine, too. I don't know. Don't know."

I picked the globe back up off the side table.

"It was healing," I added.

"Good. This is good, Del."

"You know what else? When she pulled away from hugging me, she grabbed my shoulders and told me I was going to be a great father. And that's the first time it really set in that I was going to be a dad. I don't know how I didn't think of it before, but God, I'm going to be a dad! What the hell have I been doing? I'm going to be a dad. That's all that matters, huh?"

"Sure, but I think 'what the hell you've been doing' is making sure you're doing the right thing for the right reason. Your child will not heal your marriage and you know this. That's why you're here."

I nodded.

"So, I've still got more story to tell then."

Bea finished writing a note on her paper and told me to go ahead.

"Mom and I walked up to the house in this weird haze of healing and hurt. I think that's about the only way to say that. And when we got to the house, Dad, Charlotte, Johnny and Charlie were all sitting around the table, drinking and laughing. We joined them and Dad got me a beer. Then he sat back down, and Johnny said, 'Del, we've all decided your relationship with that horse was odd. We think that horse was the only thing that actually knew you.' He smacked the table and they all laughed."

"I smiled along with them, because it was kind of true. But I also told them that that was going to change. I was looking at Charlotte when I said it, and she had a subtle grin on her face. I could tell she had been crying, but her skin was bright. She really is a beautiful woman, Doc."

"Do you believe they actually think your relationship to Sally was unhealthy?"

I sat the globe at my feet. *Sally looked up at me and let out a loud sigh. "Alright, alright. I'm coming down." The tree bark scratched against my forearm. The callouses on my hand fought against splitting open as I made my way down and untangled her rope from around a branch.*

"Yes and no. I don't believe they think it was romantic. Oh man, if they thought that, we might have a deeper problem, and I don't think you'd be qualified. Regardless of what Johnny said, it was a joke. But there was truth in it. I mean, I told you, Sally's the only other creature I could be myself around and feel fully free and open. That part was true. Sally loved me in the way I thought I needed."

"Thought?"

"Yes, thought."

"Anything to add to that?"

"I'm just starting to think there's more to love than how easily you get along."

"I see. So, I imagine you spoke with Charlotte alone."

I nodded.

"Tell me about it."

"I don't know what to say. She was especially compassionate toward me because of Sally, but we did talk about Carolyn. It was a hard but good conversation. A hopeful one. But she still needs a lot of space. I don't know how to feel about all of this, and I still don't know what to do. But I'll tell you, she seemed so strong. I've never known this side of her. I know she loves me; I can tell so deeply she does."

"Did she say anything that might help your relationship move a step forward?"

"Yes. She wants to start therapy with me. I told her about you, but she wants to go to someone else, someone I'm not seeing."

"That's smart. I agree."

"We won't start yet, she says she still wants a week or two to have space, so I guess my current step is to be patient and give her the space she needs and keep talking to you."

"Alright. That's good." Bea shifted in her chair. "Last session, I asked you to think about your *raison d'etre*. I imagine realizing you'll be a father has made this a most pressing question, yes?"

"Definitely."

"Have you got an answer for me?"

"No. I did think about it though. And I think being a father is going to help me better understand it. Because I don't exist for the kid, right? But I partly do, I suppose."

"That's not a bad way of thinking about it. Well, I look forward to your answer once it's developed.

"Before you leave, Del, I want to talk about one last thing. We haven't given names to anything you experience yet, but I think we should now, okay? Naming things puts a boundary on them. They may not be perfectly accurate, but they make actionable steps possible. Having a framework sheds off a lot of chaos."

I nodded.

"Are you comfortable saying you experience depression?"

"I don't know—I mean, one of the last things I told Sally as I told her goodbye was that I think I'm depressed. Why did I say that to a horse? I don't know, but that's the first time I've said it. Still, anytime I think about it, I think 'no, not me.' I don't relate to other people that have depression."

"Well, that's the nature of the disease. It isolates you, makes you feel alone. It pretends like it doesn't exist. If it can trick you into believing that, then it's winning. But I do think your case might be a little different."

"Really? Why is that?"

"You experience depression, Del, I think that's fair to say and might help you deal with it, but I don't think you experience meaninglessness. I think you experience too much meaning, and it overwhelms you, so you cower into a shell of a man, but I don't think this is just a chemical imbalance. Though I won't assume it's not *not* a chemical imbalance. I think you are disconnected from the narrative of your life."

I gave an absent stare. She asked me, "What do you think about that?"

"I can't put it in words or translate it into anything tangible. And the meaning just seems absurd! How could I believe in it? I've no reason to but I'm completely immersed in it. The religious possesses me. I see a crucifix and I weep. I see a Buddha and my lungs release an air of anxiety and breathe in peace. The preacher says God sent his only son to save the world, and I don't know what that means or if it's historically factual, but I know it's true. I can't control this meaning, and I can't put it into words. I don't believe in it. But it consumes me.

"And my dad thinks I'm spiritual. That's not a word I would use to describe me these days, and I wouldn't expect him to, either. What do you think?"

"Aren't we all a little spiritual in our own way?"

"That's an idea that obsessed me in college. We all have a religious inclination. That Augustinian notion."

"If you believe that, why are you no longer religious, in the practical sense?"

"Yeah, good question. I'm not sure that I'm not."

Bea bit the end of her pen. "Interesting. We will have to talk more about that in the next session. I'll make a note." She clicked her pen open and wrote on her notepad.

"One day at a time, right Del?"

"I guess so."

"I'll see you on Thursday."

She shook my hand, and I left.

Walking down Peachtree, I came to the Presbyterian church. I checked my watch to see it was 4:15 in the afternoon. I decided to go into the sanctuary and sat in a pew toward the back, facing the large cross hanging behind the pulpit. It was draped in purple cloth. As I sat there, focused on the cross, I began to wish I had gone to a Catholic Church. I wanted to see Jesus nailed there. I wanted to see him suffering with me. The empty cross didn't do much for my 'religious inclination.' It didn't give me comfort. It left me feeling empty. Alone. Lonely.

But I hadn't come to the sanctuary to have a religious experience. I was looking for Adam. Luckily for me, he walked out of the door to the right of the altar before I had to go looking for him. He saw me sitting there and grinned.

"Great timing! I was about to head home for the day. Let's get a beer?"

I agreed and we walked out of the church together.

"How are we, Del?" He softly put his hand on my shoulder blade. I must have twitched. He removed his hand.

"Well, I've just had therapy so I'm both as good as I can be and well aware that I'm not too great."

Adam laughed. "Are any of us, really?"

"I guess not."

"There's this place up here around the corner. They've got a great happy hour selection. Also, it's a speakeasy theme, so it's usually pretty empty this time of day. You need a membership card to get in, or you can talk to one of the concierges nearby. They offered me mine for free, guess they wanted clergy to feel welcome."

I knew the bar. My palms started to sweat. I was nervous to return to the place I'd first laid eyes on her.

Adam was right. The place was deserted when we walked in. The atmosphere felt completely different. There were more lights on. The bartender was dressed down in casual wear and the speakers were playing alternative rock.

Adam paid for my beer. He didn't ask what I wanted and ordered two of the same kind.

"Johnny tells me you love a good sour, this is a Berliner Weisse from an Athens brewery," he said, as he grabbed the beers from the bartender.

We sat at a booth on the opposite end of the room from the couch Charlie and I had sat not too long ago.

The beer was good. Really good. I didn't think I'd ever had a beer that I liked that much. Citrus tart on the front and a wheat-y aftertaste.

Adam noticed how much I enjoyed it and smiled. "It's good, right?"

"Really good," I said.

I pulled out my phone and texted Johnny. I told him I was with Adam and that I appreciated he was a savant of beer. Later he'd reply, "I knew you would. Drink one for me."

I grinned and looked up at Adam.

"Del, I know you've got an opinion on this, and who else would want to know but someone like me?" I raised my eyebrows as he continued, "What do you think of God?"

"Damn. Let's get right into it, huh? I didn't think you'd be such a stereotypical pastor. Not even going to let me get a good bit of beer in me before you have me question the ultimate?"

"Truthfully, this is not how I start most conversations, but I'm *actually* interested in how *you* might answer. And why waste time, right? I know you're not one for small talk."

"Fair enough." I took a swig of my beer. Truth be told, I felt relaxed. Adam was a figure of catharsis. I felt like I could say whatever the hell I wanted.

"What do I think of God, huh?" He nodded.

"I hate him," I said with a smirk, and my tongue planted against my cheek.

He nodded again, "You've been wanting to get that off your chest for a while now, huh? Well, I believe you."

It felt good to say that to a clergyman. I sat back in my chair and crossed my legs. I could feel my cheeks perked up and tightened by the smile on my face.

Adam spoke again, "You know, usually when someone has that response, I feel a little bit sad. Sad that somebody has been hurt so bad by quote unquote 'God's representatives' as to feel that way. But shamefully, I also feel like, for you, that's a shallow response. So, give me a better answer."

"No, let me ask you, how do you believe in that God? Have you seen how that God let's his people treat people like you?" I scrunched my brow and perched my lips.

"What do you mean, 'people like me?' I am God's people."

"Don't act like you don't know what I'm talking about. God's people would have you killed if they could get away with it."

"Don't be so close-minded, Del. Some of them would. Sure. But that's not God's fault. It's their own ignorance. Ignorance is the only obstacle to love. And God's people are known by their love. Not their racism, not their homophobia. Their love. Why are you so angry about this?"

"Because I was one of them!" Immediately, I felt my face turn hot and the tears had formed and began to flow. "That God made me like that. I hate him! I swear I hate him."

Adam came and sat beside me. He put his arm around me, and I knew he was crying too. "I hate that God, too, Del. He's evil. But He is not real."

Crying, for me, rare as I do–though it's been much more often recently–usually starts as a burst of anger. Anger I've held in too long. Then the tears roll out more sedated, and I'm no longer angry or frustrated or mad; I'm hurt. Hurt by this confusing existence. Hurt for existing. I feel alone. Having Adam hold me didn't make me feel like I wasn't alone, but my loneliness was less severe.

I calmed down and took a few deep breaths. Adam returned to his own seat.

"I just don't get how you can believe in a loving God. I don't see it. I don't feel it. God even seems more cruel than good sometimes."

"I know."

"Then why do you believe it?"

"I don't always, but I do right now. Sometimes, times like this, I can make the leap of faith. The rest of the time I just try to live as if it were true because of the times I've been so convinced it is."

"That's absurd."

Adam smirked. "Isn't it?"

"Totally and completely absurd. How do you do it? What does this 'leap of faith' look like? What are you leaping toward? Where will you land?"

"That's why it's a leap, Del. We don't know. God's a glimmer of light and we're creatures under the shadow of a cloud. Sometimes the glimmer catches our eye, and we can feel it's true presence. That's what we're leaping toward. The hope, not the delusion, that we have seen the light."

"And why isn't God actually just some cruel tyrant for letting this happen? For placing us at the bottom of the insufferable ocean? Or the desert canyon where we haven't got the food or the water to have the strength to make the leap? What if I don't have the strength? Wouldn't it be God's fault for not giving it to me?"

"Maybe. But our hope is that God is good—Not just our hope. God wouldn't be God unless the divine nature is good."

"I don't know if I can accept that."

"That's okay. It's not much to do with accepting it. It's about living it. St. Paul writes, 'For now we see only a reflection as in a mirror; then we shall see face to face. Now I know in part; then I shall know fully, even as I am fully known' and quotes the Greek poet, Epimenides, 'For in him we live and move and have our being.' If the Christian hope is true, if any hope of goodness and truth, beauty and love, is real, then it does not matter if you can accept it. You already live in it."

"That does me a lot of good. What am I supposed to do with that?"

"Return your gaze to the absolutes."

I didn't know what a platitude like that even meant. The irony was it reminded me of how I talked as a young college student.

"I know that sounds too abstract, but contemplating these things puts our short lives in perspective." He took a strong sip of beer, finishing it off, and told me he had to be on his way. I thanked him for the beer and gave him a rigid masculine side-hug. Before he left, he added, "You should come to our service on Wednesday night. I think you might enjoy it. I know church isn't your thing, and I don't care to make it, but your heart was made to worship, isn't that what St. Augustine wrote of?"

I nodded.

"Then you might as well aim that worship at the absolute." He gave me a genuine smile. "If you ever need relationship advice from a celibate gay minister, don't hesitate to call me. Bye, Del." He winked and left. I went straight to the bar for a second Berliner Weisse.

Beer in hand, I returned to the booth and pulled my phone out to text Johnny, "Your special friend is more 'Christian' than I expected."

He responded quickly, "Yeah, but you can tell he means what he says, and he doesn't mean what you would assume. He's not going to try to convert you. Promise. But you get used to it. Want me to bring dinner over tomorrow night?" I told him yes. He said he would be over around seven. It seemed like he was trying to limit my time alone. He'd never been so intentional with me.

I scrolled through my phone as I finished my beer. The time displayed at the top of the screen caught my attention. It was late. I needed to head home to feed Amir, and myself.

On my way to the door, I grabbed our empty glasses to take to the bar. She was there, sitting at the far side of the bar studying her drink. My eyes recognized the dark, glimmering hair and red lips. My heart started thudding against my chest. Short, hard bursts, like it was scared to make a full beat. I hid my face behind my shoulder as I walked out, but I had to go right by her to get to the door. I watched her from the corner of my eye. She turned, noticed me, and smiled. Just a stranger being polite. I smiled back. Just another beautiful, mysterious woman.

***

Amir was happy to see me when I walked in after work that Tuesday. He ran his body against my leg, tiptoed with an arched back and his tail perked up in the air. Cats are weird like that. They only love you when they need something. Quite selfish, cats. He purred relentlessly as I pulled out his food and then immediately disregarded me, turning his full devotion to the food in his bowl.

I took the dishes that had accumulated over the weekend out of the sink and hid them in the dishwasher before wiping the counters down. Then I set the table with two plates and silverware. I lit a candle and set it on the marble of the kitchen pass through, making sure to hold the flame directly to the wax, so it would appear to have been burning longer and increase the aroma in the room.

At 6:55, Johnny knocked at the door, and I let him in. He brought street tacos and limes for me to make margaritas. He told me he liked the smell of the candle. I blew it out and said, "There's no need to put it up against the odor of tacos. I'll light it again later."

"I've never seen this place so clean. What's gotten into you? You're not picking up girls from the bar and bringing them back here, are you?" He jested, but I winced.

"You know damn well I'm trying to heal my relationship with Charlotte."

"I do."

"I like my place clean. You wouldn't know. It's been years since we lived together. But, since college, this is what I like. I guess I've been too overwhelmed lately to keep it the way I want it. Cleaning never was Charlotte's thing, you know? I think she tried her best for me. She just doesn't see or understand clean the way I do. My messes don't bother me like they bother her and her messes *certainly* don't bother her like they bother me. While she's gone, I guess I'm taking full hold of the responsibility."

"Well, it's good. I like it in here. Feels cozy. I'd be worried if I came in here to a slob of mess. Should I inspect your room?"

"Not necessary. It's clean." Though, if he peaked into my closet, that wouldn't be the case.

"When Charlotte comes back, you should talk her into letting you do the cleaning then."

"*If* she comes back. You've got more hope than me."

I mixed tequila, lime juice, and Cointreau, and poured the cocktail into two glasses rimmed with salt. Johnny brought the food, and I brought the drinks to the table, and we sat down to eat.

"So, she's going to therapy with you, huh? Why aren't you hopeful? That's a good sign by me."

"Sure, but you know how I am. How long can I stay engaged before I fall away again? I don't want to pretend like I can change."

"Who said anything about changing? You're fine like you are if you'd just learn to live with it."

"I'd live with it quite fine on my own. It's Charlotte that makes it difficult. She'll forgive me, I hope. I think she will. And she'll say she accepts me like I am. My volatile self. She'll say she's okay with it. She understands. But how will I ever believe that? How can I ever feel confident I'm not doing what I've done the last seven years, tearing her apart with my apathy and isolating self-absorption?"

"I don't know, Del. You've got a therapist for a reason. Just be honest with her. She can't understand you if you aren't honest."

"I've never been one to lie to her. Carolyn's the first time I've ever really done anything to betray her, and I hid that for good reason, I thought."

"That's not what I'm saying. I know you don't lie to her. But you aren't honest, either. You've got to tell her what you need, and you've got to tell her what you feel and trust her with it. You always assumed she couldn't handle your honesty and look where that got you. It didn't do you any good, did it? Well, you'll have to do something different this time. You'll just have to trust her with yourself and believe she can handle it. Charlotte's an incredible woman, Del. I don't think you've ever really seen it. She's one of the few people I ever actually thought could put up with your bullshit, but she can't handle you if you're not being your true self. As soon as you realized you couldn't be a saint to her, you withdrew so she couldn't see your demons. Well, she knows you have demons. We all do. They can't be dealt with unless they're thrown into the light."

My face tightened into a grin.

"What?"

"You've just been spending a lot of time with Adam is all."

"Oh, shut up!" He turned his head down, but I saw the grin on his face. We finished up our food and went and sat on the balcony.

"I'd love one of those mini cigars. Care to smoke?"

"I'm out," I told him.

"Seriously? I've never known you to not have them."

"I liked them too much. Figured it would be best if I took a break. A regular cigar here and there is all I'm good for for a while."

"Is this you trying to get your life together?"

"Something like that. You know, Adam has me thinking I should go to church."

"Oh, so he is converting you, huh?"

"No, you know as much as I do that where we've gone, we can't go back."

"I agree we've gone beyond a certain form of religion, but I'm not so sure that's true of what Adam's preaching. He gets it, too. I'm not so sure he's too different from you and I."

"I don't think I'm ready to go to his church yet, you know? I'd like to go somewhere I can hide. I'm thinking I'll visit that Orthodox Church." I pointed to the gold-roofed building that had the tendency to glare into my eyes when the sunlight hit it just right. "Maybe the liturgy will speak to me. Get me focused right. Be a little therapeutic."

"Could. But Del, that's not an Orthodox Church. That's a mosque."

I squinted my eyes and looked out in the distance. Sure enough, what I had thought to be an Orthodox Church was a mosque. What I thought was a cross peaking over the tree-covered street was really a crescent moon.

"Isn't that something." I kept looking at it to make sure my eyes weren't deceiving me. "Perhaps I'll try out that mosque, then."

***

Johnny left around 9 or 9:30. I hadn't checked the clock. With Charlotte gone, only for now, I hoped, I felt like I was racing to not be alone. When she'd first left, I didn't want to see anybody, and I imagined they didn't want to see me. Now, other than Charlotte, I felt like I was more right-standing with the people closest to me than I had ever been before. Yet, I still felt an impenetrable loneliness.

I realized how much time I had been spending alone the past few weeks. Had it been weeks? It felt like weeks. All the days seemed to mesh together like the unimportant details in a film or novel. The only scenes that stuck out were the ones where I wasn't alone. I didn't want to be alone.

I sat on my couch. My eyes faced the blank television. I don't want to be alone.

***

I texted Adam and asked what he knew about mosques. He replied soon after that he had been to meetings with Muslim leaders and always wanted to visit a service. He added that he was friends with one of the imams at the very mosque out in the distance from my balcony. Then, to my surprise, he said he was free to go to a prayer service *the very next morning*. Muttering *what the hell* under my breath, I texted back that I was in. We went back and forth with the plan before I made my way to bed.

Lying there, I thought how ridiculous it was that the situation I'd got myself into had brought me closer to my family. That, and Sally's death. I thought they'd reject me. It seemed like they got a good look at me for the first time since I became an adult. They knew me now. For better or for worse, they knew me. And now they had somebody they could choose to accept. I didn't know how to think about that. Maybe there isn't more to think about. I let it be and went to sleep. I had to be up early to meet Adam for the prayer service.

***

The Wednesday morning sun had long to rise, but the bronze crescent moon glowed beneath the real moon, which was full and bright as I walked up to the building with Adam. Imam Hassan met us at the door and welcomed us in. He was a quiet man, just shorter than me. His face was stoic against his dark skin and even darker beard, but his eyes glistened like stars against the night sky out in the country.

We took our shoes off and placed them with the others before Imam Hassan brought us to a wash basin and led us through a process he called 'Wudu.' Three times, we ran water across the exposed parts of our bodies, including the inside of our mouth and nostrils. Imam Hassan smiled at us as we finished and then we followed him to the prayer area. Adam and I sat toward the back and watched as the people sat around in prayer and read from the Quran. Silence seemed respectful so we communicated with different glances in between observing the worshipping people.

A man began to sing what Imam Hassan told us would be the call to prayer. The few men that were there lined up in half a row and then two rows of women formed behind them. I looked at Adam to see if we should join, but he shook his head, so we stayed put and watched. Imam Hassan took his place at the front and led them in a xenolalic tongue of prayer. The catatonic voices hitting against the ceiling put me into a meditative state. I slipped into a daze. The chanting continued as I watched a lamb trot up to the front of the room beside Imam Hassan. The people turned toward the lamb, and, as their prayers were aimed in its direction, the lamb stood on its hind legs. Its face was bare. Its fore legs pointed out toward the heavens and its hooves angled toward the people as if blessing them. Blood began to pour from its heart. A processional cross pierced through the lamb's back.

Suddenly, everyone in the room turned into a lamb, licking the blood up as it ran across the floor. My heart began to race as I tried to snap back into reality. I turned to Adam, glad to see he was still human. He smiled at me and then pulled out a pitcher, filling it with the water from the Wudu basin. He poured what looked like blood into a chalice and had me drink it. I slowly took a sip and realized it had turned to wine. Overcome with élan, I clasped the chalice into my own hands and gulped the rest of it down.

The lamb had now turned into Christ. I knew it was him because his face was blinding and his wounds were scarred over. The sheep formed their bodies so as to always be looking at him as he walked across the room. The sheep parted ways to let him through. He stood above me, leaned down, and kissed my cheek. Then he was gone.

My team at the office seemed happy to see me when I walked in a few minutes after nine. Their eyes lifted from their computer screens, and they watched me walk across the communal floor toward my office. I sat at my desk and powered on my computer. The screen showed it was loading up, so I leaned back in my chair and waited.

One of my team members, Daniel, knocked on my open door and stepped in.

"How was your weekend?"

"Fine, halfway to next, aren't we? How was yours?"

"Well, I must have missed you yesterday and I work from home on Monday now. Anyways, I had a great weekend. It was wonderful, really. The wife and I went out to the lake on a friend's boat. Just good fun."

"Sounds like it, Danny."

My desk was a cluttered mess, so I went to organizing it. I threw some papers in the bottom drawer of my desk to be dealt with later. There was a letter on my keyboard that was unmarked but sealed closed. I ran my thumb across it to feel its contents.

"So, some of us are going out to grab a drink later. Would you want to join us?"

I looked up from the letter at Daniel.

"Yeah, I'll let you know at the end of the day. I've got a lot going on, but I'll think about it."

"Alright." He bobbed his head and walked out.

I opened the envelope with a paper knife and pulled out a check. It was a bonus signed by Jasmine for two grand.

The memo read: 'You earned it'.

I dropped it in the bottom drawer and unlocked my computer. I found I was able to be productive. To my surprise, I was enjoying the work. Around 11:30, an email from Jasmine popped up with the subject: Lunch on me.

I emailed back and said I was finishing a few details and I'd be free in less than half an hour. I finished up in fifteen minutes and shut my computer down. My desk was mostly tidy, so I shuffled a few papers around to make them straight and walked over to Jasmine's office. She wasn't there, so I headed to the break room.

Her and Daniel were sitting at the table having a conversation. They were both laughing when I walked in. She saw me and said, "Del! We were just talking about you. I guess we're all still running off the high from the past two weeks. Can y'all believe this week is already stronger than last?

"Daniel says our sales department is getting more calls from companies wanting our business just this morning than what we average in a month." Her face beamed as she continued, "We're going to have to hire more team members and I want you to help me."

"So, what were you laughing about?"

I watched as both of their eyes darted away from me and toward each other.

Daniel stumbled to find words, "It's just an ironic situation for you is all."

"It is, isn't it?" I leaned against the door frame.

I could tell they didn't know what to say and started to laugh. "It really is. Who would've thought my marital problems could turn me into a decent employee?"

"Del, we didn't mean–" Jasmine started.

"No, it's fine. I can see the humor in it. I mean, if I get things worked out with Charlotte, maybe I can do it again down the road when we need a boost."

Jasmine stood up and smoothed out her dress.

"Lunch then?"

I nodded.

Daniel had an awkward grin on his face and said, "Enjoy."

I smiled and told him we would.

We rode the elevator down to the lobby floor and walked across the street to the tavern. It was the same tavern a lot of my team members would frequent after work. I imagined it's where Daniel and whoever else was planning on going would be later that evening. The restaurant was split into two main rooms, the bar room with a few tables lined against the walls, and a more intimate restaurant section with better lighting. At night, it all felt like one space with people crowding each room, talking and drinking their beers. We sat in the dining area and the waiter brought us the lunch menu. Jasmine ordered a glass of white wine, and I ordered a red.

The waiter quickly brought us the wine and Jasmine took a sip of hers before saying, "Alright, Del. Catch me up. What's been going on since last week? I will say there's something different about you."

I smiled as she continued, "Wait a minute–do you? Are you actually enjoying working with us now? What is this?" She snickered at her sarcasm.

"I don't know," I shrugged my shoulders. "I still don't know a lot of things. I don't know if Charlotte is going to come back." I looked down at the stained wood table and the empty white charger plate, "Like really come back. We are going to go to therapy together, though. That's a good sign–I hope. But I'm learning to accept things, I think. Work has been good for me. It's grounding me. Thanks for the bonus, by the way."

"Sure, you earned it. I'm sorry for making your life the brunt of a joke."

"I honestly don't care. I mean it. Who doesn't joke a little about other people when they aren't in the room? Seems impossible not to. Of course, we *never* joke about you, Jasmine." I over-annunciated the 'never' to give it a nice sarcastic curve.

"It is funny, isn't it? In a way, I'm glad it happened. I'm glad I screwed up with Charlotte. And God, am I glad she's pregnant. I become so overwhelmed any time I think about it. I'm going to be a father! I'm damn scared, but I'm also excited, you know? This is an opportunity to right my wrongs. To right a long line of patrilineal wrongs. I wish it wasn't happening like this, but at the same time, look at me. I'm facing the music. I've accepted this burden of a life and now I can make things right. Or, at least, better.

"I sound like a life coach or something, like I've been listening a little too closely to my brother. I don't think this is a bad sense of optimism though. I think it might be real. I have to believe that."

Jasmine leaned back in her chair. "I think you have good reason to be optimistic. I'm happy for you, Del. And I'm so thrilled that it's making me more money." She winked. "So, I do have to hire more sales members and marketing analysts, and I want you to help me do interviews. You've got an eye for this business that I don't exactly have."

"Alright. I'd be glad to help."

"There's more than just that. There's more than one reason I gave you that bonus."

I nodded for her to continue.

"I think you should pursue whatever you really want from this life, and I want that bonus to give you the space to get started."

I leaned back from the table.

"What do you mean? You want me to find a different job? Jasmine, there isn't a job for me. That's the point. I work because I have to. Just let me keep working here. Besides, I can't change jobs now. I need to focus on my marriage and my kid."

"You wouldn't be switching jobs exactly. I'm keeping you on as a consultant. It would be less hours, sure, but with the way business is growing right now, I can still afford to keep you at the same salary. Plus, I can get someone else in your office space, bring in more revenue, and you can focus more on your home life. It's a win-win."

"Why? There's no reason to treat me this well, so why?"

She sipped her wine, and the waiter came to take our order. I hadn't had a chance to look at the menu, so I just told her I'd have the special despite not knowing what it was. Jasmine ordered the same and the waiter left to put our order in.

"Why are you helping me like this? It just seems so unwarranted."

"You don't think this will help me, too? I mean, you've already helped me so much, I think it's completely warranted. But I do think you'll do better work for me as a consultant. You see, Del, I'm actually selfish, and I think you're the kind of person that needs balance. I think you actually need a job just like this, but you also need to feel free to pursue something personal, some sense of accomplishment, creation, individuation, whatever you want to call it. But that's exhausting too. You need this job, just less of it. And you'll feel less stress from this job, at least, that you'll be a more motivated worker. Like I said, it's a win-win. Besides, I only gave you two grand. That's not exactly life changing money."

"If you say so, but I'm not convinced you're selfish." I was too overwhelmed to process what she was saying. The waiter brought us French dip and we ate in silence. Jasmine answered some emails on her phone as she ate. My cheeks were sore from grinning.

The French dip was perfectly cooked. The bread was crunchy on the outer layer and soft on the inside and the soup du jour was warm and savory.

"So, who will replace me as the head of the team?"

Jasmine looked up from her phone. "I was thinking Daniel."

I thought about it and agreed. "I think so too."

"You should go out for drinks with him tonight. Maybe I'll let you mention the idea to him."

"Yeah, I would like to be the one to tell him."

Jasmine paid for our meal with the business card. I thanked her for lunch when we stepped out of the tavern onto the sidewalk, and she said not to mention it. Then she told me she had a meeting in Buckhead, so she left toward the parking deck, and I crossed the street back to the office.

I told Daniel I would be able to make it to drinks later but suggested we went somewhere other than the tavern. I told him I'd even love it if he came to my place, and I made drinks. He agreed to that, and I went to my desk.

Mom called while I was working. She asked me how I was doing, and I told her about how well work was going. I didn't tell her about the prayer service, but I did say I was thinking about going to church with them on

Sunday. Her voice became noticeably more cheerful. "That would be wonderful!" she replied.

I asked about Dad. She told me he'd been a little distressed over Bucky. I questioned what was going on with Bucky and she told me he seemed depressed and lonely ever since Sally died. It was nice to know she was validating the horse's mental health. I told her I was handling Sally's passing surprisingly well. Of course, I missed her.

I was thinking about the night Sally died as the static silence pounded through the phone against my ear.

I heard Mom let out a breath before she asked, "How's Charlotte?"

"You'd know as well as me, Mom."

Another pause.

"I'm praying for you both, Del. God's got this."

I held back from rolling my eyes despite knowing she couldn't see me. "Yeah–thanks Mom."

We hung up after that.

I spent an hour replying to emails and sent an email to the entire team to update them on a few details about our new clients. I told them they were doing a fantastic job and should be happy with themselves for the work they had done.

They were all intently focused on their computers as I walked out of the office. A few of them glanced up at me and smiled. I felt myself smile back and made my way home.

I walked slowly down Peachtree. The street was bare, quietly waiting for the influx of traffic that would come around four. The sun was beaming through the limbs of the trees that lined the street. This caused little pockets of sun rays to glisten between the shade. I stopped by a park and found a bench in front of a large water fountain. The fountain flowed about twenty feet above the ground level but was itself built about ten feet into the earth. Terraced bits of brick and grass for seating funneled down around the fountain's base.

A kid, maybe three years old, was running around and through the fountain, letting it splash and soak his clothes. The water would spray directly into his face, and he would look to see if his mom was watching him explore. She wasn't. She sat on a bench adjacent to me, slouched over her phone, mindlessly scrolling away.

The kid looked at me. I waved. He smiled with the kind of smile that makes your eyes close, and I chuckled a little bit. Then he ran into the fountain to let the water blast him in the face. He did it and then looked directly at me. I smiled again and gave him a thumbs up, so he did it again. His mom noticed I was giving him more attention than she was and told him they were leaving.

I understood not trusting a stranger, but I had a feeling she felt judged by me, a stranger who happened to see her taking a break. The young kid waved goodbye as his mother dragged him toward the stroller. I waved back.

The afternoon air was growing humid, and I thought about that kid, and I thought I ought to run into the fountain and let the water crash against every bit of me. I walked down each level of the concave structure until I reached the base and let the water run through my hands. I cupped my palms and let them fill, using the water to wash off my face, then I cleaned the inside of my mouth, immediately spitting the highly chlorinated water right out. A laugh crawled out from deep within me. I looked around to see if anyone was watching. Not a soul around me. I stuck my face through the fence of water, and it blasted my cheeks in a therapeutic repetition. I felt a boyish smile form on my face. That kid really was on to something.

The fountain had succeeded in cooling me off, and I made my way home. The overspray of water had soaked my clothes thoroughly and my shoes squished with every step. I hurried the two blocks home so I could dry off and put on fresh clothes.

To my surprise, the door was unlocked. It wouldn't be the first time I'd neglected to lock the door on my way out. But it wasn't neglect; she was there, asleep on the couch. Amir was purring, pressed against her side.

I grabbed a blanket from the bedroom and covered her. She reached for my hand and intertwined her fingers with mine. I kneeled and kissed her forehead. "I've missed you," I whispered into her ear. A single tear bled through her eyelashes.

"I believe you," she said as she sat up. Amir was annoyed to be woken and strutted off to his water bowl.

"Are you back then?"

She shook her head slowly.

My chest tightened over my heart. "Why not? Why put it off any longer?"

"We need this, Del. You know it as much as I do. I don't want to keep living this cycle, and I don't want to force anything.

"I want to learn to relate to you and I hope you want the same. So, instead of just existing in the same space, we can share a story. A good story." She paused long enough for me to know she was right and to know I wanted the same thing. "We can create a life, a deeply meaningful one, and I'm not talking only about the life growing inside me."

"And what if I can't?" I felt the tears form in my eyes, "What if I can't do it? What if I can't be what you need me to be?"

"I don't need you to be anything other than yourself. To stop hiding and let me see you. Like I see you now. I know you care about me. I can feel it in your hand, and I can see it in your eyes. You want this to work, and that's all that matters. We let ourselves get too passive and that is my fault too. I hid from you, too. I'm sorry, Del. I'm so sorry."

She led my head into her lap, and I wrapped my arms around her legs. She ran her fingernails through my hair, sending a tingling feeling down my back. Holding her again made me feel human. Like I wasn't just a brain in a vat. My soul met my body fully enfleshed.

I started to chuckle in her lap.

"What?" She asked me.

I sat back and said, "I'm soaking wet!"

"Yeah..." she giggled. "Why are you wet?"

"Well, I stopped by the fountain and splashed around. God, Charlotte, I've been so miserable without you here, I think I'd be okay if we just went back to passively existing together."

"Oh, it was certainly better than being without you, but I don't want to go back to being in hell with you. I don't want to live in any hell at all."

"Well, I doubt if I'll ever make it to heaven, Charlotte." I winked at her.

She grinned. "Then let's just settle for earth, huh?"

I nodded. "That's all I want," I said, and added, "Maybe we'll learn to fight, too."

"That's what earth is all about, isn't it? Wrestling for the things we believe in and refusing to let go. That's why we were in hell together, Del. We refused to wrestle. We settled for the frigid cold of indifference. But I can take a fight. I'm stronger than you think. I can take your full ignorant self, alright? Trust me with your ugliness. I can't love all of you if you don't."

She communicated so finely and clearly and all I could reply was, "You're a damn cool girl, Charlotte," to which she threw her head back in laughter.

I looked at her sitting above me. She looked strong and I felt weak. A good kind of weak. Like I didn't have control and maybe that was a good thing. I pulled myself up and kissed her and she kissed back. I laid myself on the couch and pulled her on top of me. We kissed slowly, passionately. I ran my hand through her hair and gripped her waist with the other. She clenched my face with both hands and pressed her body into mine. It felt like we were in school again. She was the only one I wanted.

She sat up abruptly, "Are you gonna change?"

"I'm trying, love, I promise."

"No, not that. Your clothes!"

I woke up to my phone ringing. Charlotte's face was pressed firmly against mine creating a humid atmosphere of stale, comforting breath. I tapped her till she woke. She sat up so I could reach for the phone. Daniel was calling to tell me he needed my address. I mumbled 'of course,' and gave it. He said he was headed my way. I said alright and he hung up.

"Daniel," she raised her brow, "from work?"

I smiled while nodding and told her the news.

"That's wonderful!" She kissed me. "I'm proud of you." She kissed me again.

"Why don't we celebrate? I think that would be okay. It'll be like we're dating again, yeah? I'll come pick you up tomorrow." Her eyes were glimmering, and I felt like I had a glimpse of heaven. She went to kiss me again, but I wrapped my arms around her tightly and pressed my cheek into the upper part of her breast. Her arms dangled in the air and then slowly started to grip my body.

"I love you."

She kissed the top of my head. "I know."

We walked down to our lemon of a car, her arm entwined with mine. I opened the door for her, and she sat and started it.

My palms were gathering sweat, and I could feel my heartbeat increase as she stared into my eyes. There were no more words to say. Not right now. So, we just took each other in.

Beautiful as ever, I had a hard time letting her go, but she closed the door and drove off as I watched her disappear.

Tears started to swell up. I felt a great sadness. Real sadness. I was sad that I hadn't seen her sooner.

I paced slowly back to the elevator. On the ride up, I realized I missed the church service Adam had invited me to and texted him to apologize, explaining stuff had come up.

Daniel was waiting at my door when I arrived. I apologized and let him in. He was holding a bottle of whiskey in one hand and a bag of oranges in the other.

He handed me the spirit for me to inspect and give my approval. The label read 'zero proof,' so I looked at him with a raised brow.

"Been sober for three years now. That stuff will still make a damn good old-fashioned. Feel free to use real bourbon in yours."

We went into the kitchen, while I tried to wrap my mind around him being sober. I wasn't bothered by it, just caught off guard because of how much time he spent with our co-workers at the bar.

"What made you go sober?"

"Doctors told me I was drinking my life away. Said at the pace I was going, I'd be dead in ten years. Decided life was worth living and quit."

I pulled a knife out and used it to slice off two slivers of orange peel for the garnish.

"Was it hard then? To quit? Did you go to AA?"

"Hell no. I mean, that helps a lot of people. I couldn't do it, though. Wasn't for me. I did start going to church. I guess I just did the steps my own way." I dropped a sugar cube in both of our glasses and Daniel handed me the bitters from my bar cart.

"Uh–" I started when he cut me off.

"Well, I'm not a prude and you can't make an old-fashioned without them. Nobody's getting buzzed off a dash of bitters anyways."

I said alright and put a dash of bitters on each cube. I dropped the orange peels in and muddled it all together with a spoon before filling the glasses with ice.

"Why do you think going to church helped you? You believe it?"

I removed the plastic covering from the non-alcoholic whiskey and pulled out the cork. I sniffed the opening. It smelled like whiskey without the bite of alcohol. I measured out two ounces and dumped it in the first glass, and again for the second. After stirring it all together, I handed one glass to Danny, and we clinked the glasses together.

I led him out to the balcony while he tried to answer my question.

"I guess so. I don't know. All I know is it helped, so, in a sense, it is real to me. I needed to give up control of my life and let God have it."

"Step 12."

"No, that would be step 2. Really, its intertwined with all of them. I could not admit I was powerless without the Lord's help. How I see it now, at least."

I nodded, and we sat on the balcony chairs.

"What does it mean for you to let God have control?"

"It's not like he's some dictator giving orders for my every move. He doesn't control me. I just submit to his will. It's what is best for me. My preacher always quotes this guy, Calvin, saying, 'You are not your own. You are God's.' Something about that gives me peace. So what if people don't like it or just don't get it. It gives me peace."

"Understood." Church language put a bitter taste in my mouth. "Enough religious talk. I've got something pretty serious we need to discuss." I placed a grin against my cheeks so he knew it was a good kind of serious, then sipped my drink. It didn't taste anything like a real old-fashioned, but I said, "that's pretty good," and Danny beamed with delight.

"Jasmine and I have been talking, and we decided it was time for me to change roles. From now on, I'll be a consultant with the firm." Daniel was listening, but it didn't seem he knew where the conversation was heading. I watched his face to see if anything was clicking and, when nothing did, I added, "And we think you're the best fit to take my place."

"And what if I don't want it?"

"Well, why wouldn't you? It's higher pay! It's just about the same job with more leadership. Why wouldn't you want it?"

He tried to hide his laughter behind his glass. "Of course, I want it. You know how frustrating it was to watch you get promoted when I've been here ten years longer than you?"

"I'm sure it was hard. I'm sorry."

"But you deserved it, Del. You went to college, right? I didn't. That seems to matter with these people. Anyways, you're as sharp as they come and more mature than anyone senior to you at the company. The frustrating part is you didn't care. It didn't mean anything to you."

"That does seem to be my flaw, huh? My apathy runs to the core."

"Watching you these last couple weeks has been refreshing. You've got a new life to you. And now you're stepping down! I can't say I'm not sad I won't be able to see where you could've taken us."

"I'll still be consulting."

"I'm not sure that's a real job but fair enough."

"This is good news for both of us, Danny. I've been watching you and I know that you'll rise to the occasion. It is more stressful though, I won't lie to you. It was probably more stressful for me than the usual person because it prevented me from hiding as much as I could had I not been responsible for leading anybody. The responsibility is good though. Grab it and see what you can do with it. I know the job was given to me because of my ability to produce out of God knows where, but production doesn't make a good leader.

"You've got a gregarious nature about you, Danny—well, anyways. People like you, you're engaging, people will love working for you because of who you are. That's what will be fun, too. As long as you don't lose that personality of yours, they're gonna love you and you're gonna love leading them. Don't worry about what you can do or what you know, all that matters is who you are."

I hadn't prepared a speech, but there it was. I felt my words heading in that direction so I followed them to see what I would say. Words of encouragement rarely come out as eloquent as you expect, but for some reason that doesn't seem to matter in most cases.

Danny thrust his tongue into the side of the cheek as obvious as he could, "Alright, pastor."

And I went to telling him about my college studies and that, in fact, I knew a lot about John Calvin, which led to a lot of laughter.

I rode the elevator down with Daniel and walked him to his car. He shook my hand and expressed his gratitude for 'everything.' I knew what he meant. I waved goodbye as he pulled out and then went to check my mail. Among the ridiculous amount of franchise ads and bill notices was a handwritten letter, unsigned. Of course, I knew who wrote it. I waited until I was back in the condo to open it, quelling my anxiety as best as I could.

Once I was through the door, I poured a proper drink. Amir had been waiting at the door acting neglected, so I picked him up and set him on my lap as I sat on the couch.

I took a long sip and opened the letter.

With time and distance, dear Del, I've been given the gift of reflection. I'm back in Chicago now. With my husband. I realized as much as I felt unseen by him, it has often been my fault for hiding. And why did I feel like you saw me in a way he didn't? I let you. You were a stranger, even now you are a stranger. It was safe, and I was bored. Bored of the sameness of it all. I blamed him, but I see now, my husband loved me as I am. He did not care if I was not academic, you see. It was not a matter of him not respecting me, as I had felt. I was his rest. I am his rest. That's what he tells me.

Does that mean anything to you? I do wonder. As I understand him, my interest in academic things, untrained as I am, scares him. It scares him! It's not about having power over me or feeling threatened by my own self-trained intellect or him thinking I'm not a stimulating conversation partner. He just longs to be with someone *he doesn't have to be academic with.* God, if he told me sooner. He says he didn't realize this until I left him. Well, I understand him now, and I want to be that for him. He wants to be a person with me, and I a person for him. That's what helps him to not feel so alone in this world and his line of work. And even as I am that person for him, we now do talk about intellectual matters. It is really so beautiful. Our relationship has made me feel open and free.

And I hope the same for you. Do I hold anything against you? I must. It's not so easy to forgive. I do feel wronged by you and yet I can now relate to my husband because of you. I'm sure you have a more eloquent understanding of the nature of reality for why it is this way, but you were like a cigarette butt thrown in an un-swept forest, but now we're growing back, my husband and I, renewed and fresh with green life. Perhaps I care for you for this reason. Whoever you are. What I do know of you is you will appreciate the old tradition of the letter. Take that as a sign of appreciation for who you are and for our encounter. I wish the best for you, truly, and for your wife. And, I truly am sorry I destroyed your painting, but it really didn't belong on that wall.

A buildup of anxiety crashed together in one short sentence:

I hope you come to tell her all the truth,
Your dearest, Carolyn

P.S. I know how much you love a good poem.
This poem seems to come to mind when I think of you.

Emily Dickinson's Poem, *Tell all the truth but tell it slant*, slipped out on a small piece of soft, waxed paper.

> *Tell all the truth but tell it slant–*
> *Success in Circuit lies*
> *Too bright for our infirm Delight*
> *The Truth's superb surprise*
> *As Lightning to the Children eased*
> *With explanation kind*
> *The Truth must dazzle gradually*
> *Or every man be blind–*

I hadn't thought much about her by this point because I did tell Charlotte about that weekend. But here she persisted in my memory like a thorn in my side. Those few hours of acquaintance where we had been captured in a fit of romantic disfigurement persisted in torturing me. She was right. In order for me to find full healing with Charlotte, I would have to tell her the truth she needed to know. She needed to know why, and she needed to know the depth, and it had nothing to do with Carolyn. For all I knew, I was free of her. As she was free of me.

Danny said something during our second go at a religious talk that came to mind. I had ranted about the holier than thou types that went to church. He told me they weren't holy at all. Holiness, as he understood it, was acting in a way that makes things whole. That was a deeper insight than I'd expect from his kind of church. More progressive, too, which I made sure to tell him. I realized the holy act for me, and Charlotte, would be facing the whole truth, slowly, too, and not all at once. Carolyn was no longer important to this truth. It goes beyond her. I read the poem again.

The letter made me anxious, but overall, I felt good about where I was and how things were going. Carolyn's letter brought me a twisted joy. To me, the letter meant that I would be absolved of the sins that led to my encounter with Carolyn once Charlotte knew the truth. My truth. The one only I can tell. The only thing that would continue to bother me was knowing Carolyn was out there holding strong and mixed feelings about me. But that was beyond my responsibility. If I tell the truth, I'm free. Maybe writing that letter is how she set herself free.

Still, my anxiety built. My eyes refused to focus. Instead, they rapidly moved side to side. My stomach began to ache like it would after that fair ride I used to love as a kid. The one that spun so fast that gravity lost its rules. Except my eyes had lost their rules. *Why am I getting more anxious?*

Slant.

That word caused the breathlessness in my lungs. How could I tell the truth *slant*, if *I* didn't know it slant?

I did what I usually do when I wanted to manage my anxiety and tried reading from my poetry book. Of course, I couldn't open the book without flipping to my poem in the back. So, I read it again and decided, despite everything that seemed to be going wrong in my life, a lot seemed to be going right. I finished the poem. Four more lines, and it was done.

Titling poems is challenging because the name must embody the poem itself, while not giving away the content at first glance. That is, unless you are Emily Dickinson. Then you can title a poem *Tell all the truth but tell it slant* which isn't slant at all and yet, it is. That title has the opposite effect of what it pretends. The epitome of genius.

But I am not a genius, so my poem's title must remain slant. There must be a balance between concealing the message and the mood of the poem before it is read and yet, once it has been read, it should be so obviously conspicuous that the reader will think, 'Yes, this is the poem's title.' The title will first cause confusion and intrigue, but once the poem is read, the reader should be left with the *a priori* understanding that the title must have always been. There could be no other title.

Above the poem, I spelled out *Valley Peaks*, hoping this was the title that *had* to be, and closed the book. That one poem had kept me from reflecting on the work of Baudelaire but writing a few lines did me the same amount of good as reading ten poems written by someone else.

I went back to my title and crossed it out, replacing it with *Where the Valley Peaks*, paused for a moment, added a question mark, and left the book open on the coffee table.

***

In bed that night, I found myself staring at the ceiling. When I tried to close my eyes, the lamb impaled by the cross-shaped sword would flash in my mind. Thinking about the sheep lapping up the blood caused my stomach to stir. I shivered thinking about it. To think that Muslim people were drinking Christ's communion blood went against everything I had been raised to believe. It would probably revolt many Muslims, too.

I felt fear walking into the mosque earlier that morning. Living in Atlanta, I had met a good deal of gentle and kind Muslims, some more traditional in their piety than others. That didn't change the fact that I had been engrained with post-9/11 sermons throughout childhood and into college.

Imam Hassan had invited us to their Jum'ah on Friday. Adam wouldn't be able to make it, so I made the excuse that I was busy too.

My eyelids slowly fell over my eyes. As I slipped into an unconscious break, Christ met me. His lips sealed to my cheek.

***

Jasmine had me vet applications and choose the ones I wanted to set up for interviews. It was tedious work, and I didn't enjoy it, but occasionally I would come across an applicant that surprised me to the bone. The ones that showed the most amount of potential were the ones I least wanted to call. I did it anyway because that's business. It's their fault for shooting too low. I imagine had I been rejected on the notion that I was shooting too low without knowing the reasoning, I wouldn't be able to pick myself back up. Maybe they just needed a job. Maybe this was their way of picking themselves back up.

I ate lunch with Daniel. Jasmine suggested we keep close to help make the transition smooth. I liked Danny, so I didn't mind bonding. He ordered a non-alcoholic beer from the bar, and I was surprised when the bartender didn't skip a beat, grabbing a can with a '0%' label on it and pouring it into a glass for him. I ordered the same and, while the bartender grabbed my can, Daniel said he was fine with me drinking around him. I told him I already didn't drink during the day, and I wanted to try something new. Of course, I regretted it.

After scheduling a few interviews set to happen throughout the next two days, I left the office early for my session with Bea.

***

A cup of green tea was waiting for me when I walked in and sat on Bea's couch. She put her book away and turned her chair to face me. Smiling, she said, "Hi, Del. How are we today?"

I told her I was good, to which she replied, "Then why are you here?" We chuckled cordially.

"Where would you like to start?"

"I had an incredible daydream during a Muslim prayer service. I'd like to get your thoughts on it."

She raised her eyebrow and asked, "Muslim prayer service? I assume you weren't raised to be so ecumenical, no?"

I replied with a chummy, "I was not. But I went with Adam, you remember the pastor I was telling you about who's close with my brother? We went 'cause Charlotte's mom asked me to try church out again because she thought it would help me out, and I figured 'well, that's as much of a church to me as a Christian one.' It helped that I could see it from my balcony. Anyways, while we were there, watching them pray from the back of the room, I had an incredible imagining of sorts that sucked me into a trance."

"Alright. I'll certainly hear it. Daydreams, much like dreams, are often our unconscious trying to communicate with us, so we would do well to pay attention to them. I haven't asked you about your dreams, or daydreams, quite yet because I prefer to get through a few sessions. Some clients obsess so much over their dreams, reducing me to a cryptographer of the unconscious. I'm no cryptographer, and I'm no prophetess, but that's what they see me as. I can help people with their dreams, but not when they come to me like that. I'm not worried that you would do that so let me hear it, but Del?"

"Yes?" I replied.

She leaned forward. "I will tell you upfront that dreams are not meant to be fully understood, they are meant to be lived with, contemplated, and integrated. So be prepared to be comfortable with uncertainty."

I nodded.

"Alright, tell me the daydream."

I described to her in full detail the lamb, the sheep, the blood, Adam pouring me a glass of the blood, having me drink it, and how it turned to wine.

"Ah," Bea smiled. "What a wonderful image! Yes, I quite like it. A bit offensive to the Muslim community, though, no? Certainly not halal. Then again, it's not so easy to tame the unconscious."

I shrugged. "So, what do you make of it?"

"What do I make of it? What do you make of it! I don't believe this is a dream to be rationalized by analysis. We could certainly argue about the theological symbolism. Just sit with this one and don't forget it. Maybe read up on the Scriptures of Jesus' last supper and see what thoughts come to mind. You know Carl Jung would say to turn toward the religion you were raised in. I'd suggest you have a Protestant psyche. Have you read any Jung?"

"*Answer to Job* did a number on me in school."

"I'm sure it did. Surprised you didn't find me sooner. Anyways, since the dream has such a communal notion to it, the Last Supper is a good place to turn in the Gospels. Oh, and perhaps look up Tintoretto's *Last Supper*. I always preferred that one to da Vinci's."

I imagined I had a dazed expression on my face. I really thought she'd have more to say.

"That's it?" I said with frustration.

"That's it. Now don't be upset with me. I told you I'm no prophet, and I think you as well as the rest of our culture would benefit from not having to have everything laid out plain. Just accept the mystery."

"Fine." I said, in a tone laced with vexation.

"Do you feel like things have gotten better since you've started seeing me? Not necessarily because of our sessions but within that timeline."

I surveyed my knuckles, then the innocent scars on my fingers. The childhood memories connected to them crossed my mind. All the things I still carry today. I looked up to see her patiently waiting for my response. I felt the urge to say yes, but I wanted to make sure that was the truth and not just the more comfortable answer. My eyes shifted to the mandala painting on the wall above her desk. I followed the outer leaves toward the center of my psyche.

"I do," I finally answered, continuing, "It's been chaotic, exhausting, hopeless at times, but all of the chaos seems to be making way for healing to come."

"Inner healing or outer healing?"

"Are the two exclusives? I'm not sure you can have one without the other."

"You could get fired and divorced and still find inner healing."

"Ah, but I did get fired!" I said with a grin and filled her in on the previous few days.

"What do you make of your situation with her now? I know you're still hesitant to trust that things will be different, but why shouldn't they be?" Bea asked me after telling her about my last encounter with Charlotte and our 'date' this evening.

"I'm not sure. It does seem different. It seems like I have new eyes. Like nothing had to change, I just needed to change the way I see. But I realize I have a high experience of neurosis, be it depression or whatever you would call it, and I doubt there will come a time when I'm not like this. What then? How can I keep going through this healing process with my wife when I know that down the road I'm going to wake up and disappear behind my eyes into the torment of hell. And when I fall into that darkness in my brain, I'll drag Charlotte with me–" I paused before stuttering, "And my kid."

"I'm going to risk sounding cliché here, Del, but maybe it's what you need to hear. And I want to be very sensitive to your mental health because I know what feeling neurotic is like. You feel helpless, but that is just a feeling. And that feeling gets in the way of you actually getting help."

She continued, "Hell is the right metaphor, and certainly everyone around a person in hell experiences it too, but they can either be involuntarily dragged in by mere proximity or you can let them choose to join you there. The irony is, allowing others, allowing Charlotte, to join you there, in 'hell,' in the dark crevices of your mind, is the light you need. It may not be heaven, but when the people you love join you," she grabbed the small globe from her desk, "they can bring you back to here."

"That's about as cliché as you can get, Doc," I said, withholding telling her it was basically the same conversation me and Charlotte had the day before.

"Yeah, well, clichés exist for a reason," she piped back. "There's nothing wrong with clichés so long as you back them up with substance."

I felt a sly smile growing on my face. I stared at the earth in her hands. It was a raised relief globe so you could see and feel the magnitude of the mountains.

"Now, you have to tell me what's causing you to smile like that?" She placed the globe back on the desk and leaned smoothly against her chair.

"I wrote a poem."

"Ah ha! Do you want me to celebrate you? I can send in some champagne."

Bea's sarcasm was awfully unprofessional, but I wouldn't trust her nearly as much if she wasn't so candid at times. I wondered if she was like this with other analysands or was it just me? I assumed the latter.

"Alright, do you want to hear it or not? I think you'll like it, given what you're telling me today."

"Sure." She grinned. "Let me hear it."

"It's not a great poem, okay? So just focus on the content."

"No need for disclaimers, Del. Nobody writes good poetry. Not on purpose. Nobody writes bad poetry either. That's what's beautiful about the art. It's the content and the courage of the writer that connects with people, so if you think the content is good and you were honest to Being when you wrote it, then it might as well be good to somebody."

"Alright," I replied, and recited the poem. Bea didn't tell me it was good, and she didn't give any indication that it was bad. She immediately went on a rant about how green is a feminine color and represents the earth and something Jung said. Then she paused for a moment and her eyes opened wide and began to glow.

"This is your *raison d'etre*! You couldn't have given a better answer, and in dream form too! Because isn't that what poems are? A sort of written dream? Yes, Del, you read this poem every day and sit with it like a dream. Don't force the meaning but let it become incarnate in you." She was clearly satisfied with herself. I started to wonder if I would have fared just as well finding a palm reader.

"But what does that mean! How do I embody this?" My frustrations with her lack of clarity returned. Why couldn't she be more practical? "You speak in code! It's all abstractions, but they don't help at all." I realized my voice was raised and felt my face turn red. I felt like cowering.

Bea sat calmly and waited for me to gather myself.

"I'm sorry." I inhaled deeply. "You just don't get how frustrating this is. I need more clarity about what to do and the only thing you seem to encourage is more uncertainty."

She leaned back into her chair, crossed her legs, scratched her chin, and spoke, "I'm trying to encourage you to use your intuition. That's what you are good at. Doesn't the poem make that clear? You don't know the meaning of it, and you wrote it–But you feel it, don't you? So, tell me what was going on when you wrote it. Maybe that will make things a little more clear."

I thought back to the day I wrote the first part. A lifetime had passed since then.

"I thought it was going to be an elegy, not for anyone in particular, but for relating as an idea."

"Oh, what's this? An abstraction?" she interfered with snark.

"You're sort of a–" I caught myself and paused.

"A bitch?"

"I would never say that."

"Didn't you want to? Anyways, continue. I won't interrupt again."

"Alright, but even if I did want to say it I would only mean it jokingly."

She nodded. "I would too."

"And I was in a bad head space. Charlotte was out of town. I hadn't considered the idea of separating from her in any seriousness yet, but I knew we weren't connecting. In a sense, I was still heading toward the peak, and I was cold."

I continued, "Then I tried to imagine my future with the way things were going, and that's the fourth stanza. The last line of that stanza sort of came to me out of nowhere and I didn't want to write it, but nothing else would do. I wrote the first four stanzas and read what I had a few times and realized the only direction it could take was a more hopeful one, even if that meant walking back down away from the peak. I wasn't too hopeful at the time, so I didn't write it."

"So, when did you write the last stanza?"

"Yesterday."

"So, you've got some hope now?"

"I guess so."

"Alright, good. Then that's enough for today. I'll see you next week. Bring me a copy of the poem when you come."

We stood up and shook hands, as was our ritual.

As I walked out of her office, she called to me, "Oh, and enjoy your date!"

I boiled water for more green tea and fed Amir once I was home. He purred with delight and, after he ate, hopped on the couch, and gave himself a bath.

My place was warm, so I turned the thermostat down a few degrees. I paced across the living room, craving a mini cigar. I wished I was like Meursault and just smoked inside. The thoughts flowing through my mind were wearing me out. I grabbed a regular cigar from the humidor and sat on the balcony. I drank my tea and held the cigar between my lips. I didn't light it because I didn't want the smell of smoke on me when Charlotte arrived. Besides, the taste of the tobacco was better, sweeter—not unlike a complex black tea—unlit.

The interstate was backed up with traffic going southbound but, other than that, the city was unusually calm. The sun was reflecting off the bronze dome of the mosque, and I reflected on the architecture of the sacred space now that I had been inside. What was a beautiful and intricate building from the outside was rather simple and plain on the inside. The psychological implications that flowed through my mind were both positive and critical, but mostly it was just awful admiration. Awful in the original sense of the word, signaling the divine.

When I was a teenager entering college, my thoughts on religion were of excess piety. I had a distaste toward extravagant places of worship like this mosque or like Notre Dame. I was so confused by religious and non-religious people alike who banded together to raise millions of dollars to restore Notre Dame after it was devastated by fire. I thought the more judicious thing to do would be to practice 'good religion', like the book of James writes, and help the needy with that money rather than waste it on an old, gaudy building.

But now I understood that these buildings pointed to something greater. In a literal sense, they stretched toward the sky like the minaret does on this mosque, or the spires of Catholic cathedrals do, or like the steeple reaching above the mountains into Van Gogh's *Starry Night*. I always wondered how intentional that was. Nonetheless, you can tell a fake quickly when the steeple disappears into the mountains and misses the heavens.

But, the materials and intricacies of this building's design reflect the heavens, too. So, what did the simplicity of the mosque's interior say of their theology? Detachment in the eastern sense of the word? Pious devotion? In some sense, it reflected a monk's rejection of material things to only be filled with God, but in another sense, I wondered if it was similar to the plainness of the modern evangelical church architecture and their cheap theology. I don't know if that is fair. To Islam—or to Evangelicals. As far as I could tell, there wasn't a more devout group of people to their God than the Muslim community. But then I thought of the devotion of many evangelical Christians, not to God, but to their president a few years back, and still, even now, despite him being led out of the White House by none other than the state of Georgia.

It was as if they swept the demons—and some angels, too—out of the traditional Protestant church architecture, making way for a new idol to represent their God. That president was a golden calf unlike any other in the modern day. And when we didn't replace that idol with something akin to true virtue, he came back with seven cronies alongside him. And who can blame his supporters? He did what devils do best, he spoke to their fears.

The door slid open behind me. I turned and smiled. Charlotte's dove-eyes were bright and glowing; her lips, red with lipstick, curved up toward her cheeks with a slight quiver. She wore a black metal-chained choker wrapped twice around her neck. One loop was tight against her neck, the other relaxed against the top of her satin dress, light in color and flashing between yellow and gold. The dress flowed against the curves of her body leading down to the skin above her knee, finished off with black suede stilettos strapped just above her ankle.

My heart dashed against the inside of my breast as my eyes found their way back to her face. She was reaching her hand out for me to take it.

"Are we doing this?" she asked, with a slight wink. A sprite of lightning danced through my neck and down my spine.

I stood and grabbed her hand. She placed my hand on her waist and pulled me in as my lips found sanctuary against her cheek.

IV

The sunlight shimmered against her dress and directly into my eye, blinding me as I woke on top of the sheets, still wearing the clothes from the night before. I rolled out of bed, careful not to wake Charlotte, and boiled water to make coffee. I learned to cover the coffee grinder with a thick blanket to reduce the obnoxious noise it made as it shredded the beans into coarse sand. I made enough for two and poured half of it into an insulated cup to keep it hot. I drank mine on the balcony while I watched the morning traffic.

The night before, we ate dinner at an upscale place on the east side of Midtown. We laughed a lot and didn't really talk about much other than how childish we were in high school, when we were practicing at love. Charlotte swiped the check to pay while quipping about feminism. She then laughed and pulled out my credit card. From there, we walked up toward Tenth Street and stopped at a bar for a drink. I ordered a whiskey, and we split a brownie sundae. She dragged me up to dance. We were the youngest couple on the floor, but we danced. Slow and close, and she let me lead. Toward the end of Etta James' transcendent *I'd Rather Go Blind*, she pulled me in and whispered into my ear, saying we should get out of there.

She led me out to the street where we were met with a loud crashing of static coming from Piedmont Park. Lights beamed through the trees and the energy seemed to be pulling the people through the streets and into the park. Charlotte gave me that look, and we went hand in hand till we came to a field littered with people. About half of them seemed to have randomly ended up there the same as us. Our collective gaze transfixed on the stage where a heavy-set man in an all-black suit strolled out and sat behind a set of drums. He tapped the cymbals, steady and rhythmic, until the noise turned to jazz. I looked at Charlotte with a suspicious smile before she tugged my hand to join her on the ground. She sat between my legs with her body leaned into me and her face against mine and we swayed slowly to the simple *tap ta tap tap* of the drummer's grace.

A trumpet sang out into the crowd, carrying out another man, slim cut and dressed in the same black suit. He took his place to the left of the drummer, who nodded in approval. The buildup was slow, and the musicians' intentional distress between their instruments had my heart not knowing when to beat. It took half a minute before they began to play in tune and that was about the time the seductive sound of the saxophone carried out her mister to take his place to the right of the drummer. All synced together, the jazz was loud and free. The crowd could feel it, too. Many sat and swayed, while a few couples twirled around, hand in hand. Then, without notice, the lights shut out. The park went dark.

Charlotte pushed into my chest to where I couldn't tell her heartbeat versus mine. You could hear the whispers of people wondering what was going on, kids were telling their parents they were scared, everyone was at least a little bit anxious. The lights flashed on to reveal a grand piano center stage with a lady in a long, sequined gold dress. As if an alarm clock went off simultaneously in each musicians' head, they all began to flirt with their instrument in one accord. It was nostalgic, like Leon Bridges' record 'Coming Home,' but moving and powerful in its own right. The lady on the keys began to sing.

I was bornnnnn, she held on as the crowd began to cheer and clap, *by the river...*

I knew the song but not like this.

I finished my coffee, wanted more so I drank Charlotte's too, then laid back in bed next to her. She had rolled over on her stomach and took up most of the mattress, so I slid in as close to her as I could. Mostly still asleep, she lifted her left arm and laid it across my chest. I returned to the night before.

The lady on the keys played, as three backing vocalists sang with conviction that change was coming.

The pianist began to rift reminiscent of Brittany Howard, yet overtly original,

I know, I know I knowwwwww, it will come

The crowd collectively cheered.

The band resolved the song as a bulky, muscular man, suited up in a tux about two sizes too small, walked onto the stage and yelled out, "A change is coming, amen!"

He introduced himself as Reverend Drake. He explained, for those who were unaware, that this was no concert, but a protest. An organization of Atlanta churches had come together to rally against racial injustice. Some of the crowd, out of the half that showed up out of curiosity, started to trickle out. I nudged Charlotte's arm to see if she wanted to go, but she shook her head no.

It felt right to stay, though I felt awkward. Events like that can be uncomfortable for me. But, I think, maybe I should be uncomfortable. And it was worth wondering why I felt this discomfort. Or, I should ignore the feeling and just be there because the work taking place on the stage and among the people in the crowd was important.

And it's true I have a respect for the Black church that I don't have for most other American churches. Their faith could keep a man like me believing. But I question at times whether Black churches are a liberating force for the community or if it functions as a surrogate for our society, pacifying the actual needs of those on the receiving end of racism. I met a PhD student during my year in grad studies who was researching just that. I wish I could ask her what she found. No doubt, she would be a better person to ask than me. I do know the Black church's ability to hold onto faith despite the racism they experience, both conscious and unconscious, gave me pause. What was the substance of it?

How do we relate to suffering? That's the question. And, while Black people of faith are a good answer in and of themselves, we must ask if there is any redemptive value in suffering. I want to say no. But I have to qualify that because there are positive potential byproducts of enduring suffering. More resilient character, thick skin, and the ability to hope in the face of darkness, to name a few. But love must be the only redemptive force. Especially in a Christian cosmology. Suffering for the sake of suffering is meaningless, but suffering for the sake of love is the most meaningful task in the universe.

Not everyone in the Black community has the same hope, I've learned. Afro-pessimism was a formidable perspective. It was like the difference between MLK's "I have a dream" (And what's a dream if not a hope?) versus Malcolm's, "Be peaceful, be courteous, obey the law, respect everyone; but if someone puts his hand on you, send him to the cemetery." Either way, they murdered them both. They who refused to concede power.

But Malcolm X obviously had hope, too. They didn't teach us that Malcolm was a minister when I was in school. Just a Muslim. And the only thing we knew of Muslim's was that they were all responsible for 9/11. The way they compared him to King would make you think King was a patriot who loved his country just as it was (that's what celebrating MLK Day was like growing up, at least–he definitely wasn't a radical or a socialist). But Malcolm, he was a traitor to American society.

I believe Steinbeck wrote somewhere about a novel not being a novel unless it gave hope. I pictured Paul Beatty's nihilist Bonbon hearing this and laughing outright because only a white man could write such a thing. Then again, hope does not have to be naïve. And I have no intention of claiming Steinbeck to be naïve, either. Not when he too had been exploited by American society, not when he'd seen death, especially that brutal death of a coworker who fell from on high and bled out by his feet. We have all seen horrors. Nonetheless, it seems the god of our society demands poor whites work for their salvation. So yes, they have hope, but minorities are born damned. Existing only to assure the white elites of their salvation.

Reverend Drake gave a sermon on Moses and the splitting of the Red Sea. It was short, but I could tell he appreciated Malcolm more than Dr. King.

The reverend prayed 'Thy will be done,' and the band came back on.

Charlotte had been squeezing my hand during the sermon, but she loosened up with the band's chorus. We'd never gone to a rally like this together. I'd been to a few in college because 2020 happened during my junior year, and 2020 was an apocalypse with two synonyms: COVID-19 and racial injustice. For some reason, George Floyd's murder opened more white eyes than other events of police brutality and racial violence. But open eyes still haven't solved the problem.

Charlotte gave more effort to understand the problem than I did. She read the books and listened. It's not that I didn't try to do the same, I just found it easier to think of the problem in abstractions, philosophical or otherwise, but she cared in a real way. Her heart hurt.

Even though we didn't leave, I still had a nervousness, like the anxiety a Black family might feel driving through Charlottesville despite white travel bloggers writing that the town 'felt safe to me.' It doesn't feel good knowing you're a part of the problem and that some people see you as the enemy. But the discomfort is holy.

When I think of how muddled our political system is in contradiction and quasi-progress, it makes me not want to get involved. Despite my progressive sensibilities–I am a damned idealist after all–I feel lumped in with the moderates. But I don't want to be the white moderate that depressed King as he wrote in that Birmingham jail. That's not what I mean. So, as the band played in harmony, I prodded my spineless consternations to get over it. I looked at Charlotte who appeared as relaxed as can be.

I couldn't see over the crowd's lifted hands as the song ended and the next speaker made his way forward. Reverend Drake mawkishly introduced him as 'The Reverend Doctor Eighty Ellis' and said he was a minister at Peachtree Presbyterian. I recognized his voice. Reverend Drake shoved the mic into Adam's hand, who immediately spoke crisp and clear, "The Lord's good, amen?" to which I muffled under my breath as I did when I was young, "amen," while the crowd chorused loudly, "Amen!"

I must have gotten too excited about knowing the celebrity on stage. I grabbed Charlotte's arm and pointed at him while trying to tell her who he was and how I knew him. She nodded along but I was suspicious she recognized him too. The rest of the crowd had sat down in the grass and gone silent, causing my outburst to take the attention of those around us who were probably wondering why this white man was yelling at his wife like he'd never seen a Black Presbyterian.

Charlotte picked up on it before me and sat me back down, patting my arm to calm me down like I was a neglected extroverted kid that saw an ice-cream truck drive by at a funeral. I gathered myself but not before Adam saw me. He smiled. I waved, but I figured he didn't want the crowd to know he was friends with the lunatic. He flipped his Bible open and said, "You know, it's so good to be here. Backstage I was speaking in my prayer language, and I was thinking about how that would make a lot of my church members nervous if they knew I spoke in tongues, but not y'all, right? This just feels like a people of the Spirit.

"The apostle Paul writes in his letter to the church in Ephesus that we do not fight against flesh and blood but against the powers and principalities. Hear me out, now. We do not fight against the white brother and sister, but against white supremacy."

Some of the crowd clapped as he continued, "We do not fight against these white politicians who do not have our interest in mind. We keep them accountable, yes, but our fight is against the system that keeps our voices from being heard in the first place." A few people clapped.

"And we do not fight against those lost men who feel betrayed by a country that would risk their privileges, so that we may share in the lot, but we fight for our own place, where privilege is no longer related to the color of our skin, and those who have never known privilege would know equality."

The crowd was quiet.

Adam closed his Bible and gripped the edges of the pulpit. I watched him closely as he looked at the leather-bound book. Anger and sweat flowed through the crowd like a river. Adam's jawbone bulged against his cheek. From the back row, I could see his teeth locked as he bore their frustration and hurt.

"So, King's dream is dead then? Light doesn't actually drive out darkness? Was he just on a hippie trip believing that love would drive out hate?"

"It's a lost cause!" someone cried out. Some of the crowd agreed.

"Lost cause! Plunged into the depth of the abyss then. Really, people, what's the goal? If it's too late, then this whole show," he referenced the surrounding stage and lights with his hand, "then that's all it is. A show. An absurd act–

"Well, if it's absurd, it's something we can work with." His face began to grin, and my mind may have betrayed me, but I could've sworn he glanced at me.

Charlotte yawned, and I was pulled back into our bedroom as she pressed her body up against my chest and slid her hand across my side.

My mind returned to the night before. To the dark park and the bright faces of a crowd lit by the stage.

"It is absurd. James Cone knew this. We know we are people, a people, but they see us as a thing. That's the absurdity. We are a people, we know it. We assert it! And they'll know it, too. They'll soon realize that their suffering is bound to ours, that they are not free because they hold so tightly to keeping us bound. But we are free; they don't know it, they don't think it's possible, but we are free because we say so. They, in fact, have no say.

"Baldwin knew this. The fear we see today is in our realizing of our freedom and in their inability to assert our identity. They see our claiming of our freedom as revolution, I see it as facing the absurdity.

"The question, then, is what world do we want to live in? One with hope? Or one with despair? It would be the truest kind of despair, too, because there would be no hope. And hope is not a naive sense of optimism. Hope is hope. It's given to us by God. Now, God damn America for how our people have been treated but God–" The silence flushed over the crowd in a new form as he enunciated each word with a quivering firmness. The kind of silence that means people were too busy listening to make a sound. "...God refuses to damn our fellow Americans, and so should we.

"Be angry for the love of God, but do not sin," the tremor in his voice had completely disappeared, he spoke softly, and the crowd leaned in, "And do not let the sun go down without using that anger for the good of us all. Thank you." The crowd did not cheer like they did for Reverend Drake, but clapped slowly, in unison.

Adam slid off the stage and walked toward the parking lot. I grabbed Charlotte's hand, and we trotted over to catch him.

"Adam," I called out.

"I'm sorry you had to see that," he said as he turned around.

"Seriously? That was incredible. It was raw. I don't think there was anyone in that crowd who didn't gain some respect for you."

Adam shrugged and looked at Charlotte, "Hey, Charlotte." He leaned in and kissed her cheek.

"Johnny introduced us," Charlotte said, intercepting my thoughts.

"'Course he did. What's he up to anyways? Shouldn't he be here supporting you?"

Adam chuckled, "We're only friends, Del. I don't expect him to come to these things. Stuff like this can be uncomfortable."

"We're here."

"And I could see you trying to shed your skin from the stage! How did y'all end up here anyways?"

"We saw the lights leading 'em two by two toward the ark and figured we'd see what was going on."

"I've never seen a church performance like that before," Charlotte piped in.

"We get that a lot."

"What's up with the animosity between you and the reverend? I could feel it in the air between you."

Adam sighed. "The Christian message of unity gets less and less palatable with each hashtag. But I keep preaching it, 'cause I believe it. They think I'm a sellout. It doesn't help that I'm the token Black Presbyterian." He chuckled awkwardly. "Y'all want a ride?"

"We can take MARTA back," I replied.

"I don't recommend that this late at night. I gotta go by the church anyways."

Adam drove us down 10th and while he went to turn on Peachtree, I asked him to find a place to pullover because I felt like walking the last few blocks.

He threw his hazards on and stopped by the sidewalk. Patting my shoulder, he said, "Let's get breakfast in the morning, I feel like we've got a lot to chat about." He looked at me with a smile somewhere between 'good luck' and 'I'm happy for you.' "Charlotte, it was a pleasure to see you again." He kissed her hand while I stumbled out of the seat and went to open her door.

"Thank you, Adam. I'm so happy you're in our lives. The four of us should get together soon." She quickly added, "I know you and Johnny are just friends." Adam smiled and drove away.

We were left in the orange and white glow of the outdated street-lamps and the lobbies of all the buildings that never went to sleep.

"What a man." Charlotte grabbed my hand as we began walking. "He's so endearing."

"I think he's the only truly meek man I've ever met. If he said he was the messiah, I'd probably believe him."

Charlotte laughed, "I don't know about that, but I do like him."

Then I told her, "You know, he took me to a Mosque the other day, oh man, I can't believe I forgot to tell you." She stopped walking and her face went stoic.

"You did what?"

"We went to a Muslim prayer service."

"Really?"

"And I really liked it."

She had a surprised grin on her face.

"So, are you converting?" She satirized.

"No, but only because things are good between me and mom, and I won't be ready to ruin that for a while."

We ambled toward our building, and I dragged her through the small park with the large fountain, to a walkway covered in trees on one side and then a wall of fountains on the other. Antique street-lamps lined the path. I'd never been, but I imagined it was kind of like Paris.

"Good morning," Charlotte mumbled behind her closed eyes. I kissed her forehead and slid out to make her coffee.

She stumbled out of the bedroom and leaned against the kitchen door frame as I was grinding the beans. She covered her ears and held her head like she had a headache.

"I think I'm hungover."

"From what, the mock-tail at the restaurant or the doughnuts we ate at midnight last night?" I pointed to the pastry box, empty sans crumbs.

"Definitely the doughnuts." She kissed my cheek and moved to the couch.

"I'm making a declaration right now: I will never eat that many doughnuts that late at night ever again."

"You said that last time," I said through the pass-through. I brought her coffee over and sat next to her.

"Am I allowed to have caffeine?"

"I hope so, otherwise we need to get Reece on the phone and tell her she's gonna have to spend some time in rehab."

She took a sip, "I'm kidding, the doctors say I can have about nine/tenths of a cup, so I'll leave you the last sip."

"The part that's all spit? Thanks."

She slipped her head in the pocket of my chest.

"So, we should find a therapist then. Right?"

My cheek rubbed against the crown of her head as I nodded.

"I can ask Adam to recommend one. I'm sure he's acquainted with half of them in the city."

"You think he'll send us to a Christian one?"

"I'd trust him if he did."

I looked across the room where we'd danced to the record player the night before, with a clock on the wall that seemed to count minutes instead of hours.

Tick

Tick

Tick

"You know, Charlotte–" A lump in my throat caused me to stutter.

She sat up and faced me.

"We can start talking now. That way we'll be well ahead when we sit in front of our therapist. I bet they'll be so impressed too; they might put us in gifted therapy."

"And then twenty years down the road, we'll realize having a neuro-divergent marriage actually makes life harder because we don't look like the other 'healthy marriages.'"

"Exactly." I hid behind the joking my need to tell her, not about Carolyn, but what I knew to be true of myself that led to the events with Carolyn.

She gave a scrunched-nosed grin, "We should pick up doughnuts."

I chuckled, "Yeah?"

"What is it?" she asked.

"I want to be honest with you. About everything, about that weekend you were in Seattle, about Carolyn."

"We've already talked about it. Del, I understand. Listen, it hurt. It still hurts, but I'm not going to give up on forgiving you."

"It's more than Carolyn."

Charlotte let go of my hands and pressed into the couch, "What do you mean 'It's more than Carolyn'? This isn't the first time?"

"No! God, no! I've never done anything like this before."

"Then what is this about?"

I reached for her hands again. They twitched when I touched them but slowly laid steady in mine.

"It's about why I am the way that I am. Why Carolyn—why there might be more 'Carolyns' in the future."

"So you're already planning your next affair? Who the hell do you think you are?" She jerked away, grabbed the keys from the counter, and rushed toward the door.

"Charlotte, hold up! It's not like that. I don't want to cheat on you, and I have no intentions of that happening again."

"Then what's it like?" She whipped around in the door frame. "Huh?"

"She offered me an escape."

Charlotte thrust her finger at me and then cupped her face with her hand, "You're—" she lowered her voice, "an asshole."

"Not an escape from you, from me!"

But the door had already slammed in front of my face, and I was left sitting there in my pity once again. My phone was vibrating in my pocket.

***

"I'm convinced I'm an idiot," I said before I took a sip of my coffee.

"You wouldn't lose anything by reading a book or two on communication." Adam stabbed his pancakes and slid his knife through the prongs, cutting the pancakes into a pie chart before plunging one of the convex triangle slivers into his mouth. "But I know exactly what you mean. I felt the same way when I was married."

"Why'd you divorce your wife? I mean, I assume it was because-"

"I'm gay? No, she handled me coming out alright, actually. I mean, I never lost my attraction for her, and I was committed to her. Anyways, she divorced me."

"Really?"

"Yep."

"How come?"

"I let the ministry absorb me. And not in a pastoral way. I became so obsessed with God that I neglected her needs. Our communication shut down and I bottled everything up. She'd probably tell you today that I was a monk trapped in a married person's body. My ministry work suffered, too. That's what I mean by it not being pastoral. I was there for everybody in theory but nobody in practice.

"I locked myself in my office, searching for the answers to our collective existential crisis. It was self-absorbed reflection, and it didn't help anybody and made those closest to me, especially my wife, suffer. She finally got the courage to leave me. I signed the papers without a fight and went back to drowning in search of enlightenment in my office. I thought about becoming a monk, but I was convinced the ascetic life was just a front for depth and a fake sense of belonging. And I did not think I could imitate Christ by working out my salvation in the absence of the real world."

"Well, you obviously snapped out of it, so what changed? What clicked?"

"Have you read any Kierkegaard? I know you'd probably take interest in his kind of thinking."

I was amazed at his ability to delve into a conversation while still giving his pancakes due attention.

"I tried to read *The Sickness unto Death* and couldn't make anything of it. I couldn't understand a lot of dense academic stuff as an undergrad."

"Fair enough. He made himself more complicated than necessary if you ask me, but that's part of why I like him.

"Anyways, I was drowning in existential anxiety, so what better place to look for answers to my angst toward existence than the guy who fathered existentialism and the word 'angst'? Honestly, like you, I didn't understand much of what he wrote. It seemed tired and inapplicable and seemed to dig my grave even deeper. Well, I came across the opening sentence of *The Present Age* and found the enlightenment I was looking for." Adam sipped his coffee. "And a reason to stop reading Kierkegaard." He winked.

He pulled out his phone and showed me the quote that appeared on his lock screen.

The present age is one of reason, reflection, passivity, filled with fleeting flares of fiery intensity and falling acutely into restful idleness.

"What does he mean?"

"It means we think too much, and our self-reflection keeps us from doing any good."

"I don't like that."

"Truth is a sword."

"So, you gave up Kierkegaard and your intellectual pursuits and set out to inspire and love people, huh? It's that simple?"

Adam laughed, "No, ha ha. *Metanoia* is a lifelong process. I don't want to deny that 'I contain multitudes.'

"I haven't stopped reading Kierkegaard, either. 'The Dane' is brilliant, and I don't use that word lightly. In fact, that quote was the epigraph to my dissertation. My translation, too. I went back to school and did my PhD on 'Kierkegaard for the Oppressed.' Which was a leap, of course, 'cause what could this white European man have to say for people that look like me in America? Well, quite a lot, actually, as I tried to prove. James Cone was my other big influence. Basically used his work to interpret Kierkegaard for the Black experience, to understand God's imminence in my suffering.

"But I so often find myself in love with the abstract, transcendent, heavy theology of white men. I don't think that's a problem. A Black man taking comfort in the universality of God is a good thing. The problem is not enough of our white Christians take the time to listen to the Black community who can identify in a special way with the God who suffers the injustice of the cross. I'm not sure white people know anything of the cross if they ignore the injustice against people of color in this country."

I was trying my best to understand, but it had been so long since I thought like a religious person.

I interrupted, "Reverend Drake kind of reminded me of Malcolm—not that I know much about Malcolm at all." Adam raised his brow. I continued, though I was eating my words before they came out. "And you're kind of like Dr. King," I half-muttered.

"No. No." Adam leaned back in the booth and put his arm over the back rest of the laminate upholstery. "I hate that dichotomy, and I hate people being compared to King. King's his own person and so is everyone else. Besides, I try to be a healthy dose of both."

"What's that mean?"

"Cone was doing it with Black Theology. He said the 'Black' was Malcom and the 'theology' was King. He needed both to articulate the gospel in his context, and I do, too."

He continued, "It takes a certain privilege to be able to ponder God in universal terms. God is universal, that's what they understand so well, say Barth, the Niebuhrs, Calvin, Augustine, Bonhoeffer. Well, Bonhoeffer wasn't the typical white theologian, was he?"

I shook my head as if I could bring to memory anything I must have learned in school of Bonhoeffer.

"Often the problem with their understanding of transcendence, though, is they put it at odds with God's imminence as if God was at odds with Godself.

"Well, let me stop preaching at you, but I guess my sympathy for white theologians is what's caused some of the tension between me and some of my community. Not the Presbys at Peachtree, of course. They're predisposed toward abstract understandings of God, which is probably why they can look over the images of white Jesus without thinking twice. They don't have any sense of a double consciousness, it seems. But that's why I like being there, I get to show them that the abstract connects to the material and how living the Christian life can actually bring about real change in our world, our local society. And the cool thing is, there's been a change at that church. You'll feel it when you come."

He said "when you come" with certainty. *When I come*–As if he knew I was predestined to visit his church. Or, he knew how badly I longed to be a part of what he was speaking about for some personal reason I couldn't put to words.

He kept talking, though I had metaphorically left the room and entered one in my mind.

He was unaware. "It's not unfair that others like Reverend Drake think I've sold out, abandoned my 'Blackness' or that I'm too sympathetic to white Christianity, or that I do theology for fun rather than survival like they do. I still struggle with the possibility that they're right. White Christianity, a world I'm too familiar with and sometimes too comfortable, has not set us free; it's authorized our captivity, but real Christianity, that real religion we were given by Christ, I believe it will set us free, and the white Christians too, but that means I've got to be around them.

"And it's not like I'm teaching Jonathan Edwards, that pro-slavery unintegrated weak theologian," he looked down at his pancakes, "But I will commend Wesley. He knew better than to support slavery. I've got no patience for Edwards. I don't care about the time period. Wesley knew better. Christian leaders should always know better.

"You know, Malcolm X knew this, that there was a separation between Christianity and what Christ taught, and it's my hope that I can increase just a little bit of Christ back to my unique community at Peachtree. Also means I've got to constantly be aware that even I leave Christ at the door from time to time.

"Understanding God to be transcendent, though, helps me articulate how God is imminent in our sufferings, mainly in the lowly and beaten down person of Jesus Christ." He turned his head toward the ceiling light and rubbed his thumbnail ever so lightly against his freshly shaven chin.

"I guess I needed to get that off of my chest," he continued, "I've been holding it in for too long, had to empty my reserves. You're the kind of person I feel like I can do that with, too. 'Cause you've got a religious mind, and even though you can't really understand it, I know you try. Honestly, I don't always want to be understood, I just want to be heard. Thanks for listening."

I tried to mutter 'thanks' or something of the sort because it did seem like a complement, but he started to circle back around, "But I don't need anything from Kierkegaard or from any other person who attempts to explain our existence to the degree that that's possible. I've got it in me to do it myself."

Adam stared at me as I was replaying everything I overheard him say while I was trying to process what it was I was feeling inside. *I've got it in me to do it myself.* I returned his gaze and nodded.

"Tell me about school, Del," he said with a sternness that, for some reason, poked me like a dagger.

"Huh?"

"I'd like to know more about why you went to school for ministry and how you ended up a marketing analyst. I don't want the Augustinian excuse either–I want the real one."

"Well, I don't know what to tell you." But I did, and Adam saw it in my eyes. He waited for me to continue.

"My grandfather was a preacher," I started. "My mom's dad. He pastored small churches all across the Midwest. I always looked up to him. More than humble; his meek sincerity from the pulpit, the way he preached... you knew he believed what he was saying. It was powerful. My mom always told him his sermons were too long, but to me, they were never long enough.

"A truly great man, my pap. His only claim to fame was when he was interviewed in the local paper after his church was taken away in a tornado. I think that happened in Indiana, but one always thinks of Kansas when it comes to tornados, don't they?"

Adam remained rigid, compassion in his eyes, but his hands, the vertex of his elbows, were clasped, comfortably sat against his lips.

"I wanted to follow in his footsteps. My senior year of high school I dedicated my life to Christ. Gave up friends, extracurricular activities, and distanced myself from Charlotte. I was gonna be a preacher and couldn't have distractions.

"However, when I went to school to study ministry, something felt off. There were too many unresolved contradictions. And the 'love' everyone seemed to be talking about seemed more like an extra serving of ego.

"My senior year of undergrad I was wrestling with all of this, and I stumbled on a newspaper article on Christian love, and can you believe it, it was written by my own grandfather. *The Brethren Evangelist* had published him. He wrote how Christian love in the first century had undone everything we knew of love up until that point. He argued that love opened up a nearly endless amount of possibilities, and that love, Christian love, had done and could do more than words can describe. But I didn't see it at school or in the churches I tried, or in the influencers who used Christ to gain a following, and I didn't feel it anymore. I guess I realized I only believed that stuff 'cause of my mom and grandpa.

"I still had a deep need for some conceptual meaning, something to serve as an answer to the problem of this life. But I didn't feel like I could preach and pastor to people under something I didn't believe for myself. It couldn't be Marx's opium. Honestly, my school was shady, too. They groomed us to be influencers more than spiritual guides. We were being formed to be more like the CEOs of Silicon Valley than the saints of the Great Tradition.

"God still held me captive, though. And though I didn't think I was in any position to tell people about God, I wanted to figure him out.

"That's when I came back to Atlanta and studied theology."

"At Emory, right?"

I nodded. "I only lasted a semester and a half. Didn't even take my finals that spring. I found out pretty quickly that I don't think like an academic. And I didn't want to, either. I liked thinking about big ideas, *but not like that*. It didn't seem like I could find my voice. Because, quite frankly, I couldn't find my brain." I paused to sip my coffee.

"Since it was a liberal university, however, I learned pretty quickly that if there was a God, then that God would love me as I am. With that belief engrained in me, and the fear of hell gone, I became apathetic about the whole 'God' business. It was too confusing. An unnecessary headache. Besides, Charlotte was back in my life, and we were so different from the kids we were in high school. It wasn't better, but it was easier. We kind of just slipped into this rhythm, a rhythm I accepted as the burden of my life. I still had this craving to try to understand the world, that never left me. But, I pushed it deep down to focus on providing for my wife and making a living." I went quiet for a moment, but Adam didn't respond. He wanted me to keep going.

"It's funny. I never cared about making a living until me and Charlotte got back together. You know, I would've been content to be poor, reading esoteric philosophy and classic literature. I wrote a lot of poetry in my later college days. Felt like the only proper way to try to understand this life."

I stared into my coffee. "I know it seems like our relationship was numb before we were even married, but I remember how much I wanted to be a good husband. That's all that mattered to me. She's what made it easy to give up all my questions, to drop out of school, to get a real job. She pulled me down to this earth."

I glanced back at Adam who stared deeply into my eyes.

"But then you start to wonder if 'down here' is where you really belong."

Adam had a sideways grin on his face, the kind of look that says, *I know what you mean*. I sighed. "So that's it. Charlotte's the missing piece. Sort of, since I gave the whole ministry thing up before she came along."

Adam finally responded, "It sounds like you went searching for a faith of your own, and the one you were raised with didn't quite fit. It sounds like the faith you found was existentialism."

I laughed, but he was serious. "For a time, I suppose. Existence is the primary question. You learn that outside sources don't know as much as they would like you to think. But I don't know much, either."

He nodded. "You know, Kierkegaard fathered existentialism, but Sartre really gave it its bearings. Have you read him?"

"Well, I've tried to read *Nausea* multiple times. Can't say I like it. I don't care for the main character. I relate to his problems but not to him. But I am loosely familiar with Sartre's philosophy, I suppose."

"More of a Camusian Absurdist then? I was thinking about it the other day. Do we go with Plato's essentialism or Sartre's existentialism? Plato's certainly seems like the more Christian option, wouldn't you say? Our essence precedes our existence. In other words, God gives us our meaning instead of us having to go out and create it. You've got your philosophical instincts, Del, what do you think?"

My head was spinning from the stream of consciousness we'd both already shared. "Hmm." I considered avoiding the conversation. There wasn't a clear thought in my mind for me to grab hold. It would be easier to let him keep talking than share my own opinions. I started, "You do realize normal people don't jump into these discussions on casual breakfast dates, right?"

Adam replied without skipping a beat, "Are you trying to be normal now? And don't act like these aren't the things you wish people would ask you about instead of your meteorological insights. *Beautiful day for a swim, no?* Besides, aren't these the kinds of questions that bounce around your mind? Don't you want to work on extroverting that thinking a little bit instead of deflecting because you're worried that brain of yours is a little more infantile than you'd like to let on? Or is that what you found out in school?" He winked, so smooth and cocky, because he knew he had me pegged.

"Alright, sure." I took a breath and smiled. "It's both."

"Both? How can it be both? They're contradictory ideas. Opposites. This is why you've got to say what you're thinking, so iron can sharpen iron and all that jazz. Otherwise, we get too comfortable with paradoxes that go against logic. The very definition of an impossibility."

"Who's to say paradoxes are impossible?"

"It goes against reason. Black can't be white and white can't be black. One is all color, and the other is none."

"It's still both, alright?" The contradiction was now swirling around in my mind and I could see the form of it. Two opposites who know how to dance together.

I began my explanation, realizing my own thoughts in real time, "The meaning is already there, preceding my existence, but I tap into the meaning by making it. This is the same as Sartre, and Camus, I think, giving meaning to the perceived absurdity of existence.

"When you Christianize Plato's essentialism, you assume the essence is specific. Like it's pre-ordained that I married Charlotte and that's the meaning my existence was created for, but that's the real absurdity. However, looking at the Trinity, and I'm as shocked as you to be using Christian language, the idea of loving, mutual submission precedes existence–and that's what marriage represents. I wasn't created to marry Charlotte, yet we attempted to tap into that loving mutual submission that precedes time by standing before my brother and putting pagan rings on our fingers," I said, pointing to the gold circling my finger.

It's funny the things you get so used to that you forget they're even there. The ring stole my attention before Adam pulled me back.

"That's interesting, but it still sounds like essentialism if you ask me."

I looked back up. "Alright then, let me put it a different way. Let's say Plato had it right. We'll assume the Christians have it right and there is a creator out there. I think we still have to *act* like existence precedes essence and by creating our own meaning, we're actually living out the meaning that precedes our existence. Which sounds a whole lot like Kierkegaard taking his leap of faith. Or maybe just the opposite. I'm all twisted up in the paradox."

"So, essentialism?"

"Nope, both. Because the inverse is also possible. Our relationship to the universe might actually be absurd. In which case, even if we were tricked, or convinced, I should say, into taking the leap of faith, we'd find meaning despite the fact that there was no real meaning to begin with, but that wouldn't matter because, well, nothing would matter. That is, except for the apparent meaning we find in taking the leap."

"A sort of Pascal's wager, huh?"

I sucked the inside of my lip and leaned forward on the table. "No, I don't like that. Never mind. Maybe forget it. I'll keep thinking, I suppose."

I added, "You know, some Indigenous myths say ravens used to be white." I shoved a large bite of cold omelet into my mouth as the waiter came by to see to us. Adam asked for the check and, to my discontent, paid for my meal with the church's credit card.

We sat quietly for a time. Adam was good company to have because though there was plenty to say, I also felt comfortable in our shared silence. The morning was getting late outside the window. The glass was building up a storage of the sun's heat.

When I turned back to Adam, he was leaned back with his arm over the booth. He broke the silence, "You know, you remind me of Calvin with his 'one cannot know themselves until they know God.'" He paraphrased Calvin in a hushed, bold voice, as if Calvin were a wizard in a movie making a prophesy over the main character, "and also 'one cannot know God until they know themselves.'" He laughed at his cleverness.

"Ah, and don't forget the possibility that meaning-making is all but an evolutionary process to keep us alive and evolving," I added.

"Which leaves us with the question: what cares so much about life to keep us evolving than Life itself? What wills life more than Life itself?"

"Fair enough," I said with a shrug.

"'But just like Life, I'll rise.' We'll have to argue this further another time. But I do have a more serious matter I want to throw out there just to see if you'd be interested."

My interest piqued. "Go on, 'Eighty.'"

Adam smirked. "I'll have to explain that one. Well, I guess there's not much to explain. My full name is Adam Dietrich Ellis, Dietrich after Bonhoeffer." I nodded. "An interesting pacifist, wasn't he? Anyways, my great-grandfather knew him from the time he studied in New York. They went to the same church in Harlem. That man left such a mark on my great grandad. He's been important to our family ever since. So I'm given his name as if he were family. Adam Dietrich. A.D. Born to pronounce the year of our Lord."

"Incredible" was all I could think to say.

"Well, I guess that's related to what I was going to say." He took a breath and looked me in the eye, "Del, I know we're both 'pacifists to the core,'" he said as if neither of us were, "but with all of this talk of another war—and I fall on the side of a serious war sounding foolish and regressive in the modern age, but the possibility remains—" He took another breath to relax himself. "Anyways, there's a need for chaplains to be on call and I'd like to sign you up."

The final bite of omelet slid off my fork as I looked at Adam's confident face.

"Huh?" I almost laughed out loud.

"Me? A chaplain? Adam, I don't even consider myself a Christian. Isn't it a chaplain's main job to, well, pray for people?"

"No, their main job is to be there for people and hold space for their hurt and honesty. To encourage them toward the Good. So, you don't have to pray for anyone or anything, but I think sitting with somebody is just about the same as praying with them. Del, you have the capacity for this. I saw it in you, and I felt it in you, the first time I shook your hand and looked in your eyes. And with your education, getting you certified shouldn't be difficult in the least."

I shrugged him off. "I don't know."

"Just give it some thought, alright? The archduke hasn't been shot yet, so you've got time. I do think you'd find a great deal of meaning in it, whether it's waiting for you to find it, or for you to create it yourself." He winked.

"And who knows? Maybe it turns out to be your passion." He squeezed my arm and strolled out, dapping up the waiter on the way out. The waiter smiled at the bill in his hand and slid it in his pocket.

I watched Adam pass through the door. I took in the contradiction. I believed in it.

***

Work was busy. Jasmine and I interviewed three applicants. She loved all three but only one of them stood out to me. Tonya, a twenty-five-year-old from Macon. She'd graduated from Mercer with an MBA. Her brow was wrinkled beyond her age, her posture was upright. The entry-level marketing was shooting too low for her, but I could tell she'd climb the ranks quickly until she made it to a position where she could thrive. That's how I explained it to Jasmine at the end of the day. She had me call Tonya while I sat there in her office to tell her she had the job.

The phone rang for a few seconds until an older lady answered, "Hello, Tonya's phone."

"Yes, hi, I'm from the marketing firm."

"Did she get the job?"

"Is Tonya there?"

"She's changing her baby. Did she get the job?"

"She did."

"Oh, my goodness. Praise God! Oh, I'll have her call you right back. Alright honey. Goodbye." She hung up the phone, but not before letting out an excited yelp.

"Did you know she had a kid?"

"Yes, it was in her application." Jasmine laughed. "You didn't read it?"

"Applications don't tell you who a person really is," I said with smug sarcasm.

"You don't think 'mother' is part of a person's identity?" She leaned back in her chair, using her interlocked fingers as a pillow, "You're lucky you're somewhat smart because you're definitely the lazy kind."

"I'll see you in the morning, but not too early." I winked and left for the day.

I found interviewing people to be an enjoyable type of menial work. It might as well have been an escape from my personal life. But it was only a distraction that began and ended while I was there in the moment.

Charlotte was hurt by my doing and that reality walked me home. I thought about texting her and apologizing for being an idiot, but she wouldn't put up with that kind of self-deprecation, so instead I wrote that I was sorry, I loved her, and I hoped to see her soon.

Amir was waiting for me at the door, so I scooped him up into my arms, and we spent the night binging my favorite show from my teen years. Three episodes in, I filled Amir's food and water bowl. Then, I made chicken and pasta for myself and paired it with half a bottle of wine. Before drinking a third glass, I smoked on the balcony. The night had a breeze, but the wine had warmed me. Lit up apartments and offices were scattered across the city like the stars I couldn't see because of the light pollution. I went back inside and fell asleep on the couch to the sixth episode that night of *How I Met Your Mother*.

I woke up in the middle of the night cotton-mouthed. The tv was off and the comforter from the bedroom hugged me tight. I peeked in the bedroom to see Charlotte sleeping under the thin sheets. I drank a glass of water and took the comforter back to the bedroom, covered her with it, and joined her under the sheets. Leaning over, I carefully kissed her cheek. She wrapped her arm over my body and pressed into my side.

Why does she keep coming back? I wondered. Perhaps I'll never know. It's her own secret.

My eyes opened to an empty bed. A soft melodious piano came from the speaker in the living room. Charlotte was sitting on the couch reading.

"You only dog-ear the depressing poems, you know that?"

"Poems are best enjoyed when you can relate to them, I guess." She half-smiled and went back to Baudelaire. I went to the kitchen to boil water.

"I can make you coffee." I walked back into the living room to her head still in the book.

"Do you want coffee?"

She held up the book to the back page. "What's this? I didn't know you were writing poetry again. You haven't done that since–"

"We got married," I finished the sentence for her.

"It's good."

"Thanks. Coffee?"

"Sure."

I measured out the coffee beans to thirty grams and ground them up into a fine mulch. The box of filters was empty, so I threw the ground beans away and asked Charlotte if she wanted to walk down the block to the local shop.

The sun was peeking through the city scape as we strolled up to the shop by the art museum, silently, side by side. The barista made our coffee, and we sat on the patio facing the lawn. A group of elementary students went chattering by as an overworked teacher tried to get them in line. A few of the kids looked at us with big smiles, and Charlotte waved excitedly while grinning ear to ear. The kids giggled cheerfully before the teacher snapped at them to calm down.

Charlotte slid her chair closer to me as the kids disappeared into the museum. She placed her hand on mine. Tears welled up in my eyes and, as they started to drop, I cried out, "What are you doing?" I looked away, toward the street.

"I'm your wife, for better or worse, and if you're going to suffer in silence then I won't let you suffer alone."

I stared at the statue in the center of the lawn titled "The Shade." It was sculpted by the Frenchman Auguste Rodin, depicting an Adamic-style man with his head slouched to the side, his neck stretched beyond comfort. He looked like Atlas, bearing the weight of the world.

I researched the sculpture after the first time I came across it. In reality, it was Adam, reaching toward hell, rather than toward God.

If Michelangelo had Adam reaching toward consciousness (or, perhaps, God reaching toward Adam through consciousness), then Rodin had him reaching toward the unconscious. Rodin began working on the sculpture in 1880 and, sure enough, Freud would be deemed a doctor the next year. Despite his work on unconscious complexes being overly directed by his own, Freud's work was immeasurably liberating to the human psyche. For one, we began to accept the unconscious as a reality.

Later, his mentee would split with him over his own obsession with sex, at least, that's the main thing people like to think, and Carl Jung would turn his attention to the collective unconscious and our religious tendencies. Jung knew the unconscious was a hellish place. It was also a holy place. "No tree, it is said, can grow to heaven unless its roots reach down to hell," as he would say. And Rodin's Adam was doing just that, hand outstretched to the inferno below. Luckily for us, where we sat had us facing directly into his ass.

In my last session with Bea, I had described my head space with a quote from Dante:

> "So mourned I through the brute which rest knows none:
> She barred my way again and yet again,
> And thrust me back where silent is the sun."

"And what does that mean to you?" Bea asked me.
"I think–"

"Oh, please stop trying to think—you're not a thinker—what do you feel?"

"I feel hollow. Like an impenetrable shell protecting nothing inside."

"Protecting nothing inside or protecting something not worth protecting? These are two very different things."

"The latter."

"Yes, well, that is what you feel, but it's not the truth. You wouldn't need a shell if you weren't protecting something valuable."

Charlotte tangled her arm up in mine and laid against my shoulder. Her pulse beat slowly against my side. Oftentimes, when I coil up like this, my breathing becomes inconsistent. My heart rate will speed up because my lungs aren't sharing the burden of keeping me alive and my chest will tighten, making it even harder to breathe. But as Charlotte's heart tapped, my chest loosened, fresh air filled my nostrils, and my heart went to a steady drum.

"You're willing to put up with this for the rest of your life?" I asked her.

"The law kind of requires it."

"We could easily go to the courthouse and get that figured out."

"I'm not talking about a man-made law." She leaned up and kissed my cheek. "I'm talking about a divine law."

"Ah, so we should bolster our union to appease the wrath of God." My dry sarcasm granted me a chuckle from Charlotte, and I was able to smile.

"All I am saying is, there's a reason marriage is a sacrament in the Catholic Church despite the fact that they worship a celibate single man, and I'm staying with you to find out what that reason might be."

Tears creeped down my stoic face as she pulled my head into her heart.

"That's the main reason?"

"One of them." She poked my side. "You know, I don't need you to talk about your feelings to know what you're feeling, love. I know you feel things more deeply than me, if we're honest. I need you to know you have permission to feel things the way you want, and I have no expectation for you to try to put that into words. I know well enough that when it comes to feelings, words never quite do it justice, and you are a just man."

I nodded, feeling the snot and tears that had built up in her shirt covering the right side of my face. I sat up and rubbed my cheek against my sleeve. She was looking at me and smiling, laughing at the grossness of my emotional excrement.

I shook my head and turned my attention back to the statue. My mind went to Emma Jung. Carl was certainly not a faithful husband. Who knows how that affected his own neurosis? Neurosis is no excuse. No. The *ressentiment* of many men considered great has led to the mistreatment of countless strong women, Emma Jung included.

Emma Jung. Emma Jung. Could it be her strength that caused Jung's work to be given life by so many feminine figures? Could it be that Jung, coming out of his mental break, his so-called encounter with the unconscious, realized how important the feminine was, how neglected she had been–locked in the unconscious where she doesn't belong? This must be why he cared so much about the dogma of Mary's assumption (even with his Protestant psyche) because who was there other than Emma Jung? She must have been his cornerstone, and not just financially in their early days. I can hardly think otherwise.

"Alright, Mr. Underground Man, we ought to get you off to work." Charlotte stood and held her hand out for me to take. I did, but I pulled her back into my arms.

"One of these days twice two will make five and it will be quite excellent," I said, muffled against her face before planting my lips lightly, yet firmly against her cheek.

"I forgot you read that poor translation. What even is 'twice two makes five'? But it is more fun to say, isn't it? It's just like you to choose the poetic over accuracy, you know."

I squeezed her tightly in my lap, "Hey."

"Yeah?"

"We're having a baby."

She sniffed her nose and giggled, "I know," and kissed my cheek.

"We've got to name her."

"So, you think we're having a girl?"

"Almost definitely."

Charlotte pulled away and grinned a devious grin. I raised my brow, and she pressed back against me. We watched the kids play outside of the museum gift shop for a moment. She jerked back again so that we were eye to eye.

"How about Mary? Mary Ann. She'll be old-fashioned."

"What? Like your Victorian mother?"

"No, like a roaring twenties flapper girl. Oh, she's going to be fun!"

I put my hand on Charlotte's stomach, "What do you think? Are you a Mary Ann?"

"I think I felt her leap! Feel my arm, it's covered in chill bumps!"

I knew the fetus was still smaller than a tadpole, but I believed her. I ran my hand across her forearm until our hands intertwined.

"Mary Ann, it is," I replied.

"But we should have a boy name. Just in case."

"Alright, what do you suggest?"

"I think it would be nice for him to be the third. That's old-fashioned, too. Peter Robert the Third. Sounds like royalty."

"I've never cared for the tradition, but I think my mind has changed." I shrugged. "I think I might come to like it, but I won't have to for now 'cause we're having a girl."

We sat there with my arm over her shoulder for some time, and then we walked home, hand in hand. My head hurt from crying and my stomach was turning because I was terrified. Terrified of being a father. Not like the kind of fear most new parents have. That's a healthy fear of the unknown. It should be expected. My fear was rooted in what I knew. What I knew about myself. Charlotte must have noticed my thoughts getting the best of me because she stopped me about a block from our building. She looked me in the eye and told me it was going to be alright. I told her I knew that, but the voice inside my head wasn't convinced.

At our place, Charlotte told me she would stay while I went to work, and I could take the car. We decided she wouldn't move back in until after our first session together, but after work I'd take her back to her mom's place and we'd have dinner there. Part of me knew I should see Sarah. She'd asked if we wanted to invite my parents to dinner too, but I told her I didn't think that would be the best idea. She understood, and we agreed to dinner at 6.

I knocked on Jasmine's door first thing at the office. She was on a call but motioned me in. I took a seat in one of her nice, vegan-leather chairs and twiddled my thumbs while she talked.

"Alright, you too. Bye." She hung up and looked at me.

"What?"

"You better be glad I fired you."

"Well, not technically–"

"That was headquarters. They want us to merge with the D.C. branch."

"Oh, wow. I'm sorry."

"Don't be. They promoted me. But everyone remaining in office either has to move to D.C. or jump ship."

"Ah, so I really am out of a job."

"No, no. They still want you. It will be a bit of an unconventional job. They want you to fly into New York once every quarter to meet at headquarters. While you can do most of the job remote, you'll be traveling a lot. You'll be consulting the whole company." She smirked.

My laughter got the best of me. "They what?"

"Del, they've implemented the innovations you made to how we operate across the company. Literally, our branch in the U.K. is doing it."

"The hell? But it was so simple."

"Aren't the best things? Anyways, I don't need you this week. Besides, we won't be hiring anybody at this location anymore."

"What about Tonya?"

"Well, the merger could take up to a year. We'll see how she does and if she's okay to move, she'll join us in Washington. But I have a feeling that a year will be enough time for her to launch into something better for her. Or she'll take a higher position in D.C., and that'll make the move worth it. Anyways, I've got tons of logistics I need to think through. Go home, or do whatever you feel like doing. I'll probably need you next week."

I exhaled and stood up, "Alright then." I stood up to leave, "Don't you want to know how my personal life is going?"

She grinned, "No need. It seems like things are going well." She flicked her hand, motioning for me to leave.

Walking down Peachtree, I figured I'd give Adam a visit. At this point, I felt like he was paid for people like me to stop by and interrupt him.

His office door was open, so I knocked as I walked in. He looked up from his Bible and smiled.

"Ah, you really are a Christian, huh?"

He chuckled, his eyes back on the Bible, and closed the book, "Trying my best, but I'm not convinced any of us are capable of being Christians this side of heaven. Nietzsche got that right, there's only been one Christian."

I took a seat, "So it's okay if I'm not?"

"Of course. You're too close to God to be a Christian."

"What's that supposed to mean?"

"Don't worry about it too much. What's up?"

I told him about the five minutes I had spent at work that morning before coming to see him. He seemed happy for me but uninterested. Then, I told him about Charlotte coming back.

"She's a good one. A little stubborn putting up with you like that, but I think it requires a little bit of stubbornness to make a marriage work."

"What do you think of marriage being a sacrament?"

"I'm a good Presbyterian, so there's only two sacraments: baptism and communion, but I do think marriage is sacred.

"Obviously, the Bible talks about marriage being a symbol for Jesus's relationship to the church, but single, and now celibate, as I am, I'm convinced marriage is the most godly and human thing we're capable of this side of heaven. I know I use that expression a lot, but can you blame me? We're in an imperfect world, so it's nice to think there's another that is perfect, or at least more whole."

I shrugged. Adam opened one of his desk drawers and pulled out a book. I knew what it was because I had the same copy. He turned to a dog-eared page and started to read:

> *As flowers, by chills nocturnal made to pine*
> *And shut themselves, when touched by morning bright*
> *Upon their stems arise, full-blown and fine;*
> *So of my faltering courage changed the plight.*

"Dante."

Adam nodded. "How he was able to write those lines knowing he was about to enter hell, I don't know, but these words comfort me."

"*Inferno's* my preferred book in the Divine Comedy."

"How could it not be? You can be quite comfortable in your own inferno, but I'm sure you have glimmers of paradise from time to time."

"*Inferno's* the most honest of the three."

"Sure."

"Adam, how do you do it? How are you okay knowing you'll spend the rest of your life alone? Most people who stay single for the entirety of their life seem to trick themselves into believing they'll find somebody one day, but you've chosen this. How do you do it?"

"You know, I don't have a good answer. It's hard as hell. I miss being married to my wife more than I would like to admit. But, as I came to terms with my sexual identity, I felt an overwhelming sense of pressure to fall in love with a man, get re-married, and live out our days 'living off the fat of the land'," he said as he did a poor impression of Steinbeck's Lennie.

"I realized marriage, not sex, was an idol for me, and idols get in the way of living out the truth that's set before us. Affirming as I am," a tear bubbled in his eye, "you wouldn't believe the flack I get from the queer community. Not all of them, not most of them, many of them understand, especially the ones that take the time to talk to me about my decision. At the end of the day, they don't understand that I'm comfortable with my sexuality, that it's the comfort of marriage that gets in my way."

I felt like we came from opposite places. Being alone was my 'idol,' and it was per chance of luck or nonchalance that me and Charlotte got married. Or an attempt to be normal.

He continued, "It's a myth, though, that single people are alone. I don't feel alone, most of the time. I've got your brother, as weird as that relationship is. I've got you, now, and hopefully a lot more of Charlotte. I've got my church people, who I jovially trust to show more concern for me than I do for them. And even when I'm alone, I've got the spirit of Christ to comfort me."

"Yeah." I didn't know how to respond, and I didn't want to say the wrong thing.

"Sorry if that makes you uncomfortable."

I shrugged.

"But I hope my life challenges both the American ideals of the nuclear family and our rugged individualism. Being celibate, I do not have a traditional family, and being a dweller of this community," he said as he referenced the church with his hands, "I'm forced to be in communion with others, others who look and act and think so differently from me yet are committed to love the same as me."

I leaned back in the chair and examined the wooden-planked ceiling. Adam returned to reading his Bible. He flipped the page and then looked up at me. I caught his glance from the periphery of my eye and returned his stare.

"I've got something for you." He swiveled around in his chair and pulled a small book from his overloaded bookshelf and handed it to me. "It's not Dante, but I've found a lot of comfort reading these."

It was a collection of poems by Rowan Williams, the old Archbishop of Canterbury. "There's a poem in there about Nietzsche I think you'll appreciate, or possibly resonate with."

"Religious poetry isn't really my cup of tea, Adam. Don't you think it tends to lean too propagandist for the non-religious?"

"Ah, don't be so short-sighted." He began speaking in a lofty, pretentious voice, using his hands to enunciate, "He's not a religious poet, he's a poet for which religious things matter a lot."

I examined the book in my hand, flipping through the worn out, marked up pages. I read the description on the back plagiarizing Adam's description almost word for word.

In the table of contents, there was a poem titled 'Nietzsche: Twilight,' page eighty. I flipped toward it and stopped on the dog-eared page sixty-five.

"Why does the name Thomas Merton sound familiar?"

Adam looked up from his Bible, "Merton, 20th century mystic and monk. You'd like him."

I read the title 'Thomas Merton: Summer 1966.' The footnote read, "At this time Merton, the radical monastic genius, poet and social critic, was entangled in a tormenting and unconsummated love affair." I glanced at Adam, but he had returned his full attention to Scripture. One sentence had been annotated with brackets, "[Not to make sense is / what most matters.]" And:

What was I seeing,
then, that summer? light from a dead star?
<u>Not quite.</u> (Underlined by a dark pen strike.)

I looked at Adam again, but he was somehow absorbed in the book of Exodus. Of course, he was reading it in Hebrew. I had to keep from rolling my eyes. I knew a very little amount of Hebrew from the two semesters I took in undergrad, but we memorized the names of every book in the Tanakh. And, for a final, I translated a chapter out of the Song of Songs. What a strange book that is. I wasn't about to get into that conversation with Adam.

His cheeks began to show pink, so I knew he felt my stare, but his eyes continued to follow the words on the page. No doubt he was reading the prosaic tabernacle prescriptions toward the end of the book: the altar must be five cubits long and five cubits wide; the altar shall be square, and it shall be three cubits high. How engaging.

I flipped to the poem on Nietzsche, but once again, my attention was caught by another poem, 'Rilke's Last Elegy.' "The river flows in both kingdoms..." Rilke was a favorite of mine. I'd read *Letters to a Young Poet* in college and it carried me through a solemn winter. He'd opened my eyes to a different view of the world, a romantic one, a world where pain and grief are canvases for beauty. I remembered feeling all alone—despite the many interesting friends I'd made while in school, a sense of loneliness had often accompanied me during those years—when I picked up the letters Mr. Kappus had collected from Rainer Rilke. In them, he encouraged being comfortable with solitude, finding unity between the inner and outer lives, and to embrace the difficulties of life. The only irony was, as I became more comfortable with solitude, I found that embracing a deeper experience of life made it all the more difficult to relate to other people.

"What are you reading?" I looked up to see Adam leaning over his desk toward me with his hands clasped together over the Bible.

I blinked and realized my eyes had glassed over. "'Rilke's Last Elegy.'"

"Does Williams do him justice?"

I nodded. "He does."

I looked through the stained-glass window placed in the center of the north wall. "You can tell he uses Rilke's influence to write it, not so elegant, yet the use of nature to describe seen and unseen reality, life after death—" I paused, lost in the beauty of the window. "It's a beautiful image, especially 'So when you whisper into the stream, the words run / round through the moon's valleys, where we don't see...'"

"Insightful, Del. Have you considered writing your own poetry? I imagine you'd find a certain repose in being able to express yourself that way."

I chuckled.

"What?"

"Charlotte thinks the same thing. But I can't just speak in poetry."

"Of course not, people would think you'd lost your mind. But, when you can't speak any other language, that's when you fall on your native tongue, yes? English is your secondary language. You're forced to use it because that's the agreement we've made to function in society, but when that language fails, you know how to say it in poem."

"You sound more like a poet than me at the moment."

"Well, write these words down and we'll publish it. *Letters from a Queer Clergyman* sounds nice." Adam threw his head back in his chair in laughter, and I chuckled at the sight of him finding himself so funny.

"Alright," we composed ourselves, "I should probably head home and see if Charlotte wants to grab lunch." I stood up to leave and Adam came around his desk and hugged me.

"You're a good man, Del. Hardheaded as a brick and deep as an ocean. Thanks for coming to see me. Oh, and take this, I want to hear your thoughts on some of his other poems 'cause I never have insights like the one you made about the Rilke poem." He handed me the Rowan Williams collection.

I thanked him and walked out the door, down the hall, and toward the sanctuary.

My nostrils filled with the air of musty old hymnals and freshly-stained wood floors. My feet tapping against the floor echoed through to the chancel and faded against the apse. The North and South walls were lined with stained glass images depicting the history of the church, from Abraham to the missions of Paul. They were both very white, as were the depictions of Jesus, but who would expect different from a predominately white denomination in the early 1900s. I remembered that Adam had called himself a token. This denomination had undergone incredible strides to be as inclusive as possible, but, despite the lack of prejudice, the liturgy still paled in comparison to the worship styles of other churches. Western consciousness doesn't make much space for symbols, so why would anyone want to go to a church veiled in the symbolic? Especially when the clergy neglect to make space for the symbols to be encountered properly in the act of worship. I took a seat in a pew toward the back of the presbytery.

Of course, I enjoyed the symbols more than anything else the church had to offer because my capacity for literalism, and often history, too, is naught. Both are necessary, I've realized, but the literalism is so unbalanced and pervasive. I needed a break.

Above the golden cross on the altar, and behind the organ, a squared circle depicts Christ sitting on a throne, holding the scriptures with the sun shining from behind him. Why is the sun there? That's a question nobody in the church is asking, and they wouldn't like the answer either. But if they made more space for the symbols to speak, then they might understand themselves better, and they would realize that they were more steeped in Greco-Roman mythology than they were aware. Consciously, they would say they weren't at all, but it seems those non-conscious aspects of our psyche are perfectly comfortable with the existence of many gods. None of this would matter if we could take symbols for what they were and not take the literalism too, well, literally.

The wooden pew beneath my rear grew more and more uncomfortable, so I pulled out the kneeler and leaned against the pew in front of me. I found myself mesmerized by the Christ-figure glowing through the center of the mandala. Scripture in hand, the words telling of the Word of God. His throne was a rainbow, and he was garbed in red. His eyes stared at me in the way that you know he is all-knowing. I felt anxious. I looked in his eyes, and at his hand at his side, then back to his eyes. The sun behind the east wall shone most persistently through the white of his stained-glass eyes. They were alive.

The longer the hypnosis lasted, the harder I found it to breathe. His eyes pierced with conviction against my chest, giving that feeling that you should be living your life more right, more intentionally. But last time I tried to live more right, it didn't go well in the least.

"What?" The word echoed through the room.

The outburst had come from my own lips and carried across the nave of the sanctuary, slamming against the stained-glass mandala.

"What's more right?" My fists clenched against the back of the pew.

I heard a door creak open to the right of the pulpit, and I nervously stood to my feet and slid quickly out the door to the street.

I walked with long strides down the sidewalk with my head down. I didn't understand my outburst. It seemed so silly, yet my heart thumped like mad against my chest.

***

"My underground man! You're home early." Charlotte jumped to greet me at the door, throwing her arms around me. I went to hug her back, but she pulled away and asked, "What's wrong?"

I shook my head.

"Okay," she said, and hugged me tighter. I rushed to not let go and the longer I held her, the tighter she gripped me.

"Are you sure this is right?"

"What do you mean?"

I led her to the couch. "How do we know this is the right thing to do? Should we even have this baby?"

"'Should we have this baby?' What are you saying right now?"

"Wouldn't it be easier? You could still leave me and find somebody else to raise her with. What if I can't do it? What if I can't be present?"

"Del," she placed her palm against my cheek. "Only God knows what's right. Only God knows. I know you didn't mean that. I know that you want this child as much as I do."

"I do. Oh, I couldn't even imagine not raising this baby. I don't know why I said that. I'm just–I'm trying to think. I don't know what to think. I feel like my mind keeps taking me in circles. I want to have this baby. And I want to be the best husband for you that I can be. Why can't I just say that? Why can't I just say I'm scared that I can't do the things that I want? Why do I speak out of my ass? God, Charlotte, I don't mean it at all. I love you. God, I love you. Life without you is hell itself. No. I'm just scared. I'm scared I can't do this. I imagine you're so frustrated and tired of me speaking like this, but God, don't you want me honest?"

Charlotte cradled my head and said, "I do."

"I feel so weak."

"It's okay."

"I think I'm going to lay down."

She nodded and let go of me, and I went to lay in bed. I sat on top of the freshly made sheets and watched the fan twirl above me.

His eyes followed me. Each time I blinked, he seemed to grow angrier and angrier. His hand gesture could easily have been misunderstood to be a peace sign. No, it meant something like blessing, but it wasn't an originally Christian depiction. It came from the Buddhists. This mudra was a sign of protection–to show Jesus with this gesture meant he was casting all evil, everywhere, away. The eyes glowed brighter. I couldn't hide.

***

Clip-clop, clip-clop... the faint sound of hooves grew closer. *Clip, clip-clop, clip-clop.* The processional cross thrust in its back, the lamb stood by me at the bedside.

"Why don't you drink some more?" He placed the chalice under his heart and the blood flowed until it flooded over the brim of the cup.

"Take it."

I reached out my hand–

Charlotte jumped back, "Oh! I'm sorry to wake you, but do you want lunch?" I had to blink a few times before I could see her clearly. She was holding a sandwich with chips on a plate in one hand and a cup of water in the other. I sat up and took it and she came around and sat beside me on the other side of the bed.

"What time is it?"

"Just after two," she replied.

The sandwich was good. I took a few bites before asking her, "When do you want me to take you home?" Her face recoiled into a blank expression. I stuttered out, "To Sarah's, I mean."

"We should leave by 4. Your mom wants us to stop by on the way."

"You talked to my mom?"

"Yeah. She says Bucky is getting more depressed without Sally. They might have to put him down, Del."

"Are you serious?"

"He is quite a bit older than Sally was. Her youth was probably keeping him alive all this time."

"I wonder how Dad's doing."

"I'm sure he'd be a lot better if you were there." She kissed my cheek and left me alone in the room. I didn't want to get crumbs on the bed, so I took my food to the dining table and ate there. Charlotte was putting dishes away in the kitchen.

I chewed slowly; I couldn't help but think about Dad. I knew well enough that he wasn't talking to Mom about it. He'd drink a couple of extra beers every day for a few weeks and that would be it. The Robert men seemed damned to be alone no matter who they married. Probably why Johnny was keeping Adam at the same arm's length that Adam was keeping him.

I picked up my plate and took it to the kitchen. Charlotte was softly humming a song. I looked back at her and wondered why it sounded so familiar. While I placed the plate in the dishwasher, I was taken to those adolescent days in that Baptist sanctuary, with the light beaming through the stained-glass.

The Doxology?

***

We rode nearly in complete silence up to my parents. Charlotte drove. I couldn't help but admire the way she handled the gearshift. She engaged the clutch with her left foot in concert with a graceful downward pull of the shifter into fourth gear. The whole ride she shifted without a clink in the gearbox and without a jolt from the car. I thought about the time when I taught her how to drive standard back when we dated in high school. She learned quicker than I did, which I used to joke was because I was an even better teacher than my dad who taught me.

"What are you smiling at?"

"I just like watching you drive." She returned my smile and went back to watching the road. I stared for a second or two longer and then watched as we passed the suburbs and entered the rural hills.

"I'd like to see Reece soon. Can you believe we got pregnant at the same time? Our kids will be the best of friends."

"It'll be great," I replied, as I attempted to ignore the sweat that was building in my palms.

***

Mom and Dad were out in the barn with Bucky when we pulled up, the gravel crunching beneath the tires. Bucky was lying on his side; his eyes were glazed over, and he was breathing slow. Mom's eyes were bloodshot when she wrapped one arm around me and the other around Charlotte.

"Thanks for coming." She let go of Charlotte and squeezed me tight. "Oh Peter, I'm tired of all this death. It makes me sick."

Charlotte walked over to Dad, who was leaning against the stall door, and perched beside him.

"What's the vet say?" I asked Mom, releasing myself from her grip.

"He's old and miserable and decided he's done living. There's nothing to do about it. I wish your brother was here. He'd cheer us right up."

Charlotte glanced over at me and motioned for me to come over. I obeyed, walked over, hugged Dad's neck and told him I was sorry.

"Part of life, Son," he muffled.

"Part of life," I muttered right back.

Mom went to brushing Bucky's mane. We watched quietly.

Charlotte let our sulking go on for a few long minutes, then took me by the hand and walked me out behind the barn, into the wide, green pasture. The crickets were chirping somewhere amongst the swaying wheat. I straightened my breathing out while Charlotte rubbed her silk thumb against the backside of my hand.

"Why's Mom gotta be that way? Her empathy can be so insensitive sometimes."

"Del, what's important right now is being there for your dad. He's a mess. I think you should be here tomorrow. If not while the vets here, then at least after."

I nodded, but said, "Johnny would be better."

"Oh hush. Just because Johnny knows how to speak your mom's language, doesn't mean he's better for what your dad needs right now. That's silly. Pick up some cheap beer and drink with him in silence. Anything else would wear your dad out." I nodded again.

I would probably be with Bea when the horse doctor arrived, but I would come after.

We strolled a little further along without any reason why. It seemed like the natural world was pulling us deeper into her core. I felt like finding a soft place in the moss for us to lie and let time roll by. Charlotte stopped us and grabbed my other hand.

"I love you, darling." Before I could reply, she planted her lips against mine. I pressed back, pulling her closer by the hips. I felt a smile form on her lips, and my own grin tightened my cheeks.

I thought to myself, *this is what I want for the rest of my life. Now how do I not get in my own way?*

Charlotte pulled away with her eyebrows raised. "We're a team, you and me," she lectured, with a stern and raspy voice. "So, here's the game plan: I'm gonna go let Naomi's god be my god so you can go be there for your dad. K?"

"And who is her god?"

"Hospitality, of course. I doubt she'd let me help prepare any food or clean up around the house, but maybe she'll let me make some tea or coffee, but obviously she'll have to help me."

"Alright, it's a plan. I'll take tea, please."

"You'll take what I give you."

"Yes, ma'am."

"Green or black."

I grinned. "Green."

She took back my hand and we strolled back to the barn, swinging our arms in tune with the wind.

"You're a lucky man. I was going to make you green either way," she said as we came up to the barn.

Before walking back into the stable, she kissed my cheek close to my ear and whispered, "teamwork." Then, she trotted up to Mom and led her into the house. I leaned against the wood next to Dad.

There wasn't really anything to be said, so we both stayed silent. Like a couple of dogs. I knew myself too well to know he wasn't alright, though. With every slight sniffle and every saturated blink that was too quick not to notice, I could feel the rush of emotions spinning unabridged inside his head.

"Dad, you know I'm here for you."

"Yup," he grunted back.

I followed his eyes as they scanned through the three sectioned windows that sat in front of the kitchen sink. Behind the glass, Charlotte was pouring steaming water into four teacups. Mom was sitting at the kitchen table, head thrown back in the air. Laughing? Laughing.

"Truth be told, Del, I didn't think you'd be able to get married."
Surprised, I looked at Dad in earnest.

He continued, "Just the way the world is now, I was surprised is all. You're a loner like me and hell, I only got married because that's what everybody else was doing. And young, too. The only reason so many people in my generation got married was because we didn't think about it, we just did it. You and Johnny were taught to think about your life, slowly and carefully, so when you got married and not Johnny, I was surprised is all."

"What are you saying, Dad?"

"Charlotte's special. That's what I'm trying to say. I don't think you could make it work with anyone else. I'm not trying to exaggerate that, but you know what I mean."

I raised my brow.

"The fact that y'all have had these problems doesn't surprise me. Don't take that the wrong way, it's just—it takes a special kind of person to put up with the Robert way of being. We're not always easy to live with. But Charlotte, I remember when she'd come over those summer nights when you were in school." His eyes were watering up. Tears rolled down the side of his face slowly, but consistently, one after the other.

"Don't you remember?" he asked. I did remember. I remembered every moment.

"I loved watching you guys. I loved seeing how animated she made you. And I'd be happy to see you be like that again."

I nodded.

"Now, this damn horse. I don't know, Del. I ride him for the first time in years and now he wants to die on me. I guess I just gotta let life happen the way it's s'posed to. You know, when Sally died, I realized how important these horses were. After we buried her, I came in here and brushed Bucky all day long. And we talked and talked. It's weird how easy a horse can be to talk to. Anyways, it's just a horse. But he's been part of my life for just as long as you, and I couldn't imagine losing you, Son. I couldn't. Look, don't worry about me. It's just a horse." He wiped the tears from his face, and I squeezed him as tight as I could. He patted my back while a droll voice said in my head, "It's just a horse."

We went inside and Dad went up to his room while we drank our tea in silence. Then Charlotte and I were back on the road to Sarah's.
"Why'd you fly to Seattle?" I heard the words roll off my own tongue. Charlotte looked at me, then back on the road.

When she didn't respond, I let it go. She does what she wants, I thought, and looked back out the window at the red and gray dust covering our car from the Georgia dirt road.

"I went to see my father."

"Your father?"

She nodded without taking her eyes off the road.

"Why?"

She sniffed, preventing the snot from dripping out of her nose, and said, "Mom thought I should."

I waited for her to say why and when she didn't, I asked, "Why now?"

"Because I knew I was pregnant, and I thought he deserved to know."

"Before me?"

She looked away from me and toward the road, while sucking on the bottom of her lip.

"Del, it's—you have to understand. I was scared."

"Scared of what? We've been trying to have a baby for years!"

"Yeah, but—I don't want to have this conversation while I'm driving. Can we just drop it?"

"Yeah. Sure."

Pulling up the driveway, Charlotte brought the car to a stop and pulled the parking brake to a squeaking stiff lock. She opened the door and got out. I sat still, trying to control myself, but I was mad. I wanted to yell, but I wasn't the type to yell.

She walked up the sidewalk to the front door. On the front porch, she turned around and looked at me before walking in. My knee tapped incessantly against the door handle. I took a deep breath. "It was a past life. Worry about this later. She's right," I muttered under my breath, "She's right." Then I stepped out of the car and walked up the sidewalk and through the open door.Sarah smiled when she saw me walk in. I grinned back.

"So good to see you, Del." She gave me a big hug as I replied, "You too—Mom." She tightened her grip.

"Dinner's just about ready. Leo!" she called up the stairwell. A few seconds later, Charlotte's stepdad came stumbling down and joined us at the dinner table.

Sarah pulled Chicken Marsala off the stove and set it on the table before uncorking a bottle of Zinfandel.

I felt stiff sitting there as Sarah urged us to fix our plates. I started cutting the chicken and stabbing it with my fork to thrust it into my mouth, but Sarah chimed in before my food could reach its beacon, "Del, do you mind praying?"

"Hm—yes. No, I will. Sure."

She grabbed Leo's hand, and then Charlotte's. Charlotte locked her hand in mine as I weakly placed my other hand in Leo's. They bowed their heads while I looked for what to say.

"Uh, God," I began.

"Thank you," I heard myself say, but I didn't know what for.

"Thank you for the people here. For life. And for food. I pray you bless the hands that prepared it."

I looked around the table at their bowed heads. Sarah had a big grin.

"Be with my dad–and with Mom–as they mourn Bucky being put to rest tomorrow. May you bring them peace in the pain.

"I pray you turn our eyes toward what's good, what's beautiful, what's meaningful. Toward a better way to be. A way of love and hope and joy.

"Uh, and we pray this in the name of Jesus–or God." Charlotte tightened her grip on my hand.

"Amen."

Forks started to clang against plates as everyone turned their attention to the food in front of them. I slowly picked my fork back up and slid the meat into my mouth. It was good.

"So, Del," Sarah finished chewing, took a sip of wine, and said, "I know it hasn't been that long, but did you ever attend a church service like I asked you to?"

Nervous, I looked at Charlotte who shifted her eyes in a way that I knew she didn't want me to say yes, but at the same time, knew I should, "Well, I haven't been to a church service, but I've been to see our new friend, Adam. He's a minister at Peachtree Presbyterian, just a few blocks from our home."

Charlotte's face loosened up a bit, but it was only for a second because she took a noticeable breath and said with a stutter, "And Del went with Adam to a prayer service at the mosque."

"Is that right?"

I nodded, nervous for what would be said next.

"Now why would you do that?" Leo spat out.

Sarah put her hand on his and whispered for him to calm down, then asked me, "And how was it?"

"It was interesting. I enjoyed it. It was–honestly, it was one of the most sincere services I've attended."

As their eyebrows perched high on their foreheads, I added, "But I have no intention of converting."

"Well, of course not, you're a Christian," Sarah said with her head tilted to the side.

I looked at Charlotte and let out a stifled chuckle when I saw the massive, uncomfortable grimace on her face, then turned back to Sarah. I left the smile on my face and shrugged.

"I think I may go to Adam's church this Sunday. Charlotte, I wanted to see if you'd go with me?" She took my hand in hers and replied, "Of course, darling. I would love that." She kissed my cheek.

After dinner, I told Charlotte's parents goodbye, and Charlotte walked me out to the car. Her hand playfully found their fingers locked in mine.

"I'm not upset you didn't tell me about Seattle. I don't want to ever feel like you need my permission to do what you need to do." The gravel crunched under our feet as I stopped in the driveway, "But I do hope you'll tell me about the visit. I want to know. Is he still an asshole? Or did you end up forgiving him? Both maybe?"

She giggled and kissed me. "I would have told you on the balcony that day if you would've shut up. I'll tell you all about it soon, okay? He's not so much an asshole as he is lost in his own way."

She opened the car door for me to get in, but I pulled her backwards into my arms and leaned against the car. I clasped my hands against her belly. With my lips resting against her face, I found myself praying once again. I was praying that this was really it.

***

I called Charlie on the road and asked if he wanted to have a whiskey since I would be driving through. He invited me over but said I couldn't stay too long.

Reece met me at the door and gave me a hug before letting me in. "I've missed you! I feel like I haven't seen you in forever. I know it's only been a couple of weeks. I don't know what it is, but I think waiting for this baby to come is slowing down time."

I told her I understood, and she replied, "Oh, I know! Don't think I haven't called Charlotte every day to talk. We're going to be pregnant sisters. We might as well call you 'Uncle Del.'"

Charlie snorted as he walked up and handed me a whiskey glass. We went and sat out back under the amber string lights and enjoyed our drinks. Charlie was quiet and I couldn't tell if he was still offended by me, or if he had just run out of things to say. Either way, the silence was nice, but I knew there was something to be said.

"I'm sorry for what I said about your and Reece's relationship, Charlie. It was wrong. I don't know why I said it. I was probably just jealous is all. Truth is, I've always admired your relationship.

"I've found myself wishing I had what you guys have. It was just my resentment talking 'cause I wanted me and Charlotte to be like y'all. And I know it's me who gets in the way of it."

Charlie took a sip of his drink, set it down, leaned back in his chair, and watched the fan spin round and round.

"Anyways," I continued, "I should've been coming to you for advice this whole time rather than resenting you and thinking I had everything figured out better than you do. I really am sorry."

I took a sip of my whiskey, waiting for his reply.

"You know, Del, I don't think you want to have what me and Reece have. Don't get me wrong, I'm perfectly happy with my marriage, but your thinking that we're what a perfect marriage is supposed to look like is part of what keeps you from thinking you and Charlotte's marriage could be good as it is.

"Your expectations get all out of whack 'cause you see me and Reece, I don't know, talking about what's happening down at the town square during breakfast, or watching college football on Saturday's, and you think that's what you and Charlotte are supposed to have, but y'all are both pensive people, and I imagine y'all'd get along a lot better if you realized it was okay to just sit side by side and daydream about whatever it is that always has you preoccupied inside your head."

I nodded.

"Am I making sense? 'Cause I feel like I've psycho-analyzed you better than that therapist of yours probably can." He cracked a smile.

"You're getting wise with your age," I quipped.

"I'm becoming a father. Don't you worry, you'll be a sage like me in a few weeks."

"You believe we're gonna be fathers? At the same time, too?"

"Yeah, it's something. I'll be sending Charles Jr. over to your house for quiet time and library days. Not too often though, I don't want him to be a monk. And I'll come pick up lil' Petey for Friday night Braves games."

"You already know I'm not planning on naming my kid after me. Besides, I'm convinced we're having a girl. Little Mary Ann."

"I can't believe you made fun of me for my kids' names."

"What's wrong with Mary Ann? It's elegant and classic, and I find it endearing."

"No, it's a good name. It's nostalgic but not outdated. It's good. I'm just paying you back."

"I do think Charlotte and I are in a good place. I hope I can keep it this way, but I can't say I'm not nervous."

"I know what you mean, but it'll be different now. Whether it's better or worse, who's to say, but y'all have seen each other like never before. I swear Reece and I get closer after all of our fights."

"I'll tell you what it feels like. It feels like the same old wine we've been drinking is getting poured into new wine skins."

Charlie leaned forward and scrunched his face.

"Isn't that from scripture?"

I nodded.

"What's that got to do with marriage?" He asked.

"The love is the same, but it gets better with age, we just have to adapt to it as the seasons change."

"That's some poetic shit, Del. Didn't Jesus say not to put new wine in old wine skins though? You're flipping the script."

"Don't think about it too much so it stays poetic, okay? Besides, I could probably talk my way into making it work."

"Well, I want to see you try."

I thought for a moment, then said, "Alright, think a little creatively here. Take Jesus turning water into wine and mix it in with the example. Remember how they said it was the good wine, like top-shelf stuff? Jesus just made it, though, so is it new? Not if it represents Jesus. That's John chapter 2, but think of John 1 where John says Jesus has been from the beginning. Well, if the good wine is Jesus, then the good wine has always been. It just seems new."

"You're reaching, pastor." Charlie smirked and downed his drink.

"Maybe, but I like it. That old wine is eternal love, and as much as I hate to admit it, I think the closest thing we can get to tapping into that kind of love is in marriage. Charlotte has me convinced at least. The way she's forgiven me, Charlie–" my emotions overcame me, and I choked up, "It's stupid, really. God, I've been so cold to her. It doesn't make sense."

Charlie's face was beaming as I wiped my tear-soaked cheeks against my shirt.

"What are you, a sadist?" I jeered.

"No, I just like to see you express what's been pent up inside you."

"Well, don't get used to it. I'm going to try to save these outbursts for Charlotte and my therapist from now on."

"Yeah, yeah. Don't try too hard."

"Anyways, I've missed this. I'm going to head out now."

We walked back inside. Reece came trotting down the stairs.

"Del, before you go, we got you something. We were gonna wait for your birthday to give it to you, but I want you to have it now." She pulled out an antique wooden box from behind her. It was wrapped with a bronze metal that looked like vines. On the top, the metal plating had a diamond shape with my initials in the center. I took it and ran my hands over the metal and the grain. It was beautifully worn, likely crafted before the Great Depression.

"I don't know what you'll put in it, but how often do you come across your initials on something so elegant. We saw it and thought it looked like something you would have."

"Well, I love it." I gave Reece a hug and then Charlie, patting him on the back. I knew exactly what I wanted to store in it.

***

I sat the box on my writing desk and went to grab my poetry book. I was going to rip my poem out so that it could be the first of many poems I'd store in my new box. The only problem was I couldn't find the book anywhere. I gave up, assuming I was too tired to know where to look, and passed out on the couch.

Amir woke me up in the middle of the night by jumping on my stomach. I picked him up and took him to the bed with me and, after staring at the ceiling fan for a few thousand revolutions, finally fell back asleep.

***

The air was thick in my bedroom when I woke up. The sun was rising, reflecting off the windows of the building across the street. My chest felt tight, and I was only able to take half-breaths. I tried falling back asleep, moving in and out of consciousness for a while before deciding I'd just get up. It took me a while to roll out of bed, and the only motivation I had was Amir crying to be fed. The clock read "10:30." I had slept for eleven hours.

Amir cast himself into his food and I sat on the couch staring at the black t.v. screen. I needed coffee. My headache from caffeine withdrawals pounded just above my right eye as a small vein pulsated against the skin of my temple. The irony was I couldn't find the energy to make my coffee. This is my judgement for not buying an instant coffee maker like Charlotte suggested. Amir finished eating, jumped up beside me, and licked at his paws.

On the coffee table was the Rowan Williams' poetry book Adam had loaned me, sitting where I thought I had left my other book of poems. I'd look again if I could excite myself enough to make coffee.

I grabbed the book off the table and flipped to the bookmarked page with the poem on Nietzsche that Adam had recommended. I was tired of Nietzsche. Not because I didn't like him, but because he seemed to be the only philosopher anyone ever talked about anymore. At least guys my age with no more than an elective as an education in philosophy. Worse, they seemed to like him for the same reason as the nazis.

I knew I didn't understand him, so it annoyed me for others to act like they did.

Nietzsche: Twilight
At the clinic, he broke windows, shouting
that there were guns behind them, desperate
not to be shielded by the thin, deceiving skin
that looked as if it wasn't there. He liked
the opaque curtain or the open sky; not this.
His mother took him home; out for walks,
she told him, Put on your nice professor's face,

when they met friends. His head grew vast,
pulling him downwards till he could not breathe.
At night he roared; during the day, My voice
is not nice, he would whisper. White,
swollen, his skull drowned him like a stone,
his breath, at the end, the sound
of footsteps on broken glass.

I didn't know what to do with that, but I was haunted. The poet fascinated me more than the depiction of Nietzsche. Why would this religious poet write so compassionately of one man's madness, this man who said the poet's God was dead? I closed the book and went back to bed.

***

My phone vibrated while I was still asleep.
"Hello?"
"Del, my apologies, but I'm running about 15 minutes behind. I will see you at 2:10."
I checked the clock and shuffled out of bed.
"Alright, I'm running behind too. No worries," I replied.
"See you soon, then." Bea hung up.

I threw on a clean shirt and brushed my teeth, then I rushed out the door.
With a brisk walk I was able to get to her building at 2:15. The spring air was thick with humidity, showing signs of a creeping summer. Halfway there, I realized I had the car again. I palmed my forehead and sped up, telling myself it would've taken longer just to find parking. My face was drenched in sweat, so I rushed through the revolving door straight toward the restroom and wiped off with a damp towel before heading to her office. I knocked on the thick wooden door. She opened it immediately.
"Hi Del, come in, come in, have a seat." She shook my hand with both of hers and motioned toward the couch.
"So," she took a seat in her green leather chair and sat her reading glasses on the side table, "Catch me up to speed. How have you been?"
I was still catching my breath, "All over the place, really. I thought I was doing better, I was doing better, but when I woke up this morning, I

couldn't get out of bed. I didn't want to. If you hadn't called me, I'd still be there."

She leaned in.

"And my stomach is in knots," I added.

Tears began to form, but I dammed them up.

"Well, that's what I'm here for, Del. Why don't you start by telling me where your head was before you went to sleep last night?"

I thought back to the day before and didn't know where to start.

"Yesterday was a lot, I guess. I didn't have a break to process any of it. Dad's horse is sick. They're putting him down today. I'll go to be with him after this. And I had dinner with Charlotte and her parents, which was painful given the elephant sitting on the dining table... Then, I went and saw my cousin and Charlie. Oh, and I had a fight with Charlotte because I found out she went and saw her birth father, and I had no idea she even knew how to contact him."

Bea was shaking her head, "That *is* a lot."

"And somehow I lost my poem, so I couldn't bring you a copy."

"That's fine. I can take a copy by email. Okay?"

I nodded.

"Why did you go to your cousins' after dinner?"

"I felt like having a whiskey with Charlie. I thought that might help me decompress after dinner. He was kind of helpful. I mean, he's not you, but he's free, and we drank." I let out a sigh and smiled.

"Maybe I'll start mixing drinks for my patients then," she said with a coy grin. "Del, it sounds like you could use some company, but I'm not sure that company should be your therapist clenching a bill. So, I'm going to say let's cut this session short. No charge today. Go be with your dad."

I gripped the arm of the couch with my left hand as a tear drop slowly fell from my right eye.

"You know, I meant it when I said that poem contained your *raison d'etre*, and isn't it quite the perfect reason to be? So true to Being too! To me it seems you've started to live it out. And I will say, walking down a mountain looks easy when you've just reached the top and fought against gravity the whole way up. When you head toward the valley, gravity seems to be on your side, but if you give in to it, you might trip and tumble the rest of the way down. That's going to hurt–a lot–so, keep a check on your bearings and don't rush the journey," she said with a reassuring wink.

I sighed with a nod and stood up. Bea stood too and shook my hand. Before I headed for the door, a question came to my mind.

"Can I ask you something off topic before I go?"

"Of course."

"I know this will sound like it came from nowhere, but it's something I've tried to think through for a while, and I think you might have a better answer than me."

"Ok, ask away."

"First, do you think of yourself as a feminist?"

Bea laughed before realizing I was genuine. "If the inverse is misogyny, then yes, I suppose I am a feminist. I reckon I have no choice not to be. But I wouldn't stake my identity on it because supporting anyone who's been marginalized by identifying with something is useless if all it is is a claim on your identity. Who does that help? Anyways, why do you ask?"

"I've started to notice while reading how often old writers would say something wonderful and poetic and then suck out all of its force in this 21st century by making the subject 'man' rather than humanity. Perhaps it's all semantics, but when I read people like Jung or Calvin, they would say man instead of humanity and now, it leaves a distaste in my mouth, and I don't know what to do with it. Kierkegaard's guilty of it too, or somebody like Montaigne, the great French philosopher, who's quote, 'Chaque homme porte la forme, entière de l'humaîne condition' was one of my favorites in school.

Bea tipped an imaginary hat.

"But, though these men may or may not have held women in high esteem, they used the conventions of their time, so you do not know. And I'm left with a bitter taste in my mouth.

"But don't you think if these were twenty-first century men, they would know better? Do we give them that courtesy? And if we assume they would, should we rewrite what they've said to make it fit better into the modern world?"

Bea sat back in her chair as I leaned against the railing of the door.

"That's a lot to think about, Del. Certainly not a line of questioning I expected. Hmm. And I'm only a therapist, and this is not my field of study, but okay. Here's all I will say, we'd do best to not rewrite the past because then we'd erase the bitterness. The discomfort is what makes us realize we've grown. So, maybe give them the courtesy of believing they'd know better today by smiling when you come across their man-centered words because it reminds you of how far we've come."

"Fair enough. I do like that."

"Alright, but I do recommend you don't hold that as the standard judgement for how we treat humanity's past sins–if you know what I mean. There was a time when men wrote 'All men are created equal' and that did not even mean all men, let alone women. But now we realize it should be all men. And women, too. What blasphemy!"

I nodded. "Thanks, Bea."

She smiled. "I'll see you next week, Del."

***

I took my time walking home, cutting by the swelling fountain and up past the arts center toward a park that rested down in between an upper-class neighborhood. The park was formed like that of a crescent shaped valley, lined with trees that walled it in from the city. I followed the creek that ran through the center of it until it dammed up into a pond. The smell of moistened soil filtered through my nostrils. The earthiness of the air whispered in and out of my nose as the noise of traffic and construction faded to the background. The sound of leaves rustling in the wind and birds calling to their mates rushed to the fore.

I found a patch of moss that wasn't too damp and lay down with my arm as a pillow. It was the end of spring, the flowers had bloomed, the trees had reached their crescendo of green, and following the branches' lifted hands toward the heavens was the deep blue sky, unmoved by these trifles below.

As I dozed away into a dreamy daze, memories played before my mind's eye. They were vivid, possibly embellished–a trick of my subconscious–all the way back till I was two. It started with me smashing my face with chocolate cake. I suppose I remember that one because Mom has the picture of me, grinning large and messy, on her wall. Johnny and I were running around with mason jars, lightning bugs all around us. *Where did the lightning bugs go?*

I saw Sally. She was nearly full grown but so young. Out on the hill, under the tree, she was nuzzling me, but the sun was still setting. She snorted, so I finally took her back home. Then I was swinging alone on the church playground. Charlotte came up and started swinging beside me.

170

Elementary school children rushed off the bus and through the park toward their waiting parents on the other side of the fertile Eden extending out of their front yards. I was shaken out of the daze.

My phone buzzed in my pocket. Mom's text read that the horse doctor had arrived.

***

At a gas station just outside of the farm, I stopped for a twenty-four pack of light beer and drove up the dirt road toward the house. Sarah's car was in the driveway. I went into the garage and placed the beer in the extra fridge, then made my way inside the house.

Charlotte's eyes caught my attention before I noticed anything else. She nodded her head to show it was over, so I made my way over to Dad to hug him. He pulled away and said, "I'm alright, Son."

Mom hugged me next, then Sarah, then I gently wrapped my arm around Charlotte's waist who responded by pressing in against me. We spoke to each other with solemn stares, knowing there were no words to say. After the proper amount of reverential silence had passed, Sarah took the initiative to get Charlotte and Mom out the door to do whatever they had planned so I could spend some time with Dad.

We waved as they backed out of the driveway and, once they were out of sight, I turned to Dad and asked, "Beer?"

"Yep."

I grabbed two beers out of the cardboard box and put the rest in a cooler, then we drove the golf cart out to the tree on top of the hill, leaned against its bark, and drank.

The light beer went down like water. Besides a bit of carbonation and a hint of barley, it might as well have been water. Six empty cans sat in the cooler when I pulled out two more.

Number four got us talking.

We talked about the times he evaded death, some I knew, some I didn't. And I told him about the times I had done the same–things I'd never told him before. Street racing in high school, jet skiing at midnight during college, breaking into construction sites to climb the cranes.

He retold the story of when he first came home with Bucky. Mom was pregnant with me and pissed that he bought a horse without asking her.

171

He would always say he didn't ask because she would have said no. The first time Dad tried to ride him, he'd never ridden a horse before, and Bucky wasn't trained, but Dad just hopped on him and rode. They rode out through the pasture right by the forest, until Bucky saw a snake and bucked Dad off into the pine straw. Dad said he galloped around in place, barely missing Dad's head and rib cage with his hoof. He rolled out of the way and let the horse run. When he made it back to the stall, Bucky was outside, lying in the grass. So, Dad named him Bucky and hired someone to break him.

We talked about how badly he had wanted to be a bull rider when he was a teenager because of reading Hemingway, and then we talked about my obsession with planes growing up. My family thought I might grow up to be a pilot. When we'd drive through the city, I'd point at the planes just hundreds of feet above us after leaving the runway or descending for landing. They started calling me 'Del' after Atlanta's hometown airline, and I was so young, I still can't remember the times when that wasn't my name.

I bet Dad that he couldn't remember my birth name and he was inebriated just enough to joke around and say, "At least I know it's biblical. Your mom made sure of that."

"Dad, can I ask something personal?"

"Might as well."

"What's it like going to church all these years? Does it feel like Mom drags you, or are you glad to go?"

He looked at me squarely and replied, "Yes." He smirked, we laughed, and then his face tightened. "I don't know what to tell you, Del. I never feel like going, but I'm always glad when I do. Sure, I'm not sure if it's something I believe in, but it does feel worth acting like I do. But I think your giving up on it was important, too. I never really saw you as giving up on God though. Just the God we think we know. But who knows, your mom might have it all figured out and she'll get to tell us 'I told you so' as Peter tells us our fate. Ah, Peter! See, I told you I knew it."

We both finished off our beer, crushed the cans, and chucked them toward the golf cart before plopping down on the face of the hill as the sun began to slip over the edge of the world.

I checked my phone to see a text from Charlie saying he and Johnny were heading over to join us and told Dad, who was too mesmerized by the remnant the sun had left on the sky, or maybe he was somewhere off in his head. Either way, the experience he was having caused his eyes to mist.

"Hey Son," he turned to me.

I looked at him.

"Your kid–" he paused.

"Yeah?"

"Well, they're going to shit on you."

"What?"

"They'll shit on you, and I wanted you to know ahead of time, 'cause you gotta be prepared for it."

"You might've drunk too much."

"Nah Son, this is important advice. Just don't hold it against them, okay?"

"Alright, Dad."

"Let's go back and meet your brother and Charlie. Don't want them unsupervised at the house."

"Alright, but Dad," I still had things I wanted to discuss with him, and I knew this may be one of the few chances I'd get.

He swung his head around in slow motion and I wondered if we needed to call a ride-share to drive us back to the house.

"I'm still thinking about church and why I left. Maybe its nostalgia, or maybe I'm finally forgiving her for threatening me with hellfire, but you're right, I haven't given up on something being out there. I guess I just don't think of God as 'out there' but more 'everywhere.' Just is. I'm not sure if God is the right name, either, but something gives life to our being. I do know there's something about the Christian faith that once you get out of this small town, the tradition of people across the world who haven't given up on that God–makes me want to believe."

"Ain't nothing wrong with this town, boy. Don't be so close-minded. Ha!"

He started hobbling down the hill, leaving the golf cart behind. I followed him.

"You know what I mean," I called after him. "You're the one that got me out of here. You remember those weekend trips we used to take for my birthday? We'd go wherever the Braves played that weekend, even though neither of us were ever really into baseball. Why'd we stop doing that?"

"Because you left. You got out. Didn't need those trips anymore," he grunted without breaking his pace.

"Well, I've been back for a while now and I want to start doing it again."

He stopped near the hill's bottom and looked at me. "Sure, alright."

"I'm serious. Let's check the schedule and wherever the Braves play in September, we'll go."

He looked at me and smiled. His eyes did that twinkling thing people talk about and then he tripped on his own feet, rolling down the last two yards of the hill.

"Oh, god-dammit, I'm drunk!"

I managed to get my laughter under control, then I lifted him up and we stumbled arm over shoulder back to the house.

Johnny and Charlie had let themselves in and were sitting around the kitchen table drinking bourbon when we crashed through the door, laughing at our own intoxicated stupor.

"Ah, shit. Give me some of that," Dad grabbed the bottle off the table and shot it straight.

Charlie jumped up and pulled a chair out for him. Dad took him up on his offer and crashed into the chair, throwing his arms against the table. "Damn horse died."

"We know, Dad. We're here for you," Johnny replied.

I dropped an ice cube in a glass and filled it with whiskey and joined them. Dad was obviously holding back tears. I leaned over and patted him on the back, then he began to cry.

"Oh, don't mind me," he sucked snot back up his nostril, "These are mostly happy tears. Glad you boys are all here."

We gave him a moment in silence, but soon Johnny went to talking and we were back to cracking up again.

***

Mom woke me up the next morning with all the noise she was making in the kitchen. I crawled out of my childhood bed and walked down the stairs. Mom was sitting at the kitchen bar drinking coffee. Charlotte was cooking bacon and eggs in a cast-iron pan.

"Charlotte thought you men might need a wholesome breakfast to get you going this morning after last night." Mom patted the stool next to her for me to come sit. I took her up on her offer.

"Morning, love." Charlotte set a coffee in front of me from the only craft roaster in town.

"What did I do to deserve this?" I asked her.

"Not a thing, but I figured you'd need a whole arsenal after the mess we came home to last night."

Beer cans and an empty bourbon bottle were scattered across the table. The evidence was clear.

"After you get some caffeine and breakfast in you, you should have enough energy to clean up after yourself," Charlotte winked as I sipped my coffee through a smile.

"Also, where's my golf cart at?" Mom piped in as Dad's creaking footsteps stopped on the stairs.

"Haven't seen it," I remarked, looking at Dad.

"Me neither. Del, wanna go for a walk?"

Charlotte said, "Be quick! I don't want your breakfast to get cold."

Dad poured coffee from the pot into a mug, and we stepped out into the foggy, cool air.

"It'll be damn hot once that sun's risen to noon."

"How you feeling?" I asked him.

"Well, I haven't drank that much since I was probably your age. My head's pounding, but other than that I feel pretty damn good."

"I meant about Bucky, Dad. I want to make sure you don't bottle that up."

"I would never," he laughed.

"Yeah, me neither," I chuckled.

"I emptied that bottle out last night, didn't I?"

"Yeah, we did."

"That therapist of yours teach you that then? To not bottle stuff up?"

"I think she just taught me to pay more attention. Too simple, right?"

We made it to the edge of the hill and trekked up the rest of the way to the golf cart, then we drove it back and hid it behind the horse stall.

"I think I'm alright, Son. Just feels like part of my life went missing. I'm glad we got to ride one last time before this all happened so fast, you know?"

"Yeah."

We walked back in to find that Johnny, Charlie, and Reece had joined and were sitting at the kitchen table. Charlie and Johnny had slept in Johnny's old room and Reece had come to pick him up and stayed for breakfast. I cleaned off the table from last night's carnage and Charlotte helped me set the table.

Then we ate breakfast and drank our fill of coffee. We talked about our high school days, about our babies and baby names, their futures, plans for holidays and vacations. We laughed, we cried, and laughed some more.

Charlotte had her arm locked in mine with her head against my shoulder. I looked at my family around me, their faces bright, eyes glistening; I soaked in the lion's share of an air drenched in contentment, recognizing and appreciating these fleeting moments, knowing they are few and far between, knowing this moment is the most important moment of my life thus far, but that every moment comes together and culminates in moments like these, where all moments are present. Then, softly but firmly, I planted my lips like seeds in soil at the beginning of spring, full of hope and possibility, against the golden crown of my wife's head.

A Concluding Unscientific Postscript

The match sizzles as I put the flame to my cigar, puffing a few times until the tuck burns a deep red glow. The cigar is box-pressed, offering a slight discomfort, though odd delight, against my lips. The smoke rises like a stem opening into a flower. I sit to a new view. A new balcony. This city is a kaleidoscope, every glance, every angle, shows a different image of a beautiful whole, a microcosm of a culture alive within the Culture.

... If a crowd condemns a person, this is not an intrusion on their freedom; they are not compelled to act. They can remain undisturbed in their room, smoke their cigar, immerse themselves in contemplation, tease with their lover, rest comfortably in their armchair, walk their green garden—or indeed, they may even leave, for their presence is not required...

I place the book to the side. I am trying once again to read the postscript to the *Fragments*, but I can't get past the poetics of the preface without distraction. It is Adam's fault, really. He sends me these sections of his translations, and I find them so beautifully done. I print his work out and stuff them in my hard copies. Danish is not a language I care to learn, but Adam's translations are the best. In my opinion.

Using old seminary tricks, I have skimmed the book in its entirety as well as its predecessor, the aforementioned *Fragments*, but this preface I must have read ten times. I read it because I know it will cause me a distraction. Climacus, that character of Kierkegaard I find most intriguing, must have known his work was a distraction, that many a reader would come to the above quote and throw the book aside and take up their own thoughts and memories, the threads that make a life...

***

"Do you mind if I read it to him?"

I placed my hand on her thigh and nodded slowly.

Through the window, on the other side of the rectory, the expansive garden of red tulips and yellow daffodils, purple crocuses and pink azaleas swayed between three flowering dogwood trees. Underneath the trees, the lily of the valleys had bloomed into bell-shaped white flowers by the thousands. It looked as if the flowers were bowed over and shedding tears, watering and giving life to the burgeoning dogwoods. I glanced at our therapist, then back outside.

Charlotte began to read:

> *Curves of ice bore the way*
> *along the winding road.*
> *Climbing higher, one foot, another*
> *breathing harder as we go.*

***

On the balcony, the only light in the sky is the crescent moon and the orange tint from the glowing city below. A near perfect setting for losing yourself to thought.

Apathy was all I knew growing up; even God had turned His back on the world, and expected us to do the same. All we had was the hope of a new earth to come, and for this one to pass. In the meantime, our mission was to keep our head down and not get too involved with the current world before us. I went to college to help people learn to live like this and found myself morose.

I left that God behind.

But I had no reason to desert my apathy. If anything, my apathy became even more important to me. I had no reason, no meaning. There was nothing to escape from and nothing to escape to.

A sense of compassion welled up inside me for my parents, for Mom especially, because I remember when I believed the way she believes. I felt pity for her; it was out of her hands. When that's your God, how do you ever ask Him questions? How do you not act how He wants you to act?

I had to accept damnation in order to be free. How could I prescribe that for anyone else? How could I expect it?

Apathy, though, seems to be a form of suicide, a deadly sin. So, what is the cure for my apathy if letting Him go didn't work?

***

Charlotte's rhythmic voice carried on:

Further on, the cold grew strong
as earth came near silent.
By noon–besides my own–
sound had all subsided.

***

I release a cloud of smoke. It flows up against the walls and seeps around the balcony ceiling, away into the atmosphere. I think of Meursault, faced with the Absurd. Apathetic. What if he had wept at his mother's funeral? Would he have pulled the trigger then?

When I met Carolyn, she smashed the life set before me into pieces, the same way she smashed that painting. She reminded me of the game. That I had succumbed to the rules. Living an inauthentic life. Diminished. She lived by her own rules. She's still a paradox to me. A storm of a woman. Part of me will always think of her fondly. Can I be blamed for that? She reminded me that I had my own rules, too.

A new painting hangs over our couch, lit up against the wall by the amber glow of the nearby lamp. I can see it now through the balcony door as I puff on the cigar.

***

There was a light knock against the door that Sunday morning after Bucky passed. I opened it to Charlotte dressed in that mesmerizing yellow sundress. She had come to meet me for church. She promptly kissed my cheek and announced, "I've got something for you!" She pulled a large canvas out from the side of the hallway, flipping it around for me to see.

I wish I could describe it in a way that did the piece justice: the oily fog set on a pair of snowcapped mountains. Down in between the mountains, the sun was rising on a small town covered by evergreen trees. At the top of the western mountain, the moon sat like a boulder with a waning, gibbous shadow, being held up by the sun. It was as if *Starry Night's* world had continued turning and morning was coming. The town's chapel reached up between the valley, and the small cross at the top of the steeple sat in the coming orb of the sun, a silhouette against the light.

Most importantly, I'll add this description: I wept. Cried as I had when Sally died, but this was a different sort of cry. Apart from those two times–a cry of deep sadness and a cry of what? Hope? There wasn't a cry in all my life that compared. Though, I cry often these days. A bit like a tapped well.

Charlotte pulled my book of poems from her bag. "Sorry for taking this, I needed it for inspiration."

I flipped the cover to my poem and saw she had chosen its title. I gathered her in my arms. My face sank into her shoulder. I hung the painting in place of the old one and held Charlotte in my arms, laid on the couch, clenching every second I could with that painting locked in sight and her wrapped in my arms.

***

> *Clumps of snow lined the path*
> *in an eerie cemetery gray*
> *And as the sky came close*
> *I asked the clouds,*
> *"Can I do this on my own?"*

***

We strode hands locked together toward Peachtree Presbyterian, walking in the direction of the sun, which splashed across the street and through the gleeful trees. Johnny met us at the door with open arms that turned into a long hug. The bell began to ring with loud, reverberating dings, so we quickly walked through the large red doors to find people carelessly mingling. We lackadaisically made our way to the third pew from the front and sat, Johnny by the aisle, Charlotte beside him, and me.

Charlotte gripped my hand and whispered, "Why are your hands sweating?"

"Why aren't yours?" I replied coolly, jabbing my loose finger gently into her side. She smirked.

Johnny sat with perfect posture, yet relaxed, and I watched as his face began to beam. Following his eyes, I saw Adam in full garb strolling to the pulpit.

"Good morning, Church."

"Good morning!" The crowd, more diverse by all measures than I assumed, boasted back.

"Why don't we start on a high note? Turn in the hymnal to hymn #700 and sing with the choir."

The choir began to sing what the footnote read was an African-American spiritual.

"*I'm gon-na live so God can use me,*" they sang and clapped unlike any Presbyterian church I had known. It was a simple song, subverting and contrasting the authority of the hymnodist's Christian slave masters.

***

Now, I think I've lived long enough to know that Camus was right about the Absurd. As desperate as I am to plant myself firmly in what is meaningful, I cannot locate it, and all I find is silence. But how the Absurd is right, I do not know.

***

I traveled on for mystery
till I came upon the peak.
Eyes closed, I waited
to see if God would speak.

***

"Kierkegaard once wrote:

'Faith is the objective uncertainty thrust forth by the experience of the absurd upheld by inward passion...Faith is not contingent on objectivity... Faith must not resign to unintelligibility; for precisely the relationship to or confrontation with the unintelligible, the absurd, is the liminal realm of faith's passion.'

185

"What does he mean in this unintelligible passage? 'Faith must not resign to unintelligibility?' Okay, Kierkegaard, now what does that mean? Be intelligible! Right?" The crowd giggled.

Adam continued his sermon. "I often wonder if Kierkegaard wanted to be understood, or, if he wanted his words to guide us into contemplation.

"Well, I'd say embrace whatever feeling has arisen in you by these mysterious words because that might just be the point. But now I'll dumb it down for you commoners who waste your time loving your neighbor rather than memorizing the dictionary."

There was a pause before the congregation, able to take a joke, chuckled in unison.

"Kierkegaard believed subjectivity was the way to truth. How each of you has experienced God is who God is. Though, being a good Presbyterian, I must add that it is not your interpretation of that experience that is God; that's idolatry! But it is the experience itself, that is where you meet God. And this I know is true because I've lived it as one of your ministers. It has been my experience of you and all your individual experiences of God, that has shown me the goodness of God.

"It seems to me the essential question we are always answering with our lives is the one posed by Shakespeare, 'To be or not to be.' Answer the question too positively and you can be sure to live life trapped in anxieties of all kinds. If you choose to be, you'll never be enough. Your only concern will be the future. *Will* too much to be and you will not be at all.

"Answer in the negative and you can expect the numbness of depression to direct your life. If you choose not to be, even the breath of life will come as a tax. It will be too much. You will not suffer because you will not feel, but you will not live, either.

"The negative answer gives me more anxiety than the positive," He paused as the crowd once again chuckled. Adam smiled at the irony, then his face tightened again.

"Because saying no to life can lead to the big NO. The end. A final answer.

"All of life is lived between these two ends, though it is much more of a circle. The journey to the other end is sometimes just a step away. Each of us will oscillate between the two until we meet our end, but there will be sweet moments where we live in the now. The present is where life is lived. It's where we meet God. It's where we create relationships and tend to them and enjoy them.

"Shakespeare's question is not meant to be given a final answer. It's meant to be asked every day of our lives. We cannot reason our way into being, but we can start each day pondering 'what is my reason to be *today*?' Today is where we wrestle with our existence, with God. Where we do not rest content with the unintelligibility of the universe but recognize our limits in discerning its meaning. Today, friends, today is where we live.

"There's another quote often misattributed to Kierkegaard," He winked at the crowd. "'Life is not a mystery to be solved, but a reality to be experienced.' The present calls us to live with passion. With the passion of our Christ.

"When was Jesus passionate? Only on his trip up calvary's hill? No! He was passionate from the start. They'll tell you that passion means to suffer, but that explanation falls short. We were the subject of Jesus's passion from the beginning of the world. We were not His suffering, we were His joy, the joy He wanted to come and live with, even if it meant He would suffer. That, that is passion.

"What is your joy today? What's worth it for you to suffer? What is your God-given reason for being in this world that justifies all the pain?"

The congregation held Adam's words as the choir came from behind him and began to sing.

I wrapped my arm around Charlotte's backside and pulled her close to me, setting my hand softly against the small round that had begun to tighten on her stomach, and she sat her hand on mine.

***

> *As I prayed, my feet gave way*
> *and I began to walk back down.*
> *Melted streams of snow, my guide*
> *to the valley green below.*

Charlotte put the book back into her purse.

"Del, *you* wrote this?"

I stopped looking out the window and turned to our therapist, a man with long, flowing, dirty blonde hair, who wore a sweater despite it being the high heat of summer, and nodded.

"What's it's title? Every poem needs a title, doesn't it? I've always felt that titles can be a key to meaning, don't you?"

Stuttering, I said, *"In the Valley Peaks the Soul."*

"Christ! That's a title."

"Charlotte picked it."

"I got it from Keats," she added.

He turned to my wife. "And Charlotte, why is Del's poem so important to you?"

Charlotte straightened her posture. "I see him in it. Who he really is. I see what he wants. And I see what he feels. Me and our baby are down in that valley and that's where he wants to be."

Her thigh pressed subtly against mine as I gripped her leg in my hand.

"Del, is she right?"

I nodded again.

"It's not a bad poem. Not bad at all. It certainly gives me high expectations for our sessions. But I'm wondering, Del, what has you so enraptured by the garden?" He motioned through the window where we all set our attention on the courtyard flora.

"I come from modest roots. The church I was baptized in wouldn't ever spend the money or effort on such an expansive garden. I can't help but wonder what makes this church different."

"It's simple, really. If the church is the location of salvation–of course, salvation is clunky because we're not talking about heaven and hell–if it is to be the temporary location of heavenly love, then it should be the home of truth, a place of goodness, and, naturally, a fount of beauty. That garden is a representation of the earth's future restoration, so of course it's worth a bit of Caesar's coin."

"I see," I replied.

"I like the two of you, and, I must say, this has been a pleasant consultation. I can't say I've ever had a couple explain their situation with a poem."

Charlotte squeezed my hand, leaning into my shoulder.

"I will see the both of you next week so we can start to frame your story, okay?"

Charlotte and I nodded.

"In the meantime, Del, it is important that you continue finding ways to relate to your wife and to yourself."

I blinked my eyes rapidly to keep them dry as I nodded again.

"And when you can't find the words to say, pick up the pen and let them flow across the page."

We walked out of the therapist's office and into the garden courtyard, south of the church, where three olive trees were spaced out across the tall brick wall. As we walked down the cobbled path, the muscadine vines stretched across the wooden arbor overhead in a row of three, only letting the sun dance through as if being romanced by the wind. It was all so wonderfully excessive.

I saw the lily of the valley up close; their piety grounded in the dirt, flowers bowed against the dogwood and reaching toward the sky. I smacked my palm against the bark of one of the dogwoods. The tree, though the branches weren't thick, was tough and dense. The feeling of it stirred my soul.

Charlotte slipped the keys out of my pocket and pulled me to the car with a skip in her step. She opened the passenger door and motioned for me to sit. I followed her orders. She kissed my cheek, then swept around and got in through her door, slamming it closed.

"Easy," I told her.

"What? You know these old doors don't close without some force." She started the car up to a loud backfire and a cloud of smoke. Candid and sincere, our laughter softened.

"Darling, why don't we get a new car? Don't you think we get with the times and finally go electric?" I asked.

"Why not? But I do love this one. Its classic." She put it in low gear and released the clutch, guiding the car onto the road, leaving behind the burning fumes exiting the exhaust pipe.

Once we moved, I bought a hybrid pickup truck. Charlotte says the hybrid is more sustainable for now. Trucks turn out to be handy, even in the city. I get made fun of for it where we come from, but I couldn't care less. *It's not a real truck*, they say. My wife still takes the old Benz in to work at the twin towers–Atlanta's unfortunate name for the building that hosts different government agencies, including the one Charlotte now works for—since there isn't a Marta station near the new apartment.

Oh, we bought an apartment east of Peachtree Street. Charlotte's eccentric aunt gave it up for cheap. Supposedly, her real estate was becoming more of a burden than a blessing. Her words, not mine. Our home is in a building that stands four stories and overlooks a small park. A brick remnant from the 1940s. The balcony faces north, so above the short end of the railing to the west bears the city's portrait, the tall structures persisting, the cranes evermore frequent, it seems. There's a parking garage to the building's south side, which was built more recently, and there we hold two designated spots, one for the classic and one aimed to the future. We aren't resigned to Atlanta's car dependency, walking when and as often as we can, but they're nice to have when we need them.

Charlotte drove the car south down 75, taking the ramp to 20 West. Then she took the West End exit where she parked at a coffee shop we had been longing to check out. One that carried notoriety in the city, and even in the country.

We frequent that place often now.

As time and space and the smallness of the world would have it, Carolyn was there. These kinds of things happen often within the city limits. It seems, as the metro sprawls and the population rises, there is an illogically high chance you'll run into a friend at a bar or shop or café neither of you have patronized before. That is, if it is in the perimeter.

The sprawl persists. Atlanta's infamous traffic has nearly taken over the entire piedmont region of Georgia. It spreads like kudzu. The car and kudzu alike were introduced like a blinding light, salvation for the land and for the economy. But it just gets out of hand. We humans must have a proclivity for being seduced by the invasive.

Charlotte and I often escape to our parents in the quiet foothills. There they continue to resist it, but the sprawl threatens.

I digress. Nathan was there too, and so was who I assumed was Carolyn's mom.

It's funny. I rarely think of her anymore, but she does appear in my dreams. Always looking like she did the night we met. Her green eyes blazoning like a copper fire. The dreams are often bizarre and hard to explain, but always exciting. For some reason, we're always in a race, whether by plane or train or car or foot. Hardly do either of us win. Usually, I awake before the dream reaches the climax, the end of the race, and I roll over and throw my arm around my wife.

I knew they were moving back to Atlanta because a picture of her next to Nathan appeared in a local magazine. He'd found some success in his research and took a professorship at Morehouse.

I don't fully know under what terms their relationship came back together, but I imagine it was somewhat similar to the way mine and Charlotte's did. I guess they learned to see each other.

Anyways, Charlotte and I walked up to the patio, her hand locked around my elbow, and there they were sitting. Nathan was speaking and the older woman couldn't keep herself from laughing. It was a wonder Charlotte didn't see them, didn't see Carolyn. Nathan didn't notice us either, but Carolyn and I locked eyes. All she did was smile. I nodded softly and grabbed the door for Charlotte who pushed the stroller into the shop.

They were gone when we walked out with our coffees. We sat there at their abandoned table and let the sun shine on our faces.

***

We lost the baby.

There's not much I care to say about it. We would have had a girl. I was right. Little Mary Ann. We found out only two weeks before. We were supposed to have a girl. She fought for life into the second trimester. Charlotte was devastated, and so was I. She blamed herself. I blamed God. It seems my faith is strongest when I need someone to blame, but it was the fault of no one. Only the pain of life's shadows. A temporary pain that has no discernible end.

The call came while I was in New York. I was sitting next to Jasmine. We were in a meeting with the board of directors. Our first meeting. The meeting went on. Sarah called but I let it ring. My gut turned, and I knew I should have answered. When she called again, I rushed out of the room without a word.

The first thing I heard was wailing. Charlotte's cries.

"Del," Sarah started, but I knew.

"Put her on the phone."

***

Maybe Camus was wrong.

Faced with the Absurd, he turned to the temporal. His despair from looking at the finite robbed his attention from the infinite. God was a scapegoat. Religion was an excuse to live an inauthentic life. A distraction. Camus had no time for faith.

But why shouldn't we find ourselves so busy with trying to relate to people, people who are so contradictory in nature that it's almost an impossible task, that we don't have time to contemplate the absurd nature of our being? If anybody understands him, it's not me. Adam tells me Camus rejected the title of existentialist because even Camus, the self-defined 'unbeliever,' believed in human essence *a priori*. You'd think, since that's the paradox I can't overcome, I wouldn't waste a second trying to disagree with him, but every fiber of my being tells me I must rebel, even against him.

***

"Baby."

I could hear the echo of the hospital room. The sounds of Charlotte's agony, her deep, gravelly bawling, the snot she sniveled back through her nostrils, her gasping for air.

"Baby."

"Del." Her voice faint, her lungs dyspneic. "Del, I'm broken. I can't."

"It's okay. We will get through this. Charlotte, you're the strongest person I know. We will get through this. I'm coming straight to you. I'm coming. I'll be there soon. I love you, Charlotte. I'm sorry. I'm so sorry. Listen to me, baby. You are strong. We will get through this."

***

Adam says it's up to me and Charlotte to make meaning of the tragedy. Mom reminds us we will see her again one day. Dad and I don't talk about it and that's the grace I often need.

192

The grief is immeasurable. I know she would have been as beautiful as her mother. I also have a feeling she would have been wilder than either of us. Truly, we have never faced anything harder, but we're doing it together. Every day is a new struggle, but with it comes new intimacies, too.

While I've taken to studying Camus, I've been reading more of Søren Kierkegaard. I have to in order to keep up with Adam. We've started to meet every week or so to discuss whether *essence* precedes *existence*, or vice-versa. There's never any telling which side we'll take, though at the end of the day, I'm firm in my conviction: it's both.

Though I'm fighting with the *Postscript*, the Kierkegaard book I'm still drawn to the most is *The Sickness unto Death*. Possibly because of the nostalgic hold it has on me, reminding me of those college days when my eyes were big and glossy, my hair full, and the space between my eyebrows smooth.

Of course, there couldn't be a more fitting book for me, for I am a man in constant despair. Despair at not being myself, I guess Søren would say. In that way, Kierkegaard has validated my being. I've flipped through *The Sickness* many times since college, never really reading too deeply, though I will try again soon. I'm not sure I'll ever really get him, not on a philosophical level, but I feel it. Man, do I feel it. On a poetic level. I may not get him, but he gets me. There is one sentence that captured me when I first read it and still holds me today:

Man is a synthesis of the finite and the infinite, of what is temporal and eternal.

But Kierkegaard was too caught up in the infinite, wasn't he? He refused to take comfort in this life, so he had to take the leap, the leap Camus condemned as philosophical suicide. Kierkegaard was too confounded with the despair of this life, so he hoped for a world without despair. Is that right?

No, now I remember Kierkegaard dogmatically stating that faith in a future life is not faith at all; faith serves this life. Of course, I'm content to say they're both right. As far as I can tell, no two people stand closer together. They're so close, they're the other's shadow. One called it a sickness, the other called it a plague, but they both faced the same problem. At this point, I'm so confused and certain I've misrepresented them both. With all those pseudonyms, who can say where Kierkegaard stood?

Will I take my own leap or accept Sisyphus' stone? Why can I not choose both? The leap would mean to assume that this life has meaning. Finite life has infinite meaning. Have I already taken the leap? I feel like I've placed myself on the edge of the cliff, and yet, if I took another step, I don't think I'd fall. There would be no cliff. Only a shadow. Now, I've placed one foot in the shadow and one in the light. This is where I'll stay.

For a while now, I've looked to the wrong place, or at least I've taken a myopic glance in the wrong direction. Toward the infinite.

And maybe that's why I'm convinced in my rebellion against Camus, because I find there's something essentially meaningful about the absurd myth that the infinite supposedly became finite. A myth I believe most days, against my intellect. Yet nothing attracts my curiosity more than the ugliest event in history also being the most beautiful. So, I'll look closer. There's no need for a telescope, nor a microscope; I can see it with my naked eye. The finite. And I expect I'll find that the finite is more than finite after all.

***

I never did become a war chaplain. The war didn't come. Has not come. Thank God. Adam did get me certified to be a chaplain. I've wound up volunteering at Emory's hospital at times when they are overwhelmed and the chaplain staff is overworked. It's an interesting job. These people see me as so spiritual, like I'm Moses or something. I find it very funny. The best part of it is, a lot of the patients are older and have plenty of stories to tell. I hardly have to talk. Often, the religious patients pray for me. It's an odd thing, this reversal of roles. I appreciate it almost as much as the patients with whom I can share a silence. There is a pain too deep for words. I've seen it a hundred times over now, in the eyes of patients young and old. Eyes cannot hide fear. We've all used silence to hide our vulnerabilities, but at the end of speech, silence returns, and all the pain is shared.

I don't know why I do it. Adam says it's because I just can't help being a Christian. I think it's more selfish than that. I get more out of it than anyone. I grieve.

***

194

So, this is the tension I deal with, the Absurd is, and so is God. They're both so intrinsic to the human experience that it might even be that the Absurd is just God's self-disclosure. The doctrine of special revelation has expanded; the Scriptures, Christ himself, and now the Absurd, that is a witness to the revelation of God. Have I accepted heresy? No, it's not the belief that's wrong; it is absurd, whether I believe or not. Do I believe because it is absurd? Do I believe?

Though the universe responds with indifference

I

    Need

        Meaning

like I need breath in my lungs.

However, if God is encountered amidst the Absurd, God is not the cold, indifferent universe, nor is God me; God is. And I cannot complete that statement, or I've gone too far. This I know: there will be no justification for God's ways, not in this state of mind. "As the heavens are higher than the earth, so are my ways," says God. That doesn't let God off the hook.

My mind wanders to Adam bringing the service to the climax:

"This table is not my table, but the Lord's." He held up the chalice. "And Christ welcomes all of you to this table. Come and eat. Enemies and lovers, believers and unbelievers, this table is prepared for anyone, for everyone, come and be one in Spirit, and one in body."

I partook in the Eucharist, part of me a believer and the other part not. The thin grain crunched between my teeth; my tongue soured by the wine. My stomach turned as my heart pulsed new blood through my veins. An image of Christ weeping at Lazarus' tomb came to mind. For some irrational reason, I found my eyes wet with tears.

Something tells me God doesn't want to be let off the hook. Which means God must be pretty confident that all things will be made new. That all will be well.

The Absurd, then, is not a state of sin. Not exactly. If the Christian myth is true, then Christ became subject to the Absurd for us, not to save us from the Absurd, but to bring us through it.

The Absurd is not a revelation of God; that would identify God with it. Rather, the Absurd is the anti-revelation of God. Yes, God cannot be the Absurd, but the experience of the Absurd provokes the notion of a God beyond it, and Christ fills the gap.

One could say the Absurd exists to secure human agency, an agency not coerced by God. The object of faith is not obvious because the Absurd distorts our perception of reality. Humanity must be curious, curious like a child, or the Absurd will be our only reality. If I believe, I believe in defiant spite of the Absurd.

The universe is cold and indifferent; meaningless. And I need meaning. Therefore, God became a lamb slain before the foundation of the universe.

That's Absurd.

The word bounces around in my mind like the eyes of a biblical angel, but it takes on new meaning without undoing the old. Yet, the universe loses its meaninglessness.

Having not taken a puff in a long minute, I remove the cigar from between my lips. My tongue is parched from the smoke. I seek refuge in the red wine sitting on the side table. Its dry profile wets my tongue. I draw once again from the cigar. It is rounding out from my gnawing.

So, the Absurd is the very means that God uses to relate to me and, maybe, you. Now, I should clarify–

The door opens.

"Darling, put that thing out and hold your son." Peter is bouncing in Charlotte's arms with a big, one-toothed smile, arms reaching toward me.

I stub the cigar against the ashtray and take him into my arms. Sitting in my lap, he reaches for my face and paws the top of my cheekbone. The tear that forms in my eye rolls into his palm. Peter Jr. bundles his cheeks in my chest and pulls delicately at my shoulder as I pull him in tightly.

Charlotte pecks me on the lips and plops herself down in the chair beside me. She lets out a sigh of relief before throwing her swollen feet on my thigh, placing her hand on her rounded tummy. From the box with the initials PR nailed to the top, she pulls out a tattered, homemade book of ripped out pages, some from the blank pages of books, and others from the backs of church bulletins. In a god-awful array of colorful crayon, the title reads, *The Poems of Peter Robert*.

Written under the title: Collected by Charlotte Robert.

Him: *Like a lily among the thorns,*
So is my darling among other women.
Song of Songs

Acknowledgements

To acknowledge every person who had a hand in the culmination of this work is its own Sisyphean task, which I take on happily.

Matt Crenshaw, we approach beauty through different mediums, but our eyes are kin. Our high school selves would be proud of us. You killed the cover. Thank you.

Parker Durrance, for laughing at me as you watched me work out Del's thoughts on faith and the Absurd when I should have been paying attention to our theodicy seminar.

Jason Culmer, Baby Doll, thank you for challenging me to write characters I can't understand and let them speak for themselves.

I also want to extend gratitude to everyone who read early drafts of this novel. Your willingness to read my work was great encouragement along the way. Thank you to: Blake Adams, Elijah Thomason, Xloë Johnson, Joseph Lee, Max Wilson, Annie Ulle, Tori McCord, Jackson Carter, and my step-mom Kathy.

To the people who challenged me most when I first started this book:
Robby Waddell, my professor, pastor, and friend.
Chris Dixon, my therapist at the time.
Marie-Louise von Franz and Ann Ulanov, your work changed my life.
To Mom, Dad, Ron, Kathy (again) for all the ways you've supported me.

Perhaps most of all, I must thank my dear friend Christian Ham. This book likely would not have made it to print without his deep engagement as he did many, many edits and read-throughs. By now, he must know the book better than I do. Promise not to text blast you incessantly with ideas on the next one (maybe).

And, of course, Kate. I feel like I wrote you into existence with this one, but alas, no character could capture you. Our story is too great for the page.